"I need twenty-seven men. Tall, dark, handsome, smart. Preferably human. But with only two weeks until the full moon, I'm willing to negotiate on that last point."

Viola had long, dark hair, jet black eyes, and lips slicked with Chanel's Crimson Dream. She was president of the Connecticut chapter of the Naked and Unashamed Nudist Sisterhood, aka the NUNS, aka a group of female werewolves who met weekly at her Fairfield estate.

"So can you help me?"

"That depends," I heard myself say.

"On what?"

"On what you're going to do with twenty-seven men. I'm a matchmaker, not a personal chef."

Viola smiled, revealing a row of straight, white teeth. "We're not going to eat them, dear. We're going to have sex with them."

D1043029

ALSO BY KIMBERLY RAYE
(published by Ballantine Books)

Dead End Dating

Dead and Dateless

A Novel of Vampire Love

KIMBERLY RAYE

BALLANTINE BOOKS • NEW YORK

Dead and Dateless is a work of fiction. Names, characters, places, and incidents are the products of the author's imagination or are used fictitiously. Any resemblance to actual events, locales, or persons, living or dead, is entirely coincidental.

A Ballantine Books Mass Market Original

Copyright © 2007 by Kimberly Raye Groff
Excerpt from *Your Coffin or Mine?* by Kimberly Raye copyright © 2007 by Kimberly Raye Groff

Published in the United States by Ballantine Books, an imprint of The Random House Publishing Group, a division of Random House, Inc., New York.

BALLANTINE BOOKS and colophon are registered trademarks of Random House, Inc.

This book contains an excerpt from the forthcoming book *Your Coffin or Mine?* by Kimberly Raye. This excerpt has been set for this edition only and may not reflect the final content of the forthcoming edition.

ISBN 978-0-345-49217-3

Cover illustration by Marcin Baranski

Printed in the United States of America

www.ballantinebooks.com

OPM 9 8 7 6 5 4 3 2 1

For Sue Groff,
my vampire-loving mother-in-law!
You're the best.

Acknowledgments

I would like to say an extra-special thank-you to the following people who helped in the writing of this book: the Office of the Chief Medical Examiner of New York City, Dr. Charles S. Hirsch, for kindly answering all of my questions, no matter how ridiculous; the Fairfield Police Department, for answering even more ridiculous questions; friend and confidante Tammy Ramsey, for falling in love with Lil and boosting my confidence; fellow author Gerry Bartlett, for reading on a moment's notice and giving me her honest opinion. Thanks, everyone!

And many thanks to my readers who send notes and e-mails. Your encouragement means the world to me!

One

❤ ❤ ❤

"I need a man." The attractive woman sitting across the desk from me leaned forward.

Her name was Viola Hamilton and she was the latest client to come walking into the small but well-furnished office that housed my latest business venture—Dead End Dating, Manhattan's first and only hook-up service for vampires. And humans. And any other creature who could fork over my pricey (but well worth every red cent) fee.

I'm the Countess Lilliana Arrabella Guinevere du Marchette. Lil for short. The latest and greatest when it comes to matchmakers, and a five-hundred-year-old born vampire with an ever-expanding wardrobe and a serious cosmetics addiction.

Okay, *okay*. I'm a five-hundred-year-old born vampire with an ever-expanding wardrobe, a serious cosmetics addiction, *and* enough outstanding Visa charges to fund a small third-world country.

But enough about the ever-fantabulous me.

"Actually," Viola went on, "I need twenty-seven men, to be exact. Tall, dark, handsome, smart. Preferably human. But with only two weeks until the full moon, I'm willing to negotiate on that last point."

Viola had long, dark hair, jet black eyes, and lips slicked with Chanel's Crimson Dream. She wore a black Gucci jacket and matching slacks. A Cartier watch with a diamond band glittered from her slender wrist. She was president of the Connecticut chapter of the Naked and Unashamed Nudist Sisterhood, aka the NUNS, aka a group of female werewolves who met weekly at her Fairfield estate.

She was also the reason my father had nearly decapitated himself with a pair of hedge clippers last weekend. My old man detested thick, overgrown bushes almost as much as he did female werewolves, and so he religiously trimmed the azaleas that separated the two estates. Viola, on the other hand, detested short, puny vegetation and snobby, pretentious born vampires, and so she religiously put up a fight.

I, on the other hand, welcomed any and everyone with my arms wide, my mind open, and my deposit slip ready.

A smile spread across my face as I mentally calculated what twenty-seven men (preferably human) meant in terms of outstanding credit card payments.

"So can you help me?"

"That depends," I heard myself say. Wait a second.

I knew Viola could fork over the cash. I should be shouting "Yes!" After all, I'm a born vampire: the PC term for unconscionable, pompous, money-hungry, bloodsucking aristocrat.

"On what?"

"On what you're going to do with twenty-seven men." Okay, so I'm not exactly PC. Sure, I can be as pompous as any ancient born *vampere*. I am most certainly money-hungry. I'd also recently fallen off the wagon on the bloodsucking part (I'd been going for the bottled stuff up until a few weeks ago when I'd been staked in the shoulder and nursed back to health by a megalicious made vampire named Ty Bonner). *And* I am also an aristocrat (French royalty and all that). It was the unconscionable part that I had trouble with. "I'm a matchmaker, not a personal chef."

Viola smiled, revealing a row of straight, white teeth. "We're not going to eat them, dear. We're going to have sex with them." She stubbed out her cigarette in the small crystal ashtray on the corner of my desk. "And procreate. Female werewolves only ovulate during a lunar eclipse, which means we get one, maybe two shots a year to actually conceive, if any at all. Last year, we got nada. Since we females carry the actual were-gene, we can mate with any creature and still produce a were-baby. We NUNS feel a social responsibility to keep our race as pure as possible and so we prefer humans. That way we don't have to worry about any otherworldly genes mixing in with our own."

Okay, so I already knew this. Not firsthand, mind
you. While I am now a hot, hip, happening vampire,
I was raised in a very sheltered environment. Most of
my friends were born vamps and so I'd never actually
talked (for more than a few minutes) to a real werewolf.
Until now. Of course, I am as educated as the next born
vamp, and so I'd learned all about sexuality and the
various species early on. But hearing it told by a holier-
than-thou *vampere* tutor named Jacques whose lesson
had been extremely brief (other creatures weren't
deemed worthy of our precious time) and hearing it
straight from Viola (complete with details) were two
very different things. She spoke from actual experience.

"How can you keep the race pure if you mate with
a human?"

A *get real* look slid over her beautiful face. "Come
now, dear. They're *humans*. Our superior DNA obviously outranks their extremely weak genes, resulting
in a pure were-child."

Obviously. "Why not a male werewolf? Wouldn't
that be the ideal? Surely a double shot of were DNA
would really kick ass?"

"Do you know twenty-seven available male werewolves?"

"Um, not at the moment."

"Neither do we. There are a total of fifty-two members of our organization, nearly half of whom have
mates and don't need your services. I'm here on behalf of the single, uncommitted, aging NUNS. Unlike
you vamps, we only have a small window for procreation. Fifty years, to be exact. Desperation always

makes one less choosy. Besides, male werewolves are bossy and overbearing and extremely territorial. You have their child and *bam,* they're ready to pee on every tree in your front yard. While I wouldn't mind it if I found the right male werewolf, I haven't and I seriously doubt I'm going to in the next two weeks."

"Why not just go to a sperm bank?"

"We only ovulate during an actual sexual encounter. Our reproductive system requires a barrage of stimuli. One can't kiss or touch or nibble a turkey baster, dear."

"I see your point."

"We have only one requirement for a human partner: He can't be a wimp. Forget those sensitive, quiet, thoughtful, equal opportunity types that are all the rage these days. We need old-fashioned men who are blatantly physical and very domineering. Werewolves are a very aggressive race and wimpy men simply don't stimulate us sexually. The more turned on we are, the more likely we are to conceive."

"Alpha males only," I told her. "Got it."

"Wonderful." Viola smiled and opened her Christian Dior clutch. "I'll write you a check for the first half of the fee. The second is payable once everyone is matched up?"

"That's the Dead End Dating policy." As of this very moment, that is. I usually asked for a third up front, but if Viola wanted to dish out half, who was I to argue details?

Accommodate. That was my motto.

At least, it was right up there with *Shop 'Til You Drop.*

I was just about to reach across the desk and kiss this month's bills good-bye when the intercom buzzed.

"Lil?" Evie Dalton's voice floated over the line.

Evie was my devoted assistant. She had great taste in belts, lived for the latest MAC lip gloss, and could spot a fake Fendi at twenty paces. Had I been a lesbian human instead of a heterosexual born vampire with a screaming biological clock, I would have married her on the spot.

"I know you're with a client," she went on, "but could you come out here?"

"Give me just a second." My fingers closed around Viola's check.

"It's really important."

"So is this." I stared at the five-figure sum the female werewolf had scribbled in.

While it wasn't my ultimate fantasy (me plus the megalicious Ty Bonner plus this cute little number I'd spotted over at La Perla equaled dreamo supremo), it was certainly a windfall to a struggling entrepreneur.

"There are some, uh, men here to see you," Evie said.

"If Brad Pitt isn't one of them, they can wait." I smiled at Viola, slid her payment into my top drawer, and turned toward my laptop. "Let me just get you a receipt and—"

"They're not really into waiting."

"They'll have to make an exception." I punched the off button. The light blinked and the intercom buzzed again, but I ignored it.

"That's twenty-seven matches," I said as my fingers flew across the keyboard.

"Alpha matches," Viola added. "They *have* to ooze testosterone. Otherwise, we might as well forget the whole thing."

"Twenty-seven testosterone-oozing alpha matches," I corrected. "At the usual amount per match. Plus a bonus for our deluxe, ultra speedy service. Plus an additional alpha-only fee and—"

"You can't go in!" Evie's voice rose to a shriek a split second before the door crashed open and half a dozen men clad in cheap suits burst into my office, none of whom looked even close to Brad.

"Lilliana Marchette?" The question came from the first man to reach my desk. He wore a navy blue polyester number, a haggard expression, and the worst black and yellow striped tie I'd ever seen.

"She's not here," Evie shouted from the doorway. She hung on to one side of the door frame with both hands to keep from being ripped away by the rush of suits. "She left early. This well-dressed woman is her assistant. Because if she wasn't her assistant,"—she gave me a pointed, pleading stare—"she would be in big trouble."

"How big?" I asked, my gaze darting from one man to the next before swiveling back to my frantic assistant.

"Plead the fifth," Evie blurted before two of the men managed to pry her hands loose and push her back into the outer office.

"What's going on here?" I shot to my feet.

"We need you to come with us," the man with the black and yellow tie said as he flashed a silver badge and motioned to two of his men. They quickly pushed Viola out of the way and rounded the desk for me.

Detectives. Badges. Handcuffs.

The pieces started to fall into place and panic bolted through me.

"But you can't!" I wiggled away as another man (FYI, navy and red tie) reached out. "I didn't mean to put a dent in that soda machine. I was just trying to get my money back and—"

"I don't know anything about a dented soda machine."

"The jury summons," I blurted, rushing down my mental list of offenses. "I meant to call about that but my cell phone's been out and I don't like to use my business phone for anything other than—"

"It's not the jury summons."

"I didn't mean to take that towel from the gym. It just got mixed in with my change of clothes."

"Nope."

"That cab driver said it was okay if I didn't have enough cash for the entire fare—"

"Guess again." Silver flashed as black and yellow pulled out a pair of handcuffs and snapped them open. Two of his men fought to get a grip on my arms. Not easy considering I have preternatural strength and a severe allergy to polyester.

"Then what did I do?" The cuffs slid on and I found myself pulled around the desk. "Because whatever it is, I won't do again. Cross my heart and hope to—"

"—die?" the detective finished for me. "You just might."

I came up short. "Excuse me?"

"Murder, Miss Marchette. You're being arrested for *murder*."

Two
❤ ❤ ❤

The cop's words settled in just as I found myself dragged across my new Persian rug (a present from The Ninas—my two best friends in the entire universe), toward the door.

"But—"

"You have the right to remain silent," one of the suits recited somewhere to my left. "Anything you say can and will be used against you in a court of law—"

"Wait a second."

"—have the right to an attorney—"

"But I didn't do anything!" I struggled as they hauled me through the outer office. "I've never harmed another creature in my entire life! I mean, sure, I put a world of hurt on Princess Annabelle that once, but she *so* deserved it on account of she's a total slut and she'd been throwing herself at my boyfriend at the time. The Ninas pulled me off of her before I actually drew any of the red stuff!"

"—cannot afford an attorney, one will be appointed for you—"

"Please." I dug in my three-inch heels and they screeched across the hardwood floor of the outer office like nails on a chalkboard. "I didn't—I couldn't—I *wouldn't*."

"—understand these rights as I've read them to you?"

"*No*," I blurted as we burst out onto the sidewalk.

"No, you don't understand?"

"Yes, I understand, but—"

"Good."

Good? Was this guy crazy? Oh, wait a sec. He was. Because no way did I off anyone. I have been known to get in-your-face with a jerk every now and then (see the above Princess Annabelle confession), but otherwise, I'm a model citizen. I pay my bills on time (sort of). And I give to the homeless. *And* I even let people cut in front of me at the Starbucks (sure, there was that one time that was totally self-motivated on account of the guy was wearing this totally to-die-for Gucci T-shirt and I wanted an up-close look, but cutting is cutting).

Murder? Me?

"This is so *not* good." I shook my head frantically as I found myself pushed toward a waiting police car. "It's bad." I didn't even want to think about what my heels looked like after all the dragging and pulling. "Terrible."

"Chopping someone up into hamburger usually is."

Yuck.

"Now get moving," another voice said. Hands reached out and shoved me forward.

Okay, so I've always had *mucho* respect for New York's finest. They faced down creeps on a daily basis without Super Vamp abilities (most of them, anyhow), and so I would never have dreamt of making their lives more difficult by dragging my feet, or screaming, or cursing, or crying, or, say, kneeing one of them in the balls.

That is, the sane, well-bred, rational, low-key me would never have done such a thing.

But this was the desperate, depraved, about-to-be-thrust-into-the-back-of-a-police-car-and-carted-off-to-*jail*-for-chopping-some-poor-schmuck-into-hamburger-meat me. It was every vamp for herself.

My knee bent and hit a bull's-eye.

"Oohmph!" The huge guy with the death grip on my right arm let loose and cupped his crotch. He doubled over and fell to his knees.

In the blink of an eye (my own, because I really don't do pain and suffering all that well), I kneed the next guy, and the next and the next.

What can I say? I have serious issues with being locked up for something I didn't do. Even worse, I have serious issues with bright orange jumpsuits (or whatever color they're wearing on Riker's Island this time of year) and those cheesy slippers.

I flexed my arms, snapped the handcuffs in two, and whirled before anyone could draw another breath, much less realize what was happening. And then I ran as fast as my preternatural legs could carry me.

I was six blocks away before I finally slowed down. I darted into an alley that ran between a Vietnamese grocery store and a Vinnie's New York Style Pizza joint, and slumped against a brick wall.

As the breath sawed past my lips, I wondered if born vamps could actually have heart attacks. There had never been any reported cases in the long, *long* history of my race (we're talking pre-Napoleon) except my great aunt LaRue, who'd suffered chest pains a few years ago. But she'd been infatuated with Ricardo, her drop-dead gorgeous lawyer. It had turned out to be a bad case of angina. She'd been forced to lay off spicy food and so she'd fired Ricardo and hired a vegan named Scott. Problem solved. Which meant, however fast my heart was beating, I wasn't likely to hit the ground unless the cops managed to catch up, flex some collective muscle, and tackle me.

I ignored the stench of rotten vegetables and yesterday's pizza sauce and forced myself deeper into the alley. I wasn't going to think about the horrible condition of my shoes—a pair of Constança Basto sandals I'd picked up for a *steal* last week. Even more, I wasn't going to mourn my Banana Republic wooden bangle with the dangling beads that had been ripped off prior to the cuffs being snapped on—*sniffle*. There would be plenty of time for that when the cops weren't *this close* to dragging me off to the pokey.

I drew a deep breath—not that I needed it, but I'd been living in the human world and blending for so long that it was sort of a habit now—and focused my thoughts on getting the hell out of there, like, *now*.

Every nerve in my body seemed to come alive in that next instant. My arms tingled and my legs vibrated. A rush of heat started at my toes and worked its way up until I felt my cheeks flush.

I know, I know, it sorta, kinda, maybe sounded a little like an orgasm. But trust me, it didn't feel like one. Except for the vibrating legs, that is. And the flushed cheeks. And, perhaps, the hot . . . not going there.

Then again, it had been so long since I'd actually had a *mucho*, fantastic O (over a hundred years ago with an actual partner), my memory might be a little rusty.

I sniffled again. Once. Twice. A third time (hey, we're talking a *hundred* years).

I felt an overwhelming sense of crappiness wash over me. Nonexistent love life. Microscopic apartment. Newborn business barely breaking even. Sure, I had hot, happening hair (brown with enough highlights to make it look sunny-licious blond), but what was hair in the big scheme of things?

A police car rushed down a nearby street and jerked me out of my sudden funk. Panic bolted through me and I clamped my eyes shut and willed myself to change.

A loud flutter soon joined the frantic pounding of my heart. Suddenly, I felt weightless (yep, the change had its perks). I left the alley behind as fast as my tiny pink wings could carry me. (I know most bats are black, but black is so . . . black. As in dark and gloomy and so *not* my color.)

Even more testimony to the fact that I was totally freaked. No way would I risk discovery and annihilation of the entire born vamp race by morphing into a cute but totally conspicuous pink bat.

But I was free, and putting as much distance as possible between myself and the whole hamburger meat thing (yuck). And that's all that mattered at the moment.

Pigeons weren't the only ones who kicked ass when it came to homing instincts.

I reached my apartment, located on the Upper East Side of Manhattan, in just under a minute, and landed in the small, and smelly, alley that ran behind my building.

A few tingling moments later, I hurried up the front steps of my building in my bare feet. While I could morph as well as the next vamp, when I was nervous (or wanted for murder) I tended to leave behind a thing or two. In this case, my shoes and a really fab toe ring I'd bought in SoHo.

I punched in the code and rushed inside the renovated duplex that housed mostly single, corporate types and a few seniors. There were only two married couples (the Griffiths on one and the Shanks up on three) and zero children, which meant that the noise level was moderate, consisting mostly of CNN, game shows, and the occasional "Your mother is driving me crazy!"

Tonight, Mac Griffith's mother wasn't just driving his wife loony, however. She was shoveling the dirt over and burying her alive, judging from the raised voices coming from the first apartment I passed as I hauled butt toward the elevator. Several frantic moments later, I reached my front door. *The O'Reilly Factor* drifted from the apartment directly across the hall from me and a rerun of *Who Wants to Marry a Millionaire* carried up from old Mrs. Janske's just below. She was a widow who'd moved in last week, along with a zillion cats and at least three birds.

My nostrils flared as I unlocked the door to my apartment and I caught a whiff of . . . Make that a zillion cats, three birds, and an entire case of mothballs.

I made a mental note to stop by and introduce myself when I wasn't being hunted for murder. While I don't particularly like animals, I do have a weakness for a well-cared-for wardrobe.

To say my apartment was small would be paying it a compliment. It was more like minuscule compared to my parents' elaborate Connecticut estate and Park Avenue penthouse.

All right, already. It was minuscule compared to most other apartments in Manhattan, or the free world, for that matter. While small, it did have separate living and dining rooms in addition to the kitchen, bath, and single bedroom. Five microscopic rooms, complete with heavy-duty window blinds, and they were all mine. Meaning I didn't have to see my parents day in and day out.

Not that I don't love my folks, mind you. But they're my *folks* and, naturally, they make me C-R-A-Z-Y.

Or rather, they had. Until I'd moved out.

A single lamp burned from the one end table I'd managed to wedge next to my couch. I shut the door and rushed into the bedroom. I barely resisted the urge to fling myself on the king-size bed that took up most of my bedroom and bury myself beneath the covers and cry.

Cry?

Vampires do not cry, at least not in public. Besides, I figured I had, at the most, five minutes (the average cab ride between my apartment and Dead End Dating headquarters) before the cops pushed their way into my apartment. I didn't have time to shed any big ones. I needed to . . . to what?

I'd never been arrested for anything in my entire life. Except that little incident at Mardi Gras a few years back. But it wasn't like I *meant* to flash my tooties at that cop. They'd just sort of fallen out when I'd climbed up onto Nina One's shoulders to catch that handful of beads. And that's all I'm saying about that.

I was now on the run for *murder*.

Who? When? Where? Fashionably dressed victim or one in desperate need of a personal shopper? I didn't know. I just knew that the police were coming. For *me*. The sirens blared in the distance, growing closer with each passing second.

My survival instincts kicked in and I did what any

wanted, fashion-conscious vampire would do: I rushed toward the closet to snag a new pair of shoes.

Okay. Maybe I snagged an outfit, too (my shirt and blue jean mini were totally rumpled and still smelled like the alley, and *so* didn't match the lizard and suede Sergio Rossi boots that I pulled on), but I was fast.

I changed and managed to stuff half the contents of my closet, complete with cosmetics and this totally smoking rhinestone choker, into two suitcases before I heard the squeal of tires in front of my building. Car doors slammed. Footsteps thundered up the front walk.

I snatched my pillow from the bed and hauled my stuff toward the nearest window. Pulling up the blinds, I pushed at the glass, but it wouldn't budge. Talk about a fire hazard. I was definitely subtracting ten percent from next month's rent. Maybe even fifteen—

The thought shattered as the elevator door *whoosh*ed open on my floor. I gathered my preternatural strength and shoved. Wood creaked and splintered, and the whole frame sort of came apart in my perfectly manicured hands.

Maybe I'd just take off five percent.

Shoes slid and squeaked and stalled outside my apartment. The doorknob turned and the door shook just as I straddled the windowsill. I glanced down at the dark, empty alleyway below me and hesitated.

Like, I knew I was a badass vamp and all. But I was a spoiled, pampered, badass vamp, and I wasn't really used to leaping into dark alleys while running for my life. Besides, we're talking three-and-a-half-inch stiletto heels on the Rossis. Not exactly ideal for leaping tall buildings in a single bound.

"Do it." A deep voice slid into my ears a split second before something big crashed into my apartment door. Wood cracked. The hinges gave.

I gathered my stuff, closed my eyes, and leapt.

I landed with a loud *squish* that echoed in my ears and filled me with as much dread as the "I see her!" that thundered overhead.

Almost.

Glancing toward the open alleyway, I turned and headed for the ten-foot fence at the opposite end. Another impressive leap later, I'd cleared the fence and shifted into *getting the hell out of here* mode.

A few frantic seconds and several blocks later, I shoved my stuff into the back of a cab and climbed in.

The driver spared me a glance in the rearview mirror. He was in his twenties, with long blond hair pulled back into a ponytail. He wore a floral print shirt and a bored expression. "Where to?"

I clutched my pillow tighter as if it were a life preserver. "Connecticut. And I'm in a really big hurry."

He grinned and eyed the pillow. "Hot date?"

If only.

"Business meeting." When he glanced at the pillow again and flashed me a knowing look, I frowned. "Could you just get us out of here?" Sirens wailed several streets over and my heart beat faster. "Like, *now.*"

My gaze collided with his in the mirror and I saw

something spark in the brown depths of his eyes. Recognition. Attraction. Desire.

Bingo.

"No problem, lady," he told me, suddenly eager to please. He shifted the car into drive and pulled out into traffic. "You just sit back and chill. They don't call me Fast Freddie for nothing."

I was willing to bet the reason they called him Fast Freddie had nothing to do with his driving. And I soon discovered, as we crawled over the Hudson, that I was right.

I concentrated on willing him faster. Mind control was another vamp plus, as long as it was used on the opposite sex.

Go, go, go!

His smile widened and he glanced more frequently into his rearview mirror, but otherwise, we didn't so much as increase a single RPM.

Dread washed over me, along with a rush of fear that I was losing my touch with the opposite sex. (A hundred years, remember?) Sure, I'd shared a major hot kiss with vampilicious Ty and it had seemed like I still had it going on. But we're talking a *kiss*. One measly kiss that hadn't even led to a second kiss, much less wild, hot, frantic sex. Much less the satisfaction that I was totally and undeniably irresistible.

I fought against the sudden tears that burned the backs of my eyes.

I was a born vampire.

Powerful. Smart. Superior. Invincible. *Attractive*. Even if I did have major gunk on my boots.

I was not going to break down in the back of a New York cab, in front of a totally clueless and only minimally cute driver.

Of course, once I reached Connecticut, and solitude, I fully intended to let loose with the water works and wallow in some major self-pity.

That is, if the cops didn't catch me first.

Three

❤ ❤ ❤

"**A**re you a parking ticket, because you have *fine* written all over you," the cabbie said as we rolled to a stop on the well-manicured road that connected a handful of pricey estates, my parents' among them.

It was the cabbie's thirtieth cheesy pickup line in as many minutes—the torture had started after we'd left the city and hit I-95 headed toward Connecticut.

The first and classic *"Do you have a Band-Aid? 'Cause I scraped my knees when I fell for you"* had snapped me out of self-pity mode and started me rethinking my nonviolence stance.

"Come on," he went on. "Talk to me."

"I really don't feel like talking. Here," I told him, motioning to the side of the road. "Just drop me here."

"But the house is way up there." He motioned to the massive white colonial that sat in the far distance.

"There's no reason to wear yourself out walking." He grinned and winked. "You should save your strength. We could go out. Maybe get something to drink. Or a lube job."

"Excuse me?"

"With all those curves you've got, I need to make sure my brakes are in working order."

Pu-*lease*.

While the *go, go, go* hadn't worked, the old vamp magnetism was, unfortunately, alive and well.

Thankfully. In my rush to escape, I'd left my purse back at the office, along with my bank card and my Visa. Not that I could have used either without alerting the police to my whereabouts.

I know, I know. I was turning out to be sort of good at this whole on-the-run criminal business (I had my clothes and I was free). What can I say? I had a brain to go with my ultra fab body. I also had a receptionist/personal assistant who never missed *CSI*, and who never failed to give me the lowdown after each episode.

For now I was broke and destined to stay that way unless I stumbled over a stash of cash hidden in my folks' azalea bushes.

So not happening. My dad, like all other born vampires, was extremely careful and frugal (that's cheap to you and me), and so the only thing hidden in the bushes was a bear trap he'd bought last week to put a damper on Viola's next NUNS meeting.

"I know milk does a body good, but baby, how much have you been drinking?"

I drew a deep breath, forced myself not to smack

the smiling cabbie and turned on the charm. "That's a good one."

"I've got more."

"I'll take your word for it. Now pull over." *Now.*

The minute the thought registered, his hands tightened on the wheel and he eased onto the side of the road. The cab rolled to a stop.

"Thanks so much for the ride." I reached for the doorknob as he twisted around in the seat and eyeballed me.

"My pleasure. That'll be eighty-five dollars and—"

"And thanks for forgetting all about me."

"What . . ." His voice faded as I caught and held his gaze.

You will forget me. As soon as I climb out of this cab, you'll forget I even exist. You'll think you drove all the way out here to get some fresh air and sightsee. End of story. No megalicious hot babe clutching a pillow in your backseat. No trying to pick her up. No enormous unpaid fare on your meter. Nada.

He blinked and the desire in his gaze faded into confusion.

As I scrambled out of the backseat, my gaze hooked on the worn paperback sitting on his dash. *Love Smart.* Guilt niggled at me and I heard myself say "Got a pen?"

He blinked, still dazed and confused, and retrieved a pencil from his glove box.

I grabbed an old receipt off his seat, scribbled the name and number for Dead End Dating and handed it to him. "Call Evie Dalton and she'll help you find that perfect someone."

Just call me sucker.

Not that I actually *felt* for the guy. Or knew what it was like to sit home all by my lonesome and wonder if there was someone—anyone—out there waiting for me (I'm talking opposite sex, not creditors). A girl had to protect her livelihood and I needed all the clients I could get. 'Nuff said.

He stared at the number as if I'd handed him a Visa Gold card with unlimited spending and I smiled. And then I frowned because, hey, bad ass vamps didn't get all mushy just because they'd made someone's day. Especially desperate badass vamps, which is exactly what I was at the moment.

Forget the undying gratitude and the fact that I've just made your year, and scram.

I willed the thought as I climbed out, and then hustled down the road. I chanced one glance behind me to make sure he'd driven off—yeah, baby—and then I really hauled butt. My boots were literally smoking by the time I sprinted across the carefully manicured lawn that surrounded my family's three-story house.

A soft, yellow light illuminated the front door and I had a sudden vision of myself curled up in my bed on the third floor. My parents still expected me to fail and so they'd yet to turn my space into another guest room. I took a few steps up the front walk before I caught myself.

My parents' place would most likely be high on the list of my possible whereabouts. While I knew they would believe my innocence and have no qualms helping me hide, I wasn't about to put them in a position where they would have to lie. Even more, I wasn't about to put myself in a position where I would have to listen to yet another of my mother's endless lectures on why I should give up the matchmaking biz, settle down with a suitable eternity mate, and squeeze out a couple of baby vamps.

I know, right?

Anyhow, I needed to think, which I couldn't do while defending my career and/or social life and/or choice of outfit. I needed to figure out how I was going to get out of this mess. I needed to . . . *plan*.

This might come as a shock seeing as how I'm such a successful businesswoman, but I've never been much for planning. I'm more of the fun-loving, spontaneous type.

Translation: irresponsible.

At least as far as my folks are concerned.

While the very thought of coming up with a cold, hard, step-by-step actually makes me a little nauseated (which is saying a lot on account of the fact that an iron constitution goes with the whole born vamp persona), I knew it was going to take as much to get me through the next few hours, or days, or weeks—or however long it took to find out what the hell was going on and clear my name.

And that's what I had to do. While I didn't know any specifics about the murder, I was firmly convinced (an arrest warrant and a police chase will do that to you) that the authorities felt certain I had killed someone. I had to prove them wrong.

With my BlackBerry back at the office in my purse, I was going to have to rely on my gray matter to keep things straight.

Number one: Find a safe place to sleep and regroup.

My feet ached and my arms felt like cement (we're talking two suitcases *and* a jam-packed cosmetics bag) as I rounded the house and headed for the back veranda. I'd just passed a potted palm when my heel snapped in two and I stumbled. My ankle twisted and I screamed and limped toward a nearby chaise loungue. Sinking onto the edge, I set my suitcases down and examined my ankle.

Okay, so I looked at the heel of my Rossi first, but with just a few *zzz*s my ankle would be back to normal. My boot wouldn't be so lucky.

I eased off the expensive leather and wiggled my toes. The pain slowed to a dull thud and my other senses (which had been completely focused on the loss of my cherished acquisition) tuned in to my surroundings. My nostrils flared and I caught the faint but familiar scent of cherries jubilee.

See, it's like this. Each born vamp emits a scent that is uniquely his or her own. It's distinguishable only to other born vamps and it's always warm and sugary sweet. Thankfully, I was sitting downwind and so my folks couldn't smell *moi*. At least I didn't think so.

We (born vamps) are also gifted with a special talent unique to each of us. Some vamps can mind link. Others have super extraordinary mind control abilities (think earth, wind, and fire—the elements, not the R & B group) that supersede the given dose of vamp whammy we all are dealt. My great uncle Martine could actually predict the near future. He'd made a fortune casino-hopping in Vegas and Atlantic City. As for me, I had a fantabulous nose for sniffing out designer pieces at department store prices. Hence my ultra fab Rossis.

My ears prickled and my mother's voice carried from somewhere inside the house.

"Can you believe he's doing this to me?"

"It's just an invitation to tea, dear," I heard my father tell her. The rich scent of mint chocolate chip joined the cherries jubilee.

"We're vampires. We don't drink tea."

"Jack's intended doesn't know we're vampires. Neither do her parents. So tea makes sense."

"Don't call her that. She isn't his 'intended.' She's his flavor of the week. You know how Jack is. He changes his mind faster than Lilliana changes her clothes. And speaking of my darling daughter, I've called the office twice and she isn't answering."

Number two: Go back to office ASAP and turn on machine.

I wasn't sure how I was going to pull this off, but I knew it was of monumental importance. I'd scraped and clawed and killed myself over the past few months to make a name in the matchmaking business and I was right there. On the cusp of greatness.

Or at least making the rent.

I couldn't fall into poor business practices, i.e., not

turning on the answering machine, just because I was wanted for murder.

That or I could contact Evie and make sure that she turned the answering machine on. I wasn't sure how to do this, either (no cell, no money, no dice), but I intended to figure something out.

"She never answers your calls," my father pointed out.

"True, but that receptionist of hers or the answering machine always pick up at the office. I'm not getting either. I think something is . . ." Her words trailed off.

"What is it?" my father asked her.

"I . . . nothing. It's just, for a second there, I could have sworn I smelled cotton candy."

So much for being downwind.

"You're worrying too much, dear."

"Of course I'm worrying. I'm her *mother*."

Aka the CEO of Guilt, Inc.

"I'm sure Lil is fine. And if she weren't, someone would have called us by now. The boys keep tabs on her."

"Jack doesn't. He's too busy committing us to social events with every human in New York."

"It's two, dear. Three counting the girl herself."

"Three too many. I swear," she huffed, "my children are going to be the death of me."

"You're immortal, dear."

"With a weakness for stakes and sunlight. Both of which seem preferable to having *tea* with that woman and her family. Are you sure she's not a witch?"

"Jack said she's a doctor."

"There you go. A voodoo witch doctor. She's probably cast some sort of spell over him and that's why he's come to us with this silly request."

"Not that kind of a doctor, dear," my father said. "At least I don't think. Then again, that would explain why the boy came up with this cockamamie plan. Jack would never cook up something like this by himself."

I have three older brothers. Jack, the youngest, is the do-no-wrong brother.

As for the other two . . . Max is the hunky one. Okay, so they are all three hunky (we're talking male vamps, here), but Max is the oldest and so he has hunk seniority. While Rob is the smart brother. Okay, *okay*, so they are all smart (another vamp given), but Rob is the only one who managed to fly below my parents' radar. He showed up for Sunday hunts, but otherwise he stayed in Hoboken where he managed the Jersey locations of Midnight Moe's. And—and this was the biggie—he kept his women to himself.

I was trying to do the same—fly below the radar, that is—but it wasn't working as well on account of my being female and the survival of my species— not to mention the family bloodline—depended completely on me and how quickly I could find a suitable vamp and procreate.

Or so my mother thought.

"I'm just going to call and tell them no. They're *human*."

In vamp terms, human meant dinner.

"Perhaps if we go," my father pointed out, "Jack will change his mind about this human. Especially when he sees us all together. He can't ignore how different we are if it's right in front of him."

Vamp definition for different? Better.

"So you think we should cancel the Sunday hunt and go?" my mother wanted to know.

I sat up straight. *Cancel* the Sunday hunt? Would they? Could they?

"I don't see how we can do anything else. We have to let him see for himself how silly it is for him to be involved with someone like that."

Yessssssssss!

"It's done, then," Mom declared. "We'll cancel Sunday and move the hunt to Saturday."

I glanced around the veranda for the nearest sharp object. Other than the heel from my Sergio Rossi, there wasn't even anything close.

Number three: Buy wooden stake.

I tuned out my parents and pushed to my feet. Moonlight reflected off the water as I rounded the pool and limped toward the pool house.

Remember, we're talking a vamp pool house. Nix the usual umbrellas or beach towels or anything to help shield a body from the glowing ball of fire scheduled to light up the sky in exactly six hours and thirty-six minutes. I did find a few floats, however, several lounge chairs and a mini fridge with two bottles of AB-positive leftover from my parents' last party.

The small clock on the fridge indicated that it was barely eleven o'clock. *Eleven?*

Which meant I had an entire night and day to get through undetected.

No problemo. I could do this. I would hunker down and regroup. Come nightfall tomorrow, I would head back to the city and get to the bottom of the whole accused-of-murder business. And I would tend to my own Dead End Dating. I wasn't exactly sure how I was going to accomplish the last part (I couldn't just waltz into the office), but I figured that something brilliant would strike while I slept.

First things first. I stacked several lounge chairs in front of the door (it didn't have a lock) and spent the next half hour blowing up four of the massive floats and adding to my mental list of things to do tomorrow evening, like contacting Evie. I wasn't sure how, but I wasn't worried (see the brilliant comment above). I drank half a bottle of gourmet blood (chilled, but beggars couldn't be choosers) and changed into my favorite J Lo sweatsuit—pink with white stripes—and did my best not to feel sorry for myself. Stacking three of the floats on top of one another, I stretched out and pulled the fourth full on top of me to act as a blanket/shield just in case someone opened the door and caught me cry—

I shook away the thought before I could even finish, closed my eyes and gave in to the tears—er, sleep.

And that's how I stayed for the next few hours until the police showed up.

Four

♥ ♥ ♥

I almost peed my pants when I heard the wail of the siren.

Almost.

Except that I'm—you guessed it—a *vampere*. While I have the same equipment as your average human, it doesn't work exactly the same. Or, in this case, not at all (*mucho* thanks to the Big Vamp Upstairs for *that*).

Plus, the sound only lasted for a few blaring seconds, and so the J Lo suit stayed in mint condition. I was left to wonder if my imagination had shifted into maximum overdrive. Loud, obnoxious siren? Or crazy, well-dressed, lunatic vampire?

I went for number one (while I was well dressed, I wasn't ready to check myself into Bellevue just yet) and crept to the door. My ears prickled and my nostrils flared and I tuned in to the world on the other

side. The buzz of the crickets. The soft lapping of the
pool water. The hum of the pump. The footsteps—

Uh-oh.

Man-made materials slapped up the walkway lead-
ing to my parents' front door and my heart jumped
into my throat. The noise paused and I heard the
shuffling of feet and the clearing of throats.

Breathe, I told myself. I sucked in air and tried to
focus on the positive aspects of the situation. No guns
were being drawn. No handcuffs were clacking. No
one was whispering "You take the back" or "On my
count" or whatever cops said in situations like this.
There were no men surrounding the house or heli-
copters lingering overhead.

I sucked more air and tried to calm my pounding
heart.

"I'm really sorry, chief." The woman's apologetic
voice slid past the thunder of my heart and echoed in
my ears. "I thought the siren was standard procedure."

"In the apprehension of a criminal, Morris." The
man's voice was deeper, more smooth and controlled.
"This is a courtesy call on two valuable members of
our community."

"Whose daughter is a murderer."

"Alleged murderer."

"But what if she's here?"

"She's not."

"But what if she is? That would mean they're aiding and abetting, which makes them criminals themselves, which means this isn't just a courtesy—"

"There's been a mistake."

"But how can you be so—"

"She's not here," the deep, smooth voice cut in again. "Now shut up and leave it alone."

Leave. It. Alone.

The words echoed so strong and sure and forceful and realization hit.

Remy Tremaine aka the Fairfield police force's token vampire. His parents lived in a four-story colonial not too far away and were longtime friends of my folks. Our dads watched the Knicks together and golfed every Saturday night. Our mothers were both members of the Connecticut Huntress Club. Remy's *madre* collected dues while mine served as vice president and my un-official spokesperson.

Meaning, she furnished my stats (height, weight, orgasm quotient) along with glasses of refreshment at every meeting.

Meaning, I'd been set up with every eligible son, cousin, nephew, uncle, father, grandfather, and great grandfather (don't ask).

All born vampires, of course, who met my mother's standard requirements for a son-in-law. Good look-ing. *Fantastique* fertility rating. And filthy rich. While police chiefs didn't rake in the mega bucks, Remy's private security service—which provided personal bodyguards to the wealthy, as well as an impressive list of celebrities and politicians—did.

I'd been paired up with Remy on at least a dozen occasions. Not that I'd fallen for him, mind you. Yummy looks aside, we're talking man-made soles.

On top of that, while Remy looked good enough to eat, he didn't smell good enough to eat. Because of his line of work, he took a special pill developed by a top-secret agency that provided tactical weapons for the armed forces. (I told you I'd spent many an evening with him.) The pill inhibited his natural scent and allowed him to mix, undetected, with the criminal element (some of them born vamps). Since the scent was a crucial mating element, I'd never been remotely attracted to him. Even if I sort of liked the fact that he didn't remind me of a walking coconut cream pie.

As far as I was concerned, Remy was . . . Well, *Remy*. I'd known him *forever* (translation—since we'd both been baby vamps back in the old country). I'd seen him wear knickers and he'd seen me in pantaloons and powdered wigs (uh, yeah), which equaled way too much history for me.

Hello? Get over it. I could if I'd actually felt *it*. The chemistry. The heat. The *bam!*

Bam! was a must-have on my prospective eternity mate list and so I'd crossed Remy off a long time ago.

The doorbell rang and my mother's voice sounded somewhere in the house.

"I told you I heard something," she said to my father.

"Of course you heard something. The entire neighborhood heard it."

The knob clicked and the door creaked open.

"Remy? What's the meaning of this?"

"Sorry about the siren, Mrs. Marchette. Morris

here is a rookie and was just following procedure. She hit the button before I could stop her." While I couldn't see what was going on, I knew Morris was no doubt standing there with a look of pure rapture on her face because Remy *was* sort of hot and he'd obviously vamped her to keep her silent.

"Since when is it procedure to stop by for a nightcap?" my mother asked.

"This isn't a social call." He paused and my heart stopped beating. "There's a warrant out for Lil."

"I told you she can't handle her finances," my mother blurted. "Haven't I told you? Just tell us how much the parking tickets are and we'll take care of it."

"She isn't wanted for outstanding traffic violations, Mrs. Marchette."

"I'm afraid I don't understand."

"She's wanted for murder."

"I told you the constant bottled diet would eventually get to her," she told my father with the same exasperation she'd used in reference to the traffic violations. "Haven't I told you? A vampire has to hunt. End of story. Obviously we can control ourselves, but to deny the hunger completely . . . It's ridiculous."

"That's our Lil," my father added.

See, I wasn't much for hunting. Not that I couldn't, mind you. I just preferred drinking my dinner out of a martini glass and following it up with an appletini chaser. Or, my most recent discovery, a cactus margarita. Talk about delish. See, they use sugar instead of salt and this to-die-for cactus juice that's actually sweet . . .

Wait a second. Where was I? Oh, yeah. While my parents went for the bottled stuff for the most part, they did indulge in the real thing on occasion. To nurture their wilder side.

I know, I know. My wild side had most likely bitten the dust a few hundred years ago. Maybe. And maybe I'm just bottling it up in hopes of unleashing it with a megalicious vampire who can't keep his hands off me.

Hey, it could happen!

"It's just like your cousin Brigitte," my mother went on. "Remember when she decided to become a nun and gave up men and blood? She lasted all of two weeks before she drained an encyclopedia salesman and even tried to sink her teeth into the free globe."

"The globe?"

"Of course, she was out of her mind by then. If you ask me, she was out of her mind even before. Imagine, a *nun*. It's too frightening to even contemplate."

"Lil didn't lose it and drain him. She chopped him into little pieces."

"That's preposterous. Not that I wouldn't like to see our daughter do a little healthy hunting. But our kind don't kill. You know that, Remy. Besides, Lilliana cried for a week when her brother ripped the head off her favorite doll. You remember that, don't you, dear?" she asked my father.

"We had a hell of a time calming her down," my dad said. "Hell of a time."

"She would never do something so messy. She hates to get her hands dirty."

Actually, it was my clothes that I hated to get dirty.

But Mom got kudos for standing up for me, so I wasn't going to argue semantics.

"There's obviously been a mistake," my mother added. "A ridiculous mistake."

"I agree," Remy sighed. "But the evidence says otherwise. The victim was Kevin Gillespie, aka Keith Gillman."

The name drew an immediate image. I closed my eyes and saw the geeky twenty-something who'd come to my office desperate to find the girl of his dreams less than two weeks ago. He'd been a little pudgy and much too pale, but I'd agreed to help him anyway. What can I say? I love a challenge. Even more, I love a client who can pay a bonus for express service.

"He was a reporter for *The New York Times*," Remy went on. "He was . . ."

Whoa, back it up. A *reporter*?

". . . a story on the local dating scene. Posing as a secret dater, he would sign himself up for the various services, go on a few dates, and write a review. He'd been about to leave his apartment for a date arranged by Dead End Dating when Lil arrived. She gave the doorman her name and her card."

Uh—yeah. Keith had shown up at Dead End Dating wearing sandals and socks, for Damien's sake. We're talking the walking poster guy for What Not to Wear on a First Date. Which meant I'd shown up at his apartment prior to date number one to make sure he wore something decent so he didn't remain a pale, geeky, lonely subway attendant for the rest of his life.

He'd had on Reeboks and jeans and a new blue Banana Republic T-shirt I'd talked him into during our predate shopping spree. Perfectly acceptable attire for a casual night of pizza and beer and conversation with his possible soul mate.

"I knew that dating service would get her into trouble. Dating, of all things."

Here we go again.

"Born vampires don't date. And they certainly don't arrange dates for *humans*."

Or made vampires. Or werewolves. Or any of the Others who'd signed up since I'd opened up shop. Yada, yada.

"First she's the laughingstock, and now she's a wanted criminal. She might as well stand on the street corner with a sign around her neck: Vampires exist and I'm one of them."

"Now, now, dear, I'm sure she doesn't mean to draw attention to herself."

"Did you see what she wore to last week's hunt? A hot pink tutu, of all things."

It hadn't been a tutu. It had been a poet's shirt with fringe, the latest from Christian Dior and my most recent wardrobe coup.

"This is all your fault," my mother told my father. "My side of the family is the picture of discretion."

"What—"

"Now, folks," Remy cut in. "There's no need to blame each other for this unfortunate situation. What's done is done and the only way out of it is to stick together."

"Such a smart boy," my mother said. "But of course, you're right."

"I still don't see why the police are so convinced she's guilty," my father said. "Just because she was seen at this reporter's apartment doesn't mean she killed him."

Right on, Dad.

"True, but the victim took a picture of her with his camera phone just minutes before the projected time of death. She was in his bedroom where he was killed. With the murder weapon in her hand. A huge kitchen knife."

Duh. I couldn't very well let him rush off to meet his soul mate with the tags still attached to his shirt. Talk about a date killer. Oops. My bad.

"There are security cameras all over the building and no one else was seen going in or out of the apartment."

"She didn't kill anyone," my father insisted. "She might be a little out of the ordinary, but she wouldn't betray her family by doing anything that would risk exposure."

I wouldn't? I mean, of course I wouldn't. I love my family.

Most of the time, anyway.

"We raised her better than that," my mother added. "At least we tried."

"I'm sure you're right and this is all a mistake," Remy said. "I know Lil. She wouldn't do this."

Maybe I shouldn't have been so quick to cross Remy off my prospective eternity mate list. *Bam!* factor aside, you had to love a man who believed in you.

"But the city police think she's your average killer. Particularly after she resisted arrest and assaulted half the cops on the scene when they tried to take her into custody. She's in a lot of trouble and it's a given that you'll both be pulled in for questioning. It would save a lot of time and trouble if you would come down to the station with me right now and make a statement. Otherwise, you'll be opening the door to a search warrant."

"Let me get my purse," my mother said.

I listened as my parents left with Remy, and then I sank down onto the nearest float and tried not to hyperventilate.

Stop breathing, I told myself. *Just stop it. You don't need to breathe. Breathing leads to hyperventilating and vampires don't hyperventilate. Or panic. Or cry. They stay calm. And cool. And in complete control. And they plan. They figure out where they're going and how to get there and then they just do it.*

That's what I told myself, but instead of working on getting myself from point A (hiding out for a murder I didn't commit) to point B (innocence, major financial success, and a date with Orlando Bloom or Jason Allen), I kept picturing Keith in his new blue shirt getting sliced and diced and—*can't breathe, can't breathe, can't breathe.*

Maybe my mother was right.

Maybe I *had* been switched at birth, because vampire or not, I was definitely in the middle of a major panic attack.

Five

♥ ♥ ♥

Dear Mom and Dad,
   I just stopped by to say hi. Sorry I missed you
guys. Take care and I'll see you at the next hunt.
                                          Love, Jack
P.S. Don't worry about Dad's Hummer. I'm just
borrowing it.

I clipped the note to a refrigerator magnet and
grabbed the keys hanging near the back door. After
punching in the security code, I let myself out the
kitchen door and headed for the massive garage that
housed a half dozen vehicles.

After the panic attack and some shallow breathing
into an old potato chip bag I'd found in the pool
house (the maid/watcher had a thing for sour cream
and onion), I'd calmed down enough to formulate a
plan. I now had two and a half hours until sunup,

which meant I needed a safe place. Somewhere no one would think to look for me. A place that couldn't be traced back to me. Which meant I had to pay cash. Which meant I needed help.

I could wait for my parents. They would give me cash, and a lecture, and a lot of advice I really didn't need at the moment.

I could go to one of The Ninas, but they would ask a lot of questions I wasn't ready to answer at the moment.

I could go to Evie, but she didn't have any money. On top of that, the cops were probably keeping an eye on her after the fiasco at the office.

I could go to my oldest brother, Max, but he liked to lecture, too. There was my middle brother, Rob, but I really didn't want to get him involved since he prided himself on staying so uninvolved. Besides, I actually had a relationship with both Max and Rob. We talked on the phone. We shared. Sort of.

Which left my youngest brother, Jack. Jack was a womanizer and a know-it-all and a major pain in the ass. Likewise, he thought I was a pampered, self-centered bitch who squandered money on way too many clothes.

I *know.*

I should have added clueless to Jack's résumé.

I'd never squandered a penny in my life. My wardrobe was an investment, just like a horde of original GI Joes or a rare book collection or any of the other stuff offered up on eBay. As for the pampered, self-centered bitch part . . . Okay, so nobody's perfect. The point?

While we loved each other (hey, family's family), we weren't about to win any contests for the closest siblings. Which meant he was the least likely person I would go to for help. If the police didn't have my parents under surveillance yet, they weren't likely to have my youngest and most estranged brother in their sights.

At least that's what I was hoping.

When I reached the garage, I punched in another security code and stepped back as the doors slid up. I stared longingly at my mother's candy apple red BMW convertible before turning toward the blazing yellow monster that looked like a bee on steroids.

While the BMW was more my style, the Hummer said cocky male vampire eager to prove his virility with an obscenely large phallic symbol, i.e., my brother Jack.

I climbed in, gunned the engine, and backed out.

A half hour later, I was barreling toward the city. I intended to swing by Jack's, get him to advance me some cash, and leave the Hummer. Then I'd take a taxi to an out-of-the-way hotel with heavy-duty window blinds and get some much-needed sleep.

Jack wasn't at home.

I stood on his front stoop and pressed the button for the trillionth time. Nothing.

This was so *not* happening.

I pressed the buzzer again and prayed that he was just tied up with one of his numerous minions (literally) which meant he couldn't get to the door. Of course, he had super vamp strength which made this whole possibility ridiculous, but a girl could hope.

"Please," I murmured, pressing the buzzer again.

Okay, so maybe the buzzer was broken. Maybe he really was inside about to call it a night and climb into his coffin (yep, ya heard me—a coffin—Jack was such a showoff) and he just couldn't hear me.

I grasped tight to the hope, climbed back into the Hummer, and gunned for the nearest pay phone.

Seconds later, I was standing on a street corner next to a hot dog vendor. The smell of roasted wieners made my stomach jump even before I heard my brother's familiar voice.

"This is Jack. I'm not home. You know the drill . . ." *Beep.*

I hung up, drove back to his apartment, and buzzed him again with the desperate hope that he'd arrived in the three minutes I'd been en route from the pay phone. Crazy, I know. But I didn't know where else to go or what else to do.

"He isn't home." The woman's voice slid over my shoulder and I turned to see a twenty-something with long brown hair and an olive complexion. Said hair had been pulled back into a loose ponytail. A pair of black Lycra workout pants clung to her short legs. She wore an I LOVE NEW YORK T-shirt that dwarfed her small frame along with worn Reeboks. A styrofoam cup steamed with coffee in her right hand and her left clutched a morning paper.

Uh-oh.

My heart jump-started as I glanced at my watch. Exactly forty-eight minutes and counting.

I was *so* having the worst night of my life.

My frantic gaze collided with the woman's and my night got even worse. She wasn't human. Otherwise, I would have been able to see into her thoughts because, hey, that's what super vamps did. We could look into any human's eyes and see the real schmoe inside, the true self that most people tried so desperately to hide. The dark brown eyes that stared back at me now revealed nothing, but I did feel the nearly overwhelming urge to reach out and scratch her behind one ear.

My gaze shifted to her high cheekbones and narrow face, and a sudden image popped into my mind.

"You're not . . ." I fought down the smile that tugged at my lips. "You can't be . . ."

She stiffened. "A were-Chihuahua. Yeah. So what?"

"So . . ." So she had the biggest, brightest brown eyes I'd ever seen. "So . . . nothing. I've just never met an actual were-Chihuahua before."

"There aren't too many of us these days. In the past, we were practically annihilated by all the other meat-eating weres who are so much bigger and stronger and nondiscriminating when it comes to a midnight snack. But thanks to modern technology"—she held up her backpack—"we can all live together in peace and harmony. Or at least minimal tolerance."

"What have you got in there? A can of Werewolf-B-Gone? Mace for Were-Tigers?"

"A Glock and handful of silver bullets."

"That'll work, too." I eyed her. "So you know Jack?"

She gave me the once-over. "Who wants to know?"

"His sister—er, that is, his sister's cousin's cousin."

"Wouldn't that be his cousin, too?"

"Well, uh, yeah. His cousin. I'm his cousin. I really need to see him. It's a family emergency." I glanced at my watch again. Forty-five minutes and counting. "I can't believe he's not home by now."

"He isn't coming home."

"What do you mean?"

"He's never home now. He's with *her*. They're practically living together."

"With who?"

"The human." Instead of saying the word with distaste, like most of her supernatural brethren, her words were filled with envy. "He's with her *all* of the time. They spend the night at her place and then he follows her to work the next day."

"But he has to sleep."

"She stashes him someplace safe."

"And you know this because?"

"I caught them together. I was out picking up a pizza and I saw them. I couldn't help myself. I followed them to the place where she works. And then I went back the next day to ask questions. She's a resident at the medical examiner's office and she's there from sunup to sundown. She obviously stashed him someplace inside because he went in and didn't come out until that evening. They both came out." Her eyes grew bright. "Together." She blinked. "They did the same thing the next night. And the next. You probably think it's creepy that I've been watching them, don't you?"

More like pathetic. "Not at all. You were obviously hurt."

"And worried. Up until I spotted them together, I hadn't seen him for days. I didn't know if he'd been taken out by an SOB or if he'd fallen through his glass dining room table and maybe pierced himself to death." She shook her head. "I couldn't stand the thought of something happening to him. Jack's so special. He's so . . ."

"Self-centered? Condescending? Shallow?"

"Sweet. Handsome. *Sexy.* I've never met another man like him."

Her eyes grew even brighter and my chest hitched. I so understood the tears because I felt like bawling myself right about now. Forty minutes and counting.

"I can't believe he's seeing someone." A tear squeezed past her thick, dark lashes and slid down her cheek.

"Don't do that."

"What?"

"The crying. I'm not good with people who cry."

"I'm not crying." She wiped at her cheek. "You're the one who's crying."

"*I'm* not crying." I wiped at my own cheek. Whoa, I was crying. Empathy crying, of course. Crying was useless. A waste of time and precious bodily fluids.

Okay, so that sounded kind of gross, but it was definitely a waste of time.

I sniffed and wiped at the traitorous moisture. "So how long were you and Jack seeing each other?"

"Three years and fourteen days."

I arched an eyebrow. "No hours?"

She glanced at her watch. "Six hours and thirty-two minutes."

"That was a joke."

"Oh." She sniffled.

"Listen, I know a breakup can be tough. But people survive."

"I know."

"You'll get through this. A breakup, however messy or unexpected, isn't the end of anything. It's just the beginning."

She sniffled and wiped at her eyes. "We, um, didn't actually *break up*. I mean, we did, but we didn't."

"I'm not following you."

"We weren't really *together* together. I just liked him."

"And he didn't like you?" I know I sounded shocked, but we're talking *Jack*. His only requirement when it came to females was a vagina. And my oldest brother, Rob, and I had seriously debated *that* after seeing him last year with a Broadway dancer named Nick. Short for Nicole, or so Jack said. But judging from the size of her pecs, I'd had my doubts.

"He doesn't actually know me. I mean, he knows who I am and that I live in the apartment below him. I think. But he doesn't really *know* me. In the sexual sense, that is. Come to think of it, he doesn't know me in the friend sense, either. We've never actually had a conversation. There was this one time that he was coming in and I was going out and we ran into each other and sort of had a moment."

"A moment?"

"You know, one of those times when you stare into someone's eyes and it's like *hell*o? This is Mr. Right."

Ty Bonner's image popped into my head before I could push it back out and certain parts of my anatomy tingled. I knew, all right. Boy, did I ever.

Not that Ty was Mr. Right. More like Mr. Right Now. As in temporary. As in it *ain't gonna happen, sistah*.

I glanced at my watch again. "The medical examiner's office, you say? You wouldn't happen to know where that is?" She nodded and I smiled. "Thanks."

She disappeared inside and came back a full two minutes later with an address scribbled on a piece of paper. "Here you go."

"Thanks." I snatched the paper from her hands and bolted down the steps.

"I hope everything turns out okay." Her voice followed me and I stopped. "With your emergency," she added when I turned and caught her sad puppy dog stare.

"Thanks." Before I could stop myself, I'd ripped off a blank portion of the paper she'd given me. I begged a pen and then scribbled the phone number for Dead End Dating. "What did you say your name was?"

"I didn't, but it's Rachel. Rachel Sanchez."

"Here, Rachel."

"What's this?"

"The new beginning. It's the contact info for this great new dating service I just started—er, that is I'm just starting to hear about. Phenomenal things. The owner is this totally hip vampire with fab taste in clothes. She knows *everything* when it comes to hooking up singles."

"A *vampire* matchmaker? You've got to be kidding."

"Hey, if the fangs fit . . ."

"Vampires don't date."

"Not usually, but we've evolved. I date all the time." I wish. "Anyhow, you really should give it a try. You won't be sorry."

She shook her head. "I don't know. What could a vampire know about hooking up a were?"

"I happen to know for a fact that the owner, the totally fab vampire, is in the process of hooking up the entire chapter of the Connecticut NUNS."

"How do you know that?"

"I've got a friend who works for her." Hey, Evie and I were friends.

She seemed to think for a second. "A werewolf is a lot easier to match up than a were-Chihuahua."

A girl could only hope.

"I wouldn't worry about the details. They give a money back guarantee."

"It's not the money."

Be still my beatless heart.

"I just don't know if I'm ready," she added.

"I know it seems really soon, but it's better not to waste any time before jumping back into the dating scene."

"It's been a really long time since I've been out with anyone."

"How long is really long?"

"About ten."

"That's nothing. Why, I've had—I mean, they've had clients who've been dateless much longer than a measly ten years."

"That's ten dog years."

"Oh."

"And it's been even longer since I've actually had sex."

I fought down a wave of panic and smiled. "So what? There's more to life than sex." What was I saying? Sex defined my race. Born vampires stopped aging when they lost their virginity. Their search for an eternity mate hinged on fertility ratings and orgasm quotients. I didn't know if it was the same for were-Chihuahuas, but from my limited dealings with Viola I was willing to bet that sex figured pretty hefty in there somewhere.

"More than sex?"

"Sure. There's mutual interests and companionship."

She seemed to think again. "Well, it would be sort of nice to have someone to share a pizza with."

"There you go. So give Dead End Dating a call and ask for Evie. She practically runs the place." At least while I was *this* close to Death Row. "She'll be glad to help you."

"Thanks." She gave me a grateful smile. "I owe you."

"No, I owe *you*." Or I would if Rachel's surveillance panned out and I caught up with Jack.

Six

❤ ❤ ❤

Dead bodies don't normally creep me out. I mean, I *am* a fearless, bloodsucking vampire.

All right, already. So I don't really do death and destruction all that well and I haven't been to a funeral in . . . well, I've never actually been to one (add immortal to the fearless, bloodsucking definition above), so I might have been a little creeped out.

I stared into the square window cut into the massive metal door and my hand stalled. Large metal drawers lined the walls from floor to ceiling. A row of stretchers sported large, black zippered bags. The smell of disinfectant burned my nostrils.

"Are you sure she's in there?" I asked the orderly who'd led me down the hallway.

"Saw her check in for her shift myself." He peered over my shoulder. "There she is." He signaled to the only upright human in the entire room. She was a small redhead wearing a white lab coat and an ID badge that read MANDY DUPREE, M.D., RESIDENT/FORENSIC PATHOLOGY.

"Maybe you could tap on the glass and get her to come out here?"

"She just clocked in. She doesn't get a break yet and she can't leave the room unattended."

I took in a deep breath and immediately regretted it. Not only did the dead bodies creep me out, but the dead smell wasn't helping the situation.

I expelled the breath, made a *no more breathing* promise to myself, and punched the red buzzer next to the door. Dr. Mandy glanced up and I waved. A puzzled expression creased her face as she crossed the room and punched a button. The door swung open.

"Sorry to bother you. You're the Mandy who's dating Jack Marchette, right?" I asked the question, but I didn't really need to bother. The moment her bright green gaze collided with mine, I knew the answer. She wasn't just dating Jack. She was desperately in love with him and she felt certain he returned those feelings. He'd surprised her with a puppy for her birthday two weeks ago and last night he'd surprised her by licking her—

Whoops. I so didn't need to know *that*. I blinked and focused my attention on the fine arch of her left eyebrow. Hmmm . . . nice wax job.

"Why do you want to know?"

"I'm looking for Jack. You do know him, right?"

She eyed me a moment longer before she finally

nodded. "Jack's in the lounge getting me some coffee."

"Jack's getting you coffee? *Jack? Jack Marchette?*" See, here's the thing. My brother loves women, and he's obviously really good at it because he usually has one at his beck and call twenty-four/seven. *Not* the other way around.

"Who are you?" she asked me.

"I'm his . . ." I thought about giving her the cousin spiel, but Jack wasn't likely to play along since he didn't yet know the trouble I was in. "I'm his sister."

A smile erupted on her face. "You're Lil?" At my nod, she grasped my hand and gave it a warm squeeze. "I've heard so much about you. It's so good to finally meet you in person."

"You've heard about me?"

It was her turn to nod. "Of course, silly. You and your brothers. Jack's really crazy about all of you."

"He is?"

"You guys are all he talks about."

"We are?"

"Of course. He's such a family man."

"He is?" Okay, so like I knew I was asking dumb questions, but this was one of those life-changing moments. My entire family unit as I knew it, complete with a pain-in-the-ass brother who couldn't stand me, was disintegrating right before my eyes.

"His strong sense of family is one of the things that attracted me to him. He's so loyal and protective and—there he is!"

I turned just as Mandy pressed the button and the door swung open. Jack stood there, a steaming cup of coffee in one hand and a long-stemmed red rose in the other.

Forget life-changing. This was a *Twilight Zone* moment.

"Hey, baby." He handed Mandy the coffee and the rose and gave her a lingering kiss.

I cleared my throat and the kiss ended. Jack turned. His expression went from dreamy to puzzled. "Lil? What are you doing here?"

"I'm being hunted by the cops for chopping some guy into little pieces."

He grinned. "Funny, sis."

"No, I'm serious."

"Lil can't stand the sight of blood." As soon as Jack said it, he and Mandy both burst out laughing.

"But she's a vampire." The statement seemed to make them laugh that much harder.

"Hey, I'm serious." I frowned and tapped Jack on the shoulder. "Hello?"

"No, really." Jack wiped at his eyes. "Why are you here?"

"That's why I'm here. I'm being hunted and I need your help."

Jack shook his head, but Mandy sobered up. "I think she's serious, Jack."

"Murder? That's the craziest thing I've ever heard."

"You and me both," I told him. "Regardless, it's

true. I'm on the lam. A fugitive. A *murder* suspect."
My vision clouded and I blinked frantically. Hello?
I was not crying now. Here. In front of Jack. The
last time I'd let loose the waterworks, he'd laughed
at me. Then again, I'd been five and he'd been seven
and he'd shattered the head of my favorite porcelain
doll.

The thought made my vision blur all the more. I
sniffled. "So can you help me?"

"What do you need?"

No laughing. Definitely a good sign. I swallowed.
"I need cash. Lots of it."

While Jack headed off to the ATM, I chatted with
Mandy while she undressed and prepped a body for
temporary storage until the scheduled autopsy.

Talk about creepy, and slow. The second hand on
the clock seemed to drag as Mandy arranged and
zipped and my muscles started to ache. While I couldn't
see outside because we were in a secure, windowless
room, I could feel the sun creeping toward the hori-
zon. My strength drained away and my eyelids drooped
and I silently begged for Jack to hurry the hell up.

"You look like shit," he told me when he finally
walked back into the room just a precious fifteen
minutes before sunrise.

Okay, I knew I wasn't about to win any Miss Vamp
America contest, but I didn't look *that* bad. "Geez,
thanks a lot. I love you, too." I opened the thick envelope he handed me.

"I drained the cash from four different machines. I hope it's enough."

"It's plenty." My eyes met his. "I owe you."

"Forget it." His gaze narrowed as he eyed me. "You really should lie down."

"I will just as soon as I find someplace safe." I glanced at the wall clock. Thirteen minutes and counting. Yikes! I stuffed the envelope into my pocket. "I've got to get out of here."

"You'll never make it," Mandy said as she slid one of the drawers closed with a loud *clunk*.

"I saw a small hotel just a few blocks over."

"Mandy and I went there," Jack added, "to, well, you know, and we spent fifteen minutes at the registration desk alone."

Can you say too much information? "I'll make it," I told him. When he shook his head and shrugged, I added, "I have to make it."

"Not necessarily." He and Mandy exchanged glances and the meaning hit me like a punch to the stomach.

"I know what you're thinking and don't," I told him, but he said the words anyway.

"You could crash here."

Ewwwww.

At my horrified expression, he smiled. "Man, but you're squeamish."

"Damn straight I'm squeamish. We're in a room full of dead people. No offense," I told Mandy.

"Sis, you're a vampire." He walked over to one of the drawers and tugged the handle. It slid free, exposing an empty drawer that consisted of a body-length stainless steel table. "Get over it."

"I'm a born vampire. Meaning I've never kicked the bucket."

"You're still dead by society's standards."

"That is totally beside the point."

"Being?"

"They're *dead*."

"And you will be too if you don't find a place to crash for tonight. Don't be such a wuss. I've done it." He gazed adoringly at Mandy, who'd turned to retrieve some clean sheets from a large utility shelf on the far side of the room.

I know, right? My *brother. Gazing*.

"You're totally freaking me out," I told him.

"There's nothing freaky about it. It's just a sliding coffin. Our kind have slept in them for years. Hell, Dad still does."

"Dad's eccentric, and I'm not talking about the drawer. I'm talking about you and Mandy." I lowered my voice and glanced at Mandy. She didn't skip a beat as she retrieved the linens and carefully refolded one that had come loose from the top of the stack. "Think about it, Jack. You've gone from crashing on fab Egyptian cotton sheets and a pillow-top mattress to crawling into a morgue drawer. For a woman." A *human* woman, I added silently.

He smiled. "Mandy's a resident."

"And?"

"And she puts in a lot of hours, which doesn't really facilitate a relationship. So we work around it. If I crash here during her shift, that means she gets to kiss me good night and good morning, and I don't have to waste time going home."

"You live ten minutes away."

"Ten minutes away from Mandy is ten minutes too long."

Okay, so now he was *really* freaking me out.

I checked his forehead. Cool as usual. Not that vampires could actually get sick, but I had to make sure. Because if it wasn't some bizarre virus affecting only macho, condescending, womanizing male vampires, then it could only mean . . .

I felt my smile spread from ear to ear. "You're in love."

My expression was infectious and he beamed. "You bet."

"Do Mom and Dad know? I mean, I know they know about Mandy, but did you say that you—"

"No," he cut in. "Not yet. I told them about her and I've set up a meeting to introduce them to her parents. We figured we would tell them then."

"At tea?" At his questioning glance, I added, "I overheard them when I was hiding out in the pool house."

"They were talking about meeting us for tea?" An anxious light fired his eyes. "What were they saying? Are they coming? They have to come. I mean, I know they don't *have* to, but they have to. They're my parents, right? They should want to meet the woman that I want to spend eternity with—"

"Relax," I cut in. "They're coming, but they're not exactly happy about it."

Relief swept his features. "They don't have to be happy. They just need to show up."

"What about me? Can I come, too?" If I wasn't dead or playing bitch to a cell mate named Big Mama.

I forced aside the last thought and clung to my new-found hope. Money. Safe place. After life was good.

"Why would you want to come? You hate tea," Jack told me.

"True, but I love seeing Mom freaked when it isn't my fault."

He grinned and eyed the stainless-steel tray. "Are you going to get on or not?"

"Not." Even as the word slipped from my lips, I knew I had no other choice. The sun was just coming up. I couldn't risk walking out of the building right now. I had to crash here. I could look for an empty room, or maybe a broom closet, but both would be too accessible while I was at my weakest.

They didn't call it the sleep of the dead for nothing. Once I zonked out, I would be completely vulnerable, and if I did manage to wake up at the first sign of danger, I would be too weak to defend myself.

I needed someplace that was dark and quiet and, most of all, secure until sunset. And I needed it right now.

"Can I at least get a blanket or something?"

"Mandy?" He called Mandy over. "Lil wants a blanket."

"We don't keep blankets on hand, but I've got these." She held up the sheets. When I nodded, she added, "I could get a few more and we could double them up to make it a little softer." When I nodded, she smiled and turned toward the utility shelf. "Give me just a sec."

"I can't believe I'm doing this," I told Jack as I spread out the half dozen sheets Mandy handed me before climbing onto the stainless steel table.

"It's really not that bad. And I'll be right next to you."

"No, you won't," Mandy told him as she came up behind him. "They put a suicide in your usual spot." She slid her hand up his arm. "But I cleared out a new spot for you right near the autopsy room. And"— she smiled—"I even brought you your favorite pillow from home." She handed him the white wedge of fluff.

"Aw, thanks, babe. That's so sweet."

Like I know the whole exchange sounds sort of creepy what with the whole morgue setting and all, but I felt a warmth in my chest anyway.

Not that I was in any way condoning my brother's relationship with a human. He should have fallen for a born vampire who could give him baby vamps and, more important, give my parents some grandchildren to take the heat off of *moi*.

But, hey, I'm a matchmaker. Love is what I do.

"Here are a few more sheets to cover with," Mandy said. "Don't worry. You'll be safe here. The only time the drawers are opened is when a body's being transferred or taken to autopsy, and it's part of my job to sign everyone in and out."

"So you're the drawer opener?"

She smiled. "Among other things. I dictate who gets put where and when. I also assist in the autopsy room as part of my residency. That's how I met your brother. He was a car crash DOA. We bagged and tagged him and put him in that top drawer right over there. That was early in the morning when I'd just arrived. Later that day, I was doing my evening check when I heard the drawer open. I looked up and there he was. It was love at first sight."

"That's after she passed out from shock," Jack said.

"Jack revived me and explained the situation."

"And you were cool with it?"

"Of course. I've always suspected that vampires exist. I've even fantasized about them. Jack's my fantasy come true."

"That's so sweet, babe."

"You're sweet." She snuggled his arm and inhaled. "Literally. He's so yummy. I could smell him forever and never get tired of it."

"You can *smell* him?"

"I couldn't at first, but after we . . ." Her words faded away, but her thoughts didn't and I found myself glancing at the clock again, eager to focus on something other than the vivid image of Mandy and my brother and—

"Would you look at the time?" I blurted. I snatched the pillow from Jack's hands and stretched out on my back. "You don't mind, do you?"

"Yeah, I do."

"Love hurts, bro. Love hurts." I wedged the pillow up under my head and tried to ignore the cold feel of the tray seeping through the sheets.

"Pretty comfy, huh?" Jack asked.

"You're deranged."

"Just close your eyes and sleep."

"I'll close my eyes," I said as he started to slide the drawer in. "But I can't imagine I'll get any sleep."

"You're a vampire. Trust me, you'll sleep."

"Says you," I replied just as the drawer slid completely shut. Metal clicked. Blackness settled around me. My heart chugged like a freight train racing for the next stop.

Ka-thunk, ka-thunk, ka-thunk . . .

Sleep? Yeah, right.

I was in the morgue, for Damien's sake. On the run for a murder I didn't commit. I had no money of my own. On top of that, the damned tray was as hard as a rock. And cold.

I shifted for a more comfortable position and forced myself to take a mental detour away from the misery of my predicament. Instead I headed for my triple M fantasy—Mexican beach, megalicious bounty hunter, and mango margarita.

Now that was more like it. I had sand. I had rays. I had a really killer Italian leather bikini.

Ty loomed over me, blotting out the warm sun as his hands trailed over my body. Leather fell away and the bikini landed in a heap next to me. He reached for the frosty glass and the mango concoction dribbled onto my bare stomach. The sticky juice slid over my heated flesh.

He smiled again and then he leaned down. His tongue flicked my . . . *Zzzzzzzzzz!*

Seven
❤ ❤ ❤

"The decedent is a twenty-six-year-old white female transient found in an alley near Fifty-second Street by other transients. Apparent cause of death was strangulation."

The voice slid under the cover of sleep and wiggled its way down next to me. Ugh. My neighbor was watching another *CSI* rerun.

Now I like *CSI* as much as the next person. Sort of. I mean, my receptionist, Evie, is somewhat of a junkie and I have to admit that I don't totally understand that. But overall, I think it's all right. In a morbid, depressing sort of way. I mean, geez, a dead body here, a dead body there. It's enough to make the average person rethink the whole people-are-basically-good-if-you-can-get-past-all-the-crap concept.

I desperately needed to drag my ass out of bed and knock on the wall. But exhaustion still tugged at my arms and legs and the only thing I really wanted to do was stay right where I was, my feet nice and toasty under the sheets.

"There don't appear to be any ligature marks on the victim's throat."

Duh. She didn't die of strangulation, buddy. If it were that easy, the ratings wouldn't be so high.

"Vessels around the mouth and nose appear intact."

Another big surprise. The nails, guy. Check under the nails.

"There are no apparent signs of bruising on the extremities. Nails are well manicured and appear intact."

Atta boy.

"Are you sure this victim was ruled a strangulation?"

"That's what the file says, doc. Said the body had all the classic signs."

"To a rookie, maybe. If this woman was strangled, I'm Britney Spears. There's something else going on here."

Uh, *yeah.*

A camera clicked and the flash *cha-chunk*ed. Once. Twice. Loud. Talk about a building association meeting just waiting to happen.

"Let's get ready to open her up and take a look." The doctor traced the Y path of incision with a blunt edge. (I definitely needed to get a life, right? I shouldn't know this stuff.) "Looks good," the man said. "Let's make the first cut." He touched the tip of the scalpel to the victim's breastbone and white-hot pain rushed through the victim, straight to her brain.

Wait a second.

That was *my* brain.

My eyes snapped open and I found myself staring up into the face of a middle-aged man with glasses and a receding hairline.

He screamed and I screamed.

Yeah, I know. Not a totally vampy thing to do, but we're talking a *scalpel*.

Blood oozed from the small cut as I scrambled from the stainless steel table. Metal clanged and instruments scattered.

"Holy shit!" The man holding the camera lost his grip as I hit my feet. The Polaroid sailed to the floor and shattered. "She's alive."

Even more, she was *naked*.

Like, I'm totally proud of my body, but I don't make a habit of walking around *au naturel*, and so this freaked me out almost as much as getting sliced and diced.

Frantic, my gaze darted around until I saw a stack of folded sheets. In the blink of an eye, I'd wrapped myself in one and was desperately looking for an exit while the pathologist and his assistant stood there, stunned. Then my brother rushed in, Dr. Mandy on his heels.

"I'm so sorry," Mandy blurted. "I was on break when they came to get the homeless woman that was brought in yesterday. They misread the files and took you and—I'm just so sorry. Ohmigod," she shrieked. "You're bleeding!"

"It's all right, babe." Jack slid his arm around her. "It wasn't your fault."

"It was. I should have been more careful, but I was really dragging. I needed coffee and they're not supposed to check anyone out unless I'm there."

"It's somebody else's mistake. You did your best."

"You're not mad?"

"Why would I be mad? You didn't do anything. You can't help it if someone else breaks the rules. You're still as conscientious, as dedicated as ever."

"That's so sweet."

"You're sweet."

"No, you're sweet."

"Excuse me?" I hiked the sheet up more securely under my arms. "I hate to interrupt this warm fuzzy moment, but I'm naked *and* bleeding, and these guys want to chop me into little pieces."

"Oh, they don't chop you up. They just open you up and remove the internal organs."

"Oh. Well, that makes me feel much better. Not!" I stepped toward my brother. "I was on the sharp end of a scalpel while I was asleep and totally vulnerable."

"That's a touchy situation for us," Jack told Mandy. "Lil's upset."

"And mad."

"But not at you," Jack assured Mandy. "She's just upset in general."

"Your ass. You said I was safe."

"I thought you were." Mandy sniffled. "I'm really sorry."

Her eyes brightened and before I knew it, I heard myself say, "It's okay."

"Really?"

"Really. I'm sure you didn't purposely set me up for an autopsy. That would totally kill your chances at impressing my folks."

She smiled. "Exactly."

"She didn't have a pulse," the receding hairline said, his trembling voice drawing everyone's attention. He'd finally zoned back to the situation at hand. "I checked myself and she didn't have a pulse and now she's talking and bleeding and *talking*."

"This is some weird shit," the camera guy muttered. "Twisted."

"She had no body temperature, either. I checked that myself, too." The hairline shook his head as if trying to make some sense out of everything. "She was cold. Ice cold."

"You try sleeping in a refrigerator," I said. His eyes widened and he stumbled backward.

"I—I have to call security."

"Lil," my brother said. "Could you do something please?"

Me? What was I supposed to do—oh, yeah.

I took a deep, calming breath, ignored the burning in my chest, and fixed my gaze on receding hairline who was backing his way toward the door.

"Don't move," I said as I stared deep into his fear-filled eyes. He stopped. His expression went from shocked to surprised. "You're not really here. You're in the lounge taking a nap and all of this"—I motioned around us—"it's all a dream." I smiled and gave him a seductive look. His features eased and a hungry light fired his gaze. "A fantasy. An X-rated fantasy."

The guy *had* seen me naked.

"W—what are you?" the camera guy mumbled.

"I already told you." I shifted my attention to him where he cowered between two large metal shelves. "A fantasy."

"You're not *my* fantasy . . ." His words faded along with the brightness of his gaze. I got a glimpse of a skinny woman with mousy brown hair and lots of freckles. His wife.

My own fear eased and my heart gave a little double thump.

"I'm what happens after one too many salami sandwiches." Okay, so I got a glimpse of today's lunch, too.

"You mean, like indigestion?" the camera guy asked.

My brother snickered and I shot him a shut-up-or-I'll-make-forever-seem-like-a-*really*-long-time look.

"Exactly," I told the man. It wasn't very glamorous, but hey, I was a matchmaker, not a home wrecker. Besides, you had to give props to a guy who fantasized about his significant other.

"At least they waited until evening for the autopsy," I said a few minutes later as Mandy led me into the ladies' locker room, after she'd doused my half-inch cut with antiseptic.

I know. Vampire. Immortal. But Mandy was

freaked and I didn't blame her. I was sort of frantic myself even though I knew that twenty-four hours from now I would be back to my usual perfect self.

"Don't forget these." Jack ducked his head into the locker room and set the suitcases he'd retrieved from the Hummer just inside the door. He winked at Mandy and then the door closed.

Still wrapped in the sheet, I sat on a bench while Mandy grabbed one of my suitcases and hauled it over to me.

"A few minutes more and I would have been history," I added.

"Dr. Morrow likes to stay ahead of schedule." She set the suitcase on the bench and unlatched it. "He's a real go-getter and he's gunning for a promotion. You weren't scheduled until tomorrow morning. The transient, I mean. She wasn't scheduled until then, but he figured he would get her out of the way this evening before he called it a day." She eyed the sheet I clutched around me. "I'm really sorry about your clothes."

"I've got plenty more." I swallowed against the lump in my throat, flipped open the suitcase, and retrieved a pair of jeans and a sequined Guess T-shirt.

"Take your time. The second shift doesn't check in for a few more hours." She flashed me an apologetic smile and left me to change.

A few minutes later, I met Mandy and my brother in the hallway.

"You can stay at my apartment," Mandy told me as we headed for one of the rear exits. "I've got a large storage closet that's pretty dark."

"My apartment will probably be too risky since I'm your brother," Jack added. "The police are sure to check me out."

I'd thought the same thing. But if they met the were-Chihuahua or anyone else who might have seen Jack and Mandy, they would be paying her a visit as well. Which meant chilling in Mandy's large, dark storage closet might not be the smartest thing to do, either.

I shook my head. "Thanks, but no thanks." I handed Jack the keys to my parents' Hummer and patted the ATM envelope stuffed into my front jeans pocket. "I've got cash now, and the night is young. I'll find someplace until this mess gets sorted out."

Jack gave my shoulder a squeeze. "I'm sure if you lay low long enough they'll find the real killer."

Maybe.

And maybe they would just keep looking for me.

The last thought followed me down the back alley and around to the side of the building where a cab waited. Darkness had fallen, and the city had come alive in a blaze of lights.

"Where to?" the driver asked once I'd stowed my luggage and climbed into the backseat.

The question swam in my head for several minutes as I contemplated my options. I couldn't go to my family. And I couldn't go to my friends. I could go to an out-of-the-way hotel room for now. While I would more than likely be safe, there was still a chance that I would wake up to find myself handcuffed and in custody.

If I woke up at all.

The cut on my chest burned and I shuddered. I could run and try to hide, all right, but there was no guarantee that I would be *safe*.

Unless . . .

"Lady? You okay?"

"No." I shook my head. "I'm not. Not yet." But I might be, with a little help from a certain tall, dark, and megadelicious bounty hunter.

Eight

❤ ❤ ❤

"Are you sure this is the right place?"

"You said Washington Street, lady. This is Washington Street."

I stared at the worn numbers printed next to the large steel door that led to what had once been a massive warehouse. My stomach clenched because I knew I was about to realize my worst fear.

Okay, so it wasn't my *worst*. But it ranked right up there with pale blue polyester pants, a management position at Midnight Moe's, and vamp detectors at Barney's.

We're talking a ten on my holy-shit-o-meter.

See, Ty is a major babe. Good looking. Sexy. Tasty. Whenever I'm around him, I tend to let my desperate need for a few fantastic orgasms do my thinking for me. Not a good thing since I've given up meaningless sex and mindless biting, and that's all Ty and I could ever share on account of his being a made vampire and I'm a born vampire and, well, it's just one of those tragic Shakespearean things. Forget taking him home for the weekly hunt. My parents would stake first and talk later. As for me . . . I am so totally saving myself for The One.

I know. Major goober alert. But after five hundred years of instant gratification, I want to give eternity a try.

And so Ty was definitely O-U-T.

But while I knew all the reasons why it shouldn't happen, I seemed to forget about them whenever he and I were in the same room. Or floating midair and watching kinky sex acts (a story all by itself).

So you can see how desperate I was to even consider cohabitating with him. But I needed a safe place and someone who didn't top the police's she's-gotta-be-here list. Ty, with his mucho connections to the New York Police Department, not to mention the FBI, surely cruised below everybody's radar. The guy hunted criminals for a living. No way would the police think he might harbor one.

A desperate, sex-starved female vamp with fantabulous taste and a weakness for violence? A great big fat yes, as it turned out.

I'd called and explained the situation to him (in great detail, complete with several surprised gasps and lots of justified indignation). And, okay, so I'd cried a little, too, but I've been under major stress and so it only stands to reason that I would be understandably *upset*. We're talking murder.

He believed me, of course, even before the water-works. How could he not? We're, like, mind-fused. See, ever since I'd tasted his blood, I'd found myself mentally linked to him. I could hear his thoughts when he wanted me to, and he could hear mine.

I wasn't one hundred percent comfortable with this new ability and so I'd pretended otherwise and blurted out the whole story. I'd asked for a place to stay. He'd agreed and given me his address.

Turns out, he lived in the heart of New York's meatpacking district. I know, right? It sounded totally rough and tough (which fit Ty to the proverbial T), but the place had recently evolved into one of the trendier sections of the city. The district was now home to gourmet restaurants, art galleries, fab boutiques, and even a few name designers, including one of my ultra-faves, Carlos Miele over on West Fourteenth. We're talking *chic*.

And so on the ride over, I'd actually entertained the possibility that Ty wasn't the yang to my yin. Maybe, just *maybe,* he was merely a (horrified gasp) retro sexual (think metro sexual with oodles of trendy style) masquerading as a cool and macho bounty hunter.

While I'm ridiculously attracted to cool and macho, guys with pedicures and more hair products than me just don't punch my buttons. I could so totally room with a retro sexual for an unspecified period of time (until I could figure my way out of this mess and prove my innocence) and keep my fangs to myself. No *problemo*.

But a bona fide, hard-edged, rugged, *naturally* sexy alpha vamp?

Problem.

"Ain't no stars out tonight," the cabbie said as my nerves started to buzz and the initial panic I'd felt when I'd first called Ty welled up inside me. "It's kinda dark."

"Very." Not that it hindered me. My vamp vision cut through the shadows and drank in the monstrous warehouse.

Obviously the chic stopped several feet away, because this small section of Washington Street looked virtually untouched by New York's trendsetters. The porch light had been knocked out. Shadows crowded near the large, garagelike door. Rust caked the hinges. Graffiti covered the metal walls. The place screamed alpha.

Big problem.

I took a deep, easy breath, paid the cabbie, and climbed from the backseat.

"You want me to wait here, lady?" he asked as he retrieved my luggage from the trunk. "In case you need to make a quick getaway?"

I swallowed a *yes* and shook my head. "No, um, thanks." I turned to stare at the building again. "I'll be fine."

Or so I desperately hoped.

"I don't mind waiting," the guy—Norm, according to his license hanging on the partition—told me. "You're a really pretty lady and it just wouldn't be right to leave you out here all by yourself."

Okay, so I knew he was just responding to my vamp charm, but there was something really sweet about the offer.

I stared into his eyes and read the details swimming in his head. Norm Walker. Fifty-seven years old. Proud father of five. Even prouder grandfather of eight. Happily married to one Earline Walker, his high school sweetheart. While I was the prettiest thing since sliced bread, Earline had given birth to his kids and cleaned his house, and made pot roast once a week for the past thirty-eight years.

Does Norm totally rock or what?

I smiled. "I'll be fine." *I will,* I added silently, or so I hoped. I gave Norm an *I'm just a really great dream and you'll forget all about me tomorrow* look, gathered up my luggage and walked to the front door.

"You sure?" Norm leaned out the window.

"Positive." *Go home,* I willed silently. *And don't forget to stop and pick up some flowers for Earline. And candy. And offer to give her a foot massage.*

Hey, we're talking five kids *and* pot roast. It was the least I could do.

"Well, okay then." Norm didn't look very convinced, but another long, lingering glance from me and he finally nodded, slid back across the seat, and gunned the engine.

I ignored the urge to turn and bolt after the cab as it rolled away.

So what if Ty wasn't a retro sexual? There was still hope. Maybe he just looked cool because I didn't really *know* him. Sure, I knew he smelled good and felt good (all hard lines and solid muscle) and kissed good and had a very tasty blood type, but what did I *really* know?

Seeing him decked out in all his bounty hunter coolness was a lot different than seeing him in his natural element. What if the hot, sexy bounty hunter was just an illusion? A carefully constructed image to hide the fact that he was (please, please, please) a total slob?

What if there were empty bottles of blood sitting everywhere? What if he walked around burping all the time? Better yet, what if he answered the door wearing a wife beater, baggy boxers, and mismatched socks?

I pressed the intercom button next to the door, and Ty buzzed me inside. The warehouse was three stories, and Ty lived on the top floor. I followed a narrow hallway to a freight elevator at the rear of the building and headed for the third floor.

Ty answered the door wearing a pair of worn, faded jeans and nothing else.

Uh-oh.

The luggage slipped from my hands and landed at my feet. My mouth went dry.

He had broad shoulders, muscular arms, and a six-pack that would make Brad Pitt (à la Troy) envious. His dark, shoulder-length hair hung around his face in casual disarray, as if he'd been running his hands through it. A small scar bisected the edge of one eyebrow and my fingers still tingled from the feel of it. (Yesss, I'd felt it before, but, unfortunately, in a totally nonsexual situation.) Wait a second. Did I say *un*fortunately? Kill the prefix. He'd kept his distance and I'd kept mine. *Fortunate*, no *un* involved.

His blue gaze was bright and electric as it met mine. My hands immediately trembled. My tummy flipped. Electricity fairly sizzled in the air between us and my nipples immediately perked up. Oh, and a few other areas snapped to attention, as well.

I blinked against a sudden rush of tears and his image swam in front of me.

"Hey," his deep voice slid into my ears and one strong hand touched my shoulder, "it's okay. This is all just a mistake. A bad mistake."

"You're telling me." I sniffled and blinked his image back into focus. Bad move. As the details grew clearer, my panic mounted, along with my lust. How in the world was I going to do this? I was standing on his doorstep, about to waltz inside and share the same space with him—*the* mega hot, half-naked made vampire who'd inspired more than one erotic fantasy with his whole bad ass, alphalicious cowboy image—and I wasn't going to bite him. Yeah. Right.

My eyes misted again.

"Take it easy." Before I could so much as sniffle, he pulled me inside the apartment and led me over to a small living area. "There's no reason to get upset." He eased me down onto a leather sofa. "We can figure a way out of this."

We could? Of course we could. We were mature adults. There were oodles of things we could do to deal with the situation. We could respect each other's personal space. We could sleep in separate rooms. He could wear clothes. I could wear a blindfold.

"I put in a call to this guy I know in the department." He walked back to the door to retrieve my luggage. "He'll give us a hand."

"Does he know how to braid a garlic necklace?" Wait a sec. Ty was a vamp, meaning he couldn't wear the blasted thing. Talk about a no-win situation.

He set my bags inside the doorway and shut and locked the door. "What did you say?"

"Never mind." I settled on the soft leather while Ty plopped down in a nearby chair. Far, far away, or so I was trying to convince myself. The scent of him—fresh air and freedom and a hint of danger—teased my nostrils.

Yum.

Wait a second. No yum. This was not a yum situation and Ty was not going to sweep me off my feet and we were not going to have wild, monkey sex on the comfy-looking bed sitting across the room. And we certainly weren't going to have a major drink fest to go with it.

This was the opposite of *yum*. Bad situation. Wrong man. Major trouble. *Ick.*

I forced myself not to take one more traitorous breath. I was going to deal with this and make the best of it. So what if Ty was alpha to the bone? I didn't have to fall for him. In fact, I could so totally hook him up with Viola, who was practically salivating for a rough and tough macho male.

One down, twenty-six to go.

Then again, Viola *had* specifically requested a human, which put Ty completely out of the running and off limits.

Thankfully.

I frowned at the sudden relief that swamped me and shifted my attention to the massive apartment. The ceiling dangled a good twenty feet above us. Floor to ceiling windows consumed one wall. We sat smack-dab in the middle of the room where a living area had been set up with a dark blue leather couch and two black leather chairs. A chrome and glass coffee table sat between them. A matching chrome and glass entertainment center stood sentry nearby covered with enough electronics to make the average human male orgasm on the spot. A big-screen television sat next to it.

To my left was the kitchen area, complete with stainless steel appliances and an island stove. To my right, the bedroom. A massive king-size bed dominated the corner. A deep, sapphire blue comforter covered the mattress. A half dozen black and blue–clad pillows had been stacked near the headboard. It looked comfy and infinitely masculine like the rest of the loft. My stomach hollowed out and my mouth went dry.

I forced myself to swallow and shifted my attention back to Ty. His gaze drilled into me and a knowing light gleamed in his neon blue gaze. "Nice place."

"It serves a purpose."

"Professional decorator or did you do it yourself?"

He gave me an odd look. "Most of it was already here. I brought in the bedroom furniture and the sound equipment a few weeks ago."

"You can't have too much sound equipment." Did I mention that my capacity for intelligent conversation is severely limited when surrounded by so much testosterone? I'm not sure if that's a born vamp weakness (like sunlight and stakes) or my own personal glitch. "So, um, who is he? This guy with the department? Friend? Relative?"

He gave me another odd look. I didn't blame him. Come on. *Relative?* Ty was, like, over one hundred years old and a made vampire on top of that. Meaning, his relatives were more than likely six feet under. And made vamps weren't known for forging deep, meaningful relationships. They plundered the earth and fed. End of story. At least according to my folks.

His dark eyebrows drew together. "You didn't hit your head during the arrest, did you?" Something strangely close to concern glimmered in his gaze and warmth curled in my tummy. Before I could reply (with so much warmth, I was a little tongue-tied), he shook his head. "What am I saying?"

That maybe, just maybe he *cared* if I hit my head? That the thought made him positively crazy because he had intense feelings for me?

Holy crap. This was it. The moment of reckoning. We'd kissed and flirted and I'd known all along that there was more to it. Sure, the situation was hopeless, but it was still a situation. We were Romeo and Juliet (with fangs, of course) all over again. I'd felt it. But he'd never said anything to confirm my feelings and prove that it wasn't just my overactive imagination and desperately deprived hormones.

But now, in the face of such danger, he couldn't contain his true feelings a moment longer. Like, I know most vampires felt only hunger, greed, lust, inflated self-worth, and did I say hunger? But I wasn't thinking about that right now. I was lost in a moment of happy and I wasn't going to kill the mood with reality.

My ears perked and my heart paused, and Ty opened his mouth.

Nine
♥ ♥ ♥

"*I want you.*"

"*I need you.*"

"*I can't exist without you.*"

The possibilities echoed through my mind and I smiled.

"I keep forgetting you're a vampire." His voice was deep and incredulous and not at all passionate.

My smile widened. Okay, so it wasn't exactly what I'd had in mind, but it sent a rush of happy through me anyway.

"You are," he said. "I mean, you *do* have fangs." He stared. "I think. So no concussion, right?"

I nodded. Just a nasty, life-threatening incision that I wasn't about to mention. Because if I actually told him, he would probably want to see it and I wasn't subjecting myself to *that*. It was one thing to see concern glimmering in his eyes and quite another to have him inspecting my chest.

Romeo and Juliet, I reminded myself. Aka doomed.

"So what about the guy?" I asked again.

"He's a high-ranking official in the homicide unit. I've helped him close a few unsolved cases and he owes me a favor. He's going to give me the details on this situation so we'll know exactly what we're dealing with." He stopped looking at me, thankfully, and reached for a laptop sitting on the coffee table amid a clutter of magazines—everything from *S.W.A.T. Gear* to *Guns & Ammo*.

"Does he know I'm here?"

"He owes me, but not that big. He just thinks I'm looking into it on my own. The *Times* is offering a reward for the arrest and conviction of the murderer, so it figures that I would be interested."

"How much?"

"Fifty thousand dollars."

Fifty thousand dollars? That's all I was worth? "I would think they could afford at least a hundred thousand."

He glanced up, a grin crooking his sensuous mouth. "It doesn't sound like much, but in my line of work it's sure to bring everyone crawling out of the woodwork, which is the point. The more people they have looking for you, the less likely you'll be able to elude the authorities."

"I thought the justice system was all about being innocent until proven guilty?"

"You're just a suspect at this point. The prime suspect. From what I've been told, the evidence is pretty incriminating, but since I don't know specifics yet, I can't say exactly how bad things look. Obviously bad enough for the judge to issue an arrest warrant. Until they figure out their mistake—which I'm sure they will—they're on a manhunt and you're it."

I sat up straight and gathered my control. "Okay, so what do we do?"

"*We* don't do anything. You're going to lay low while I gather information." When I started to open my mouth, he pinned me with a hard stare. "I mean it, Lil. The minute you walk out of that door, the cops will be all over you. You have to stay here."

"But I have things to do—"

"Inside," he cut in.

"I have a business to run—"

"Understood?"

"I don't—"

"Otherwise, you can find someplace else to stay."

I swallowed my argument and nodded. "Okay, I'll lay low and . . . What do people do when they lay low?"

"They relax. Take it easy." His gaze softened as it raked over me. "You look really tired."

"I haven't gotten much sleep what with being on the run and almost being autopsied." When he arched an eyebrow, I shook my head. "You don't want to know."

"Actually, I do, sugar." The admission seemed to surprise him as much as it surprised me. Before I could respond (not that I could, mind you; I was too busy trying to process the fact that he'd called me *sugar*), he shook his head and pushed to his feet. "The sofa folds out."

"That'll be just fine."

"I wasn't suggesting it for you. I'll take the sofa. You take the bed."

"What about all of these windows?"

He walked over to the entertainment center and punched a button. Black curtains slid from the corners and shrouded the massive room in total darkness. He walked over and fastened the part where the material met. After tugging to make sure the edges wouldn't come apart, he turned toward me. "It was either this or spray paint the windows and I couldn't deal with that."

It was my turn to arch an eyebrow. "Claustrophobic?"

"Something like that."

"Vampires aren't claustrophobic."

"I wasn't always a vampire."

My gaze went to the scar that puckered the small area near his eyebrow. My fingertips itched as I remembered the feel of the rough skin.

Bad fingertips.

I turned toward the sofa and started to move the leather cushions. "I'll just get settled—" The words stalled in my throat when I felt him come up behind me.

"Sounds like a good idea, but you're in the wrong spot. You're taking the bed, remember?" His voice was slow and deep and oh, so stirring.

"But it's your bed." My gaze swiveled to the king-size setup in the far corner and panic rushed from my toes up. There seemed something desperately intimate about sleeping in the very same spot that Ty slept in day after day. In nothing but his jeans. Or worse, in nothing but his . . .

I shoved a pillow into his arms. "You should really sleep in the bed. I don't want to put you out."

"You're not putting me out." He shoved the pillow back at me.

"Of course I am. It's a terrible imposition to have someone kick you out of—"

"Lil."

I shoved another pillow at him. "—your own personal space and it really isn't fair of me to just barge in and upset your routine and—"

"Lil." He didn't just say the name this time. He touched me and my body went completely still. "I want you to have the bed."

"But that just wouldn't be right." Or easy.

He seemed to think. "True," he finally said. "That would be pretty wrong. I mean, I do like my space."

"Exactly." Okay, so maybe he wasn't totally clueless and hell-bent on torture. "It just isn't fair."

He nodded. "The only really fair thing to do would be for both of us to sleep in the bed."

I whirled so fast that I made myself dizzy. "Enjoy the sofa." Sadistic jackass.

I ignored the grin that curved his sensuous lips and turned toward my luggage stacked near the door. A warm chuckle vibrated from his throat and followed me all the way to the cluster of Gucci.

My hands trembled and my nipples tingled as I reached for one of the bags and started toward the one and only door other than the one I'd come in.

I stepped inside the bathroom and went straight to the sink. I spent the next few minutes splashing cold water on my face and reminding myself why I shouldn't be attracted to Ty Bonner.

Made vampire. Off-limits. My parents would go ballistic. Wait a second, that was in the plus column.

The negative?

Made, my brain screamed again. But with my body buzzing and Ty's steady pulse echoing in my ears (damn my vamp hearing), the thought didn't really register. He was obviously attracted to me (I could still feel his lips from our one and only kiss) and I was desperately attracted to him. It only made sense that we would end up having hot, wild, meaningless sex.

Meaningless. Oh, yeah. There was the negative. *Meaningless* meant temporary and temporary was a big, fat no-no. I wanted a solid, long-lasting relationship even more than I wanted hot, wild sex. I *did.*

I reached for a towel and patted my face. I brushed my teeth, then my hair, and dotted a pale pink MAC gloss on my bottom lip for that full, pouting effect. (While I didn't want to want him, there was no reason why he couldn't want me.)

There. Fresh and ready for bed.

To sleep, mind you.

The bathroom door creaked open and I padded toward the bedroom. I set my case next to the nightstand and eyed the bed. My mouth went incredibly dry and I headed for the kitchen, passing Ty along the way.

I wasn't going to look at him, I told myself as I opened a few cabinets until I found a glass and shoved it beneath the faucet. Even when I heard the slide of leather as he pushed to his feet and sensed his presence directly behind me. *No looking.*

I gulped water and then I looked. I couldn't help myself. He was right there and I couldn't *not* look, not without coming off like a snot, which I wasn't. Not unless you were the bitch slut who'd stolen my first boyfriend, that is.

His gaze traveled down the length of me and back up again. His attention snagged on my sleep shirt and he arched an eyebrow. "Hello Kitty?"

I glanced down at the pink cotton and damned myself for not dipping into my La Perla stash. But who would've known I would end up here?

He grinned and I stiffened. "There's nothing wrong with Hello Kitty. Granted, if you hate cats, you might not understand the whole cute and cuddly concept, but it was the only thing handy when fleeing Death Row. Besides, it's comfortable."

He reached out and his fingertips caught the edge of my sleeve. "It's soft."

"That, too."

His skin brushed mine as he rubbed the fabric between his fingers for a few tantalizing seconds before letting his hand fall away.

"You should turn in. The sun's almost up."

Which totally explained my lack of common sense

at the moment. I was at my weakest during daylight, my strength zapped until I could fall into a rejuvenating sleep. Otherwise, I never would have contemplated hot, wild, meaningless sex with Ty Bonner.

At least that's what I told myself as I set my glass on the counter and put some much-needed distance between myself and the dangerously sexy vamp.

But as I walked toward the bed, my panic didn't ease. His scent filled my head and wrapped around me as I crawled between the sheets. Cotton slid against my skin, stroking and stirring as I adjusted the covers and buried my head beneath the pillow. Ugh. It was going to be the longest day of my life, which spoke volumes on account of the fact I was five hundred years and holding.

And I thought being wanted for murder was stressful?

Ten

❤ ❤ ❤

It wasn't the *longest* day of my life (which had occurred a few months ago and involved a murderous
vampire, a missing Dead End Dating client, and back-
to-back *Jerry Springer* reruns), but it ran a close second.

After I turned in, Ty stretched out on the sofa. My
strength drained away as the sun climbed higher outside as, I'm sure, did his. But unlike the hunky made
vamp, I couldn't seem to fall into a rejuvenating sleep.
Instead, I spent the next few hours tossing and turning and trying not to glance in Ty's direction. Then
yet another hour with my eyes clamped shut, my
mind replaying the previous night's events. Add another forty-five minutes counting designers and listening to the steady thump of Ty's pulse. Plus another
fifteen narrowing down the list to my top three faves
and then yet *another* hour wishing the rhythmic

thump, thump, thump would move a little closer. (I'm superficial and weak? So sue me.)

When I did finally doze off (we're talking early afternoon), it was a restless sleep, a rarity for vampires because we normally sleep like the, well, *dead*. But we're talking major stress, a set of Ty-scented sheets, and a pair of ruined Rossis (yes, I was still mourning the loss). Seriously, what hormone-deprived, fashion-conscious bloodsucker—or sipper, in my case—could zone out under those circumstances?

Which was why when I opened my eyes the next evening, I was too tired to breathe, much less rip off my clothes and throw myself shamelessly at Ty Bonner.

He'd pulled back the heavy drapes to reveal the floor to ceiling windows. A faint orange glow outlined the surrounding buildings. The faint shadow of the moon was already visible despite the fact that it was just this side of sunset. Dusk crowded into the massive room.

My gaze cut through the shadows to the man who stood on the far side of the room in the middle of the kitchen area. He still wore only jeans, but they were black this time. The denim outlined his muscular legs and cupped his (big swallow) ahem, package. Dark, silky hair sprinkled his broad chest from nipple to nipple before narrowing to a fine line that bisected his six-pack abs and disappeared into his low-slung waistband. He'd obviously just stepped from the shower because a few drops of water still clung to his shoulders. He'd combed his wet hair back away from his chiseled face. His bluer-than-blue gaze twinkled when it collided with mine.

Okay, so I wasn't *that* tired.

His sensuous mouth crooked into a grin as he held up what looked like a wine bottle and motioned me over.

I wasn't going. That's what I told myself. Then again, who was I kidding? I was *this close* to a majorly hot babe who wanted me even closer. Even more, I needed sustenance, which wasn't a possibility if I barricaded myself in the bathroom to escape temptation and repair the damage that several hours of bed wrestling had wrought on my hair.

I threw my legs over the side of the bed and forced my feet toward the kitchen.

"Want some?" he asked as I walked up next to him.

I swallowed. "More than you'll *ever* know."

He grinned and held up the bottle—an imported blood type from Garnier's, an upscale, vampire owned and operated deli on the West Side. "I was talking about a drink."

"So, um, was I."

His grin widened. "*Liar.*" The deep voice resonated in my head.

I frowned. "That's not funny."

"What?"

"You know what."

"I don't know what you're talking about." He feigned innocence and turned to retrieve a glass from a nearby cabinet.

Okay, so maybe I could hear him and he didn't know I could hear him. Please, please, *please*.

"*Sorry, sugar. No dice.*"

My frown deepened. "You're really annoying, you know that?"

He winked. "The feeling's mutual. So you like yours warm or cold?"

"Warm, please. What about you?"

His grin was slow and oh-so heartstopping. "I'll take it anyway I can get it, *darlin'.*"

He uncorked the bottle, poured a glass, and then turned to nuke it in a nearby microwave.

"I . . . that's nice." *Nice?* Okay, so my capacity for speech was on the fritz thanks to the *darlin'* comment. And the grin. Definitely the grin. I gave myself a mental shake and searched for something semi-intelligent to say. "I never would have figured you for a bottle man," I said just as the microwave *dinged.*

"I'm not. But I keep a bottle on hand just in case. I like to be prepared." When he turned back to me, his smile was gone. His gaze glowed with a heat that upped my otherwise cool body temperature several degrees. He held out the crimson offering. "Drink up."

My gaze snagged on the inside of his wrist and I traced the path of a thick blue vein until it disappeared beneath the muscle of his strong forearm.

I swallowed and suddenly the thought of actually touching my lips to the sweet red heat sparked a rush of panic. "I need coffee," I blurted. When he stared at me as if I'd ordered *well done,* I shrugged. "It's my evening routine. Coffee revs me up." Yeah, right. But I so didn't trust myself to *drink* drink right now. The hunger was fierce enough on its own.

Already, my palms itched and my throat burned and my insides felt tight and needy. At the first sip, it would grow even worse. Overwhelming. And I feared I wouldn't be able to sate it before . . . *Before.*

"You do have coffee, don't you?"

He shook his head. "Sorry."

And here I thought the guy was irresistible.

"What sort of vampire are you?"

"The kind that doesn't drink coffee. In case you haven't heard, we vampires usually indulge with something else." He held up the bottle in salute before downing a long swig for himself. His gaze grew even brighter and more intense and my stomach went hollow. "It's much better for you than caffeine." His voice was deeper and more husky when he spoke this time.

And much more stirring.

"Diet Coke," I blurted. "Do you have any Diet Coke?"

He bared his fangs and gave me a semi-ferocious look. "Do I look like a man who drinks Diet Coke?"

Not exactly. But when it came to pecs, he put Lucky—the shirtless construction worker in their most famous commercial—to shame.

"All right, all right." I threw up my hands. "Regular Coke?"

He gave me a *what planet are you from?* look before shaking his head.

"What about tea?"

"I'm afraid not."

"Hot chocolate?"

"Sorry."

"Gatorade?"

"Nuh-uh." He took another long swig before he glanced at his watch. "Listen, I've got to go." He shoved the cork back into the bottle and set it on the counter next to the glass.

"You can't be full already?"

"No." His gaze collided with mine. "Not even close." Silence stretched between us for several moments as he stared at me, into me, leaving no mistake as to his meaning.

Oh, boy.

"Then again, you're probably really busy. You should go. Really." *Before I do something totally lewd and lascivious.*

His gaze collided with mine and a grin tugged at the corner of his mouth. "Stay inside and keep the door locked."

The moment he moved away, my anxiety doubled and I had a rush of helplessness. It was the same feeling I'd had on the autopsy table. Irrational, I know, what with me being a Super Vamp and all. Nonetheless, it was there. Insecurity swamped me and urged me to lunge forward, wrap my arms around Ty, and beg him to stay. That, or beg him for a really phenomenal orgasm.

I kept my feet rooted to the spot. I do have *some* willpower. "What if the police show up and try to beat it down?" Unfortunately, said willpower didn't extend to my mouth.

"They won't. They're convinced you're hiding out in Connecticut near your folks." When I stiffened, he added, "Your folks are fine. The police questioned them, but came to the conclusion that they didn't know anything. But the cops are still betting you'll turn up nearby, so they're watching and waiting."

"How do you know?"

"Sugar, I know everything."

"Would you stop doing that?"

He grinned and walked toward the chest of drawers that sat near the massive bed. He pulled open the top drawer, and retrieved a black T-shirt. Muscles rippled and flexed as he hauled the cotton over his head and pushed his arms through.

I gathered my courage and averted my gaze, and found myself staring at the glass of red heat he'd poured for me. The scent curled through the air toward me and my nostrils flared. Need gnawed at my belly and crawled its way through my chest and into my throat. I swallowed against the rising burn and fought the urge to lick my lips. My attention zigzagged back to Ty, who'd dropped onto the corner of the bed to pull on his boots. Muscles rippled and flexed and . . . I swiveled back toward the blood. Then back to Ty. The blood. Ty. Blood. Ty. Blood—

Stop! Where was a Starbucks when you *really* needed one?

"I'm working on a few cases." He opened the bottom nightstand drawer, retrieved a large handgun and holster, and I stiffened.

Not that I was scared of the thing, mind you. I'd just never seen the need for a gun. After all, I'm a vampire. *Mucho* powerful. With an extra sharp pair of incisors and a fantabulous collection of MAC lip gloss. Ditto for Ty. Minus the lip gloss, of course.

To me, guns seemed like such . . .

An inconvenience.

A waste of money.

A macho phallic symbol to mask an underlying fertility rating that was less than impressive.

Even more, they were an easy way to blow off a certain body part if, like my great uncle Paul, you weren't smart enough to turn on the safety before stuffing the thing down your pants. Sure, it had only been a temporary setback (we vamps have great rejuvenating capabilities), but it had still put him out of commission for quite a while. And, according to great aunt Zelda, the "incident" had been responsible for several performance issues that had prohibited them from conceiving a sibling for their one and only son, Ivan. Which meant Ivan was a spoiled, arrogant, pompous bastard.

Then again, that just meant that he fit right in with the rest of the born male vamp population.

Ty hooked the holster over his shoulder and I heard myself say, "I didn't think you carried a gun."

"I usually don't. But I either take it with me or leave it here with you."

On the other hand, we vamps aren't exactly invincible. Superman had his Kryptonite and we have sunlight. And stakes. And any and all sharp objects capable of piercing the heart. If Ty were facing down a dangerous criminal, it would be in his best interest to have a "little friend" as backup.

"Make sure the safety is on," I told him.

He gave me an odd look, but I was happy to note that he checked the safety before sliding the gun into its holster.

He walked back toward me and retrieved his wallet, which sat on the coffee table. "Stay inside," he said again as he stuffed the leather fold into his back pocket.

"No problem. I've got tons of work to do. Speaking of which, can I borrow your laptop to check my e-mail?"

"No checking e-mail. Not until we know exactly what's going on. I want you to keep as low a profile as possible. I'm sure the cops are monitoring your online accounts. Even if they can't trace your whereabouts, they'll know you're still out there. We want to make them think you've disappeared completely from their radar."

"Like maybe I've left the country?"

He nodded. "Anything to throw them off track until we can figure out how to fix whatever's happened."

"What about the phone? Can I use the phone? I really need to call my assistant. We've got a lot of work right now and she's—"

"No. Just take it easy and forget about work."

"Excuse me? For your information, I've killed myself to gain a pretty respectable client base. I can't just forget about them for an indeterminate amount of time. Do you know what a lull will do to my momentum?"

"I doubt sitting on Death Row will help much, either."

He had a point. Still. I shook my head. "I can't *not* work."

He looked ready to slide his hands around my neck and squeeze. "Fine. Call her. But make sure you time it. Don't stay on for more than twenty seconds."

"Twenty seconds? But that's barely enough time to say hello, much less go over our scheduled workload—"

"Thirty seconds tops," he cut in. "Anything longer and they'll be able to trace the call."

"But I need to check my voice mail."

"Thirty seconds."

"It takes longer than that just to punch in my password."

"*Thirty,*" he ground out, "or I might as well turn you in myself."

"You wouldn't do that."

He eyed me. "Wouldn't I?"

No. Yes. I held his gaze for several long seconds before I finally nodded. Not that I felt one hundred percent certain that he would. I just wasn't one hundred percent certain that he wouldn't. "Thirty seconds," I grumbled.

"Good. And keep—"

"—the door locked," I finished for him. "Yeah, yeah, I got it."

He stared at me long and hard before his expression softened. "I'll be back around two. Just behave yourself until then and we'll talk." He winked and then he was gone.

I locked the door and barely resisted the urge to pick up the phone and call the cops myself.

Thirty seconds? Was he crazy in addition to being totally megawatt hot?

I dropped to the sofa and stared at the cordless phone sitting on the coffee table. I thought of Viola and the desperation I'd seen in her eyes. And then I thought about the big, fat check that had been left in my desk amid the chaos of my arrest and escape. And then I thought of at least a zillion other things I needed to discuss with Evie.

Thirty seconds?

Totally impossible.

I simply couldn't do it.

I wouldn't.

But thirty seconds *was* longer than the initial twenty. On top of that, while Ty had limited the call length, he hadn't limited the number of calls. I wasn't an expert, but I'd seen enough cop shows to know that the good guys couldn't trace short and sweet no matter how many. I could make as many phone calls as I wanted which beat, hands down, the one phone call from jail. It wasn't the ideal way to do business, but a vamp had to do what a vamp had to do.

I smiled and reached for the phone.

Eleven
❤ ❤ ❤

I pinched my nose the minute I heard Evie's familiar *Hello?* "Yes, this is Mrs. Vanderflunkinpitt"—the voice came out very high-pitched and nasal—"from your local telephone provider. We received a service call stating that you were having difficulty with your phone line in Room A."

"We don't have a phone line in—"

"The trouble started yesterday evening. Big trouble."

"Lil," Evie's incredulous voice asked. "Is that—"

"I promised your owner—a Miss Lilliana Marchette—that we would deal with the problem ASAP and we are. We're fixing everything as we speak. Just proceed with business as usual while we make the necessary adjustments to get things back to normal."

"What did you say your name—" *Clunk.*

I let loose of my nose and counted the seconds on

Ty's digital clock until a full minute had passed (I wasn't sure how long it took to fully disconnect, but I wasn't taking any chances) and hit redial.

"Vanderflunkinpitt," I said when Evie picked up the phone. "Mrs. Vanderflunkin*pitt*." I emphasized the last syllable and silently begged her understanding.

"Oh." Two seconds ticked by. *"Oh."* Evie's voice perked up. "Well, um, thank you. I was, um, really worried about the, er, problem with that line. That's my favorite line and I've grown really fond of it and I don't know what I would do if it were out of commission permanently."

"You and me both."

"But you're okay? I mean, you're sure the line is all right? It isn't permanently damaged or traumatized or anything like that?"

"Nothing a new outfit won't fix." Open mouth, insert designer-clad foot. "New wiring," I blurted, "Nothing new wiring outfitted to the, um, initial wire won't fix. You just keep things running on your end and take care of new clients and I—that is—we will do our part on this end with the pre-existing ones. That is, we'll make sure your phone calls get through. And make sure to go to the bank. I—that is—*we* usually charge an arm and a leg, so you'll need lots of funds, particularly that extra large check from your latest client. Not that I know the exact amount or anything, it's just that Miss Marchette mentioned it when she placed the service call and I've got a good memory for these things."

"I'll take care of—" *Click.*

"Sorry," I told Evie when she picked up the phone the third time. "I must be losing signal on this end." I crackled for effect. "Take care and I'll see you—that is, we'll contact you as soon as we can. In the meantime, just tell Miss Marchette when she calls from Costa Rica where she's on special assignment until her communication problems are fixed, that Vanderwalkenpitt is on the job."

"I thought is was Vanderflunkinpitt?"

"Whatever. Just keep things going."

"You're the boss. I mean," she rushed on, "you're obviously the boss at your service center because you sound so authoritative and in control. You're not *my* boss, of course. She's, um, in Costa Rica, probably basking in the sun and buying really cool souvenirs."

"Exactly. Don't worry about anything," I reassured her again. "Everything's going to be all right."

I hope.

The thought lingered in my head as I made more phone calls to everyone on my close, personal friends list—The Ninas. Francis and Melissa. The Ninas.

I know, I know. Depressing. But at least I didn't have to keep pinching my nose or thinking up stupid names. Besides, it wasn't the quantity of friends that mattered, it was the quality. And I happened to think that mine were right up there with a silver lamé Fendi and a Tiffany bangle bracelet.

I set the phone on the coffee table and ignored the urge to push to my feet and pace. Pacing would mean that I was worried and I was not—repeat *not*—worried. Everything *would* be okay. It was just a matter of laying low until the police realized their mistake.

If they realized it.

They would, I promised myself. Meanwhile, I was going to forget all about chopped-up undercover reporters and Death Row and the way the handcuffs had felt when they'd snapped around my wrists.

Relax. Ty's deep voice echoed through my head.

He was right. I needed to relax. Even more, I deserved to relax. I'd been under nonstop stress since opening Dead End Dating and so this confinement could be viewed as a good thing. This was my time. I could rest. Regroup. I could even take a nap if I wanted, provided I could calm my hormones down long enough to think about sleeping rather than the fact that I was stretched out in Ty's spot, in Ty's bed, in Ty's apartment.

Okay, so I wasn't going to take a lot of naps, but the point was I *could.* Just like I could take a long, leisurely bubble bath and give myself a facial and do my toenails and watch oodles of cable TV.

Why, before I knew it, it would be daybreak and another night closer to freedom. I pushed off the couch and made a beeline for the bathroom.

It turns out that Ty didn't actually have a bathtub and I didn't actually have any facial scrubs, much less a pedicure kit. I ended up taking a quick shower (he definitely needed a new hot water heater), before pulling on my favorite terry bathrobe and planting myself on the sofa, remote in hand.

I channel surfed for the next thirty minutes before

finally settling on an infomercial for a breakthrough exercise machine called the Boob Buster. Tell me about it. I followed several women as they increased their bra size with a measly commitment of forty-five minutes a day, six days a week, before I switched to MTV.

I found myself watching a show called *Pimp My Ride*. Hello? Where were the music videos?

Here's the thing, I don't actually watch television very often. And when I do, it's usually something I've specifically recorded—*Dr. Phil, The Bachelor, The Bachelorette, Lost,* QVC's designer hour—you know, the really important stuff I simply cannot miss.

Forget the TV. You can still relax.

I leaned my head back and stared at the darkness just beyond the windows. The stars twinkled and the moon lit up the skyline. A far cry from beach-basking in Costa Rica, but that was the point. With any luck, the police had been tapping Evie's line and maybe, just maybe, they might take the Costa Rica comment seriously.

I closed my eyes and tried to imagine what it would really feel like. Warm, I knew. I tuned in to my skin and tried to conjure the sensation, but nothing came. While I'd felt the sun's effects before—drained and powerless because I'm a born vamp and all that—I'd never felt the breezy, airy sensation of being outside, fully exposed to the sun's rays.

The closest I'd ever come had been this really cool papier mâché lamp I'd bought down in SoHo. It had been a hanging light shaped like the sun. I'd suspended it in the corner of my apartment and stood under it many times and thought about the real thing.

Not that I wasn't happy being a denizen of the dark, mind you. I love my life. Absolutely, positively, completely and totally *adore* being a vampire and all its perks—enhanced senses, super fashion sense, and primo shape-changing abilities.

But sometimes (don't tell my folks) I still wonder what it would be like to be, you know, *human*.

I lifted the edge of Ty's forgotten duster, which lay draped over the back of the couch, and ran my palm over the cool material. While he couldn't walk in the sun any more than I could, he hadn't always been so limited. I conjured an image of him poolside at a posh resort, a mai tai in one hand and a bottle of suntan oil in the other.

While I could totally get into a slick, coconut-scented version of Ty, the mai tai thing (complete with a little umbrella) sort of blew the big, bad alpha bounty hunter image.

I wrinkled my nose and let go of the jacket.

Then again, such a scenario might prove helpful. The next time I wanted to rip off my clothes and do a little mattress dancing, I could picture him with a plastic umbrella drink. Even worse, I could put him in a Speedo, wearing some of those paper sunglasses they hand out at the eye doctor's office. I'd had a client walk in just a week ago wearing a pair of those because—quote—they served a purpose and saved him from having to spend his hard-earned money to buy some real ones—end quote.

I know, right? Needless to say, I'd yet to find a woman who didn't want to smack the cheapskate in the first five minutes, much less one willing to sit through an entire date with him.

I pictured a cheap sunglasses version of Ty wearing a Speedo, but since he was ultra-hot, the skimpy bathing suit didn't have the desired effect. Add forty pounds and back hair. Yep, I wanted to smack him, all right.

I flipped open Ty's laptop and double-clicked on a word processing program. I spent the next ten minutes keying a list of possible meet markets for Viola's twenty-seven alpha males. When I finished, I made a few more notes on some pre-existing clients, including Esther Crutch, an old maid made vampire desperately looking for love. Or at the very least, companionship. Surely Ty knew some other made vamps like himself? I made a note to pick his brain for possibilities when he came home and then spent the next half hour Internet surfing.

Unfortunately, I'd left my purse back at the office which meant no credit cards, which meant no shopping, which meant no W-A-Y. I was bored out of my mind in a matter of minutes.

I stretched out on the couch, determined to kill a few hours with a nap. Easy, right? I mean, the couch was totally nonsexual and in no way connected to Ty's half-naked, sleeping body. Except, of course, for the fact that he'd slept on it the night before while I'd been in his bed. And he'd definitely been half-naked with just his worn jeans and sexy grin. I sat up. I *so* wasn't going to be able to do this.

I walked toward the windows and stared out at the surrounding view. It was early in the evening—barely seven o'clock—and cars zipped up and down the street. People walked here and there, some coming home from work, others heading out. In the apartment building across the way, I caught a glimpse of a man and woman cooking dinner. Another man sat Indian-style in the middle of his floor, his palms upturned, his face a passive mask of yoga contentment.

I'd just tuned in to a twenty-something female with a cell phone in one hand and a giant slice of pizza in the other when the sensation hit me. My arms prickled and awareness zipped up my spine. My gaze swiveled to the street below. A group of women headed for the corner. A businessman walked the opposite way, a newspaper under one arm. A taxi idled at the curb several feet away while a woman held a small boy with one hand and dug in her purse with the other.

There were no suspicious-looking characters dressed in black. No sharpshooters staring at me from the opposite rooftop. Nothing looked frightening or out of the ordinary.

Yet, I felt it. Fear and an insistent niggle that something wasn't quite right.

That, or paranoia.

I decided on number two, shook away the strange sensation, and turned my mind back to the matter at hand: finding something—anything—to do. I paced from one end of the apartment to the other. I turned on the stereo and Fuel blasted from the speakers. I tried dancing, but heavy metal rock ballads didn't lend themselves to bumping and grinding, so I ended up lip-synching.

Before I gave in to the impulse to clean (I *know*—I needed out in the worst way), I headed for the bedroom area. Two a.m. was a *long* way away and I just couldn't make it. After rummaging in Ty's drawers, I walked toward the bathroom, my arms full.

A few minutes later, I eyed my reflection. (The whole thing about vamps not having a reflection? So not true. Thankfully. I mean, can you imagine an eternity of not being able to apply a decent coat of lip gloss?)

But I digress.

I eyed myself from various angles. Where rest and relaxation hadn't been enticement enough to stay in, this was.

Since going out in my usual, fashionable glory was completely out of the question, I'd done my best to come up with an effective disguise. Ty was more the cowboy type—nix any baseball caps lying around— and I wasn't in a hurry to draw unnecessary attention to myself. Therefore, I'd bypassed the black Stetson and gone for a red and black Harley handkerchief I'd found in his top drawer. I'd tied my hair up into a ponytail, wrapped the handkerchief around my head in my best biker chick imitation, and donned a spare pair of his sunglasses. I'd slipped on one of his black T-shirts that swallowed me up and fell to mid-thigh.

A pair of old sweats covered my bottom half. The only thing that hinted at my fantabulous taste was my shoes (I couldn't very well wear Ty's size twelves). I had on my black Nine West ankle boots I'd scooped up back at my apartment. Not ultra-expensive, mind you, but they'd been handy and they did go with everything.

Except for sweat pants.

No way was I setting foot outside Ty's place dressed like this.

I toed off the boots, padded back to the couch, and finished watching *Pimp My Ride*. By the time the third episode of *Date My Mom* (don't ask) came on, I'd pulled on the boots and was back to eyeing my reflection.

Okay, it *was* sort of retro looking. Especially if I knotted the T-shirt at the waist and rolled the sweatpants to midcalf and added a few bracelets . . . There. Not too bad. It's not like I was going out cruising for a man. Not my own, that is. Besides, I still had the underlying vamp magnetism to outweigh the semilameness of my outfit and tip the scales in my favor.

My decision made, I took one last look in the mirror and killed the television. I left Ty a quick note and let myself out of his apartment. I had places to go and people to see and the night was still young.

First on my list of must do? Pay a visit to Dead End Dating.

I know. Dangerous with a capital D. But I'd left my purse (complete with my favorite bronzer and blush duo) and business cards during the arrest and so I really had no choice. Besides, I was going to be extremely careful. I would be in and out before anyone was the wiser.

At least that's what I was telling myself.

Twelve

♥ ♥ ♥

Via taxi, Ty's place was approximately ten minutes from Dead End Dating. Via cute, pink, furry bat, it took two and a half, which included dodging a drive-by courtesy of two high-flying pigeons.

I landed in the narrow alley that ran behind the building that housed Dead End Dating, an interior decorating company, a small CPA firm, and a mom-and-pop health food store. My body vibrated and hummed and quickly the frantic beat of wings faded into the steady pound of my own heart. I glanced down and stared at the tips of my Nine West boots. Present and accounted for. Whew. See, sometimes all the trappings didn't always make the transition. Then again, I'd gotten quite a bit of practice perfecting my technique in the last forty-eight hours.

The air was sharp with the scent of empty vitamin containers and whole wheat. Add a box of old toner cartridges (wasn't recycling a tax write-off?) and the one breath I'd been foolish enough to take had me wrinkling my nose.

I eyed a small ledge that protruded at the top of the building and my body lifted. I floated the three stories up and retrieved the spare key I'd hidden beneath the loose edge of one of the bricks.

A few minutes later, I unlocked the back door and twisted the handle. It didn't budge. I was just about to up the vamp muscle when I felt it again—that same awareness zipping up and down my spine, making the hair on the back of my neck stand at attention. My senses immediately tuned in to my surroundings—the distant sound of traffic, the hum of a nearby air conditioner, the faint sound of voices coming from inside the vitamin store at the far end (they were doing nightly inventory). Normal. There was nothing out of the ordinary. Nothing except the way my stomach clenched and unclenched.

Not out of fear, mind you.

Nope, this was more like full-blown panic on account of the fact I'm not in any hurry to have to pull another Houdini and knee a bunch of cops.

I glanced from one end of the alley to the other. My gaze sliced through the darkness. A trash Dumpster towered at one end. A cat tiptoed through the shadows a few feet away. The animal's head swiveled and her gaze caught mine. Recognition sparked and she shrank back, giving a slight hiss.

Okay, so this is, like, why I don't have a cat. Vamps aren't really cat people. Sure, we'll adopt the occasional stray, but for the most part we're a bunch of dog lovers. When we morph, it's usually a Doberman or an Alaskan husky or, my father's particular favorite, an intimidating jackal. (My pops was mucho impressed with *The Omen*. I *know*. Creepy or what?) Anyhow, animals can sense our otherworldliness. The cat took one look at me and made a quick getaway. Unfortunately, the strange sensation of being watched stayed with me.

Because there was an entire team of black-clad S.W.A.T. officers staked out on the surrounding building tops, all watching *moi,* a hardened, wanted criminal? Was there a roomful waiting on the other side of the door to slap on some cuffs and haul me off to the pokey? Then again, maybe I was being a total drama queen. Possibly the only thing on the other side of the door was a handful of my closest friends waiting to scream "Happy Birthday!"

My over-panicked brain voted for numbers one and two, my ego cast its ballot for three. Reason nixed them all because (a) I would have seen the S.W.A.T. members with my ultra-vamp vision, in addition to hearing and smelling them, (b) same goes for anybody inside DED, and (c) my birthday was months away.

I shook away the sensation and twisted the knob again. Hinges creaked and whined. Wood groaned. I made a mental note to pick up a can of WD-40 just as soon as things returned to normal. Closing the door behind me, I stood completely still and let my senses tune in to the darkness. Thank the Big Vamp Upstairs for night vision, otherwise I would have been forced to turn on a light, which would have been the kiss of death. While I felt certain the police didn't expect me to return (in their eyes that would be ultra stupid), they would still be keeping an eye on the place (think Columbo staked out in an old Chevy, munching a sandwich out front, rather than *The Unit*) for lack of any other leads.

I'd hoped to find everything exactly where I'd left it, but no such luck. The police had taken my computer and iPod, as well as my cell phone and file cabinet. I retrieved a batch of business cards from the spare box in my bottom drawer and paused to take a few swigs of the imported blood, which looked like just another bottle of fine red wine, in a nearby fridge. Cold, I know, but I was running on empty since I'd declined to drink at Ty's place for fear of losing control and giving in to my inner slut.

I took a last, long drink before recorking the bottle and putting it back in its place. Then I stuffed the DED cards into an empty envelope and walked into the outer office. Evie's computer was missing, as well, along with the small terminal we'd set up in interview room A, aka the storage closet. The only thing the police hadn't confiscated were the telephones and answering machine. Yeah! A message book sat next to Evie's phone and I glanced at the latest entry from that afternoon.

Rachel Sanchez. The were-Chihuahua. I smiled, tore off the message, and stuffed it into the envelope.

I opened Evie's bottom drawer in search of the one shining ray of hope amid so much gloominess. See, last month Evie had been totally stressed over her dad coming to visit, which meant she hadn't gotten her usual eight hours, which meant she'd needed an extra pick-me-up midday, which meant she'd headed to Starbucks during our peak hour and had been in such a hurry that she'd forgotten to get a lid for her cup.

Long story short, she'd dribbled mocha latte on the computer keyboard while trying to answer a new call and key in the latest client. Talk about multitasking. Anyhow, the system had blanked out and we'd had to call a repairman. He'd been able to retrieve some of our data, but not all. After he'd quieted me down (I'd sort of whimpered), he'd suggested backing up to a data pin in the future.

All right, already. So I'd bawled like a baby. My professional life had been on that computer. Talk about a low moment.

I'd picked myself up, as usual, and taken the guy's advice. Now we were a totally hip, totally conscientious matchmaking firm that backed up religiously.

My hand dove between a box of tampons and a can of hairspray and started to search. I unearthed a spare lip gloss, a bottle of clear nail polish (was there anything that stuff couldn't fix?), a chocolate-dipped spoon, two packs of Equal, a data pin, a mini curling iron—yes!

I planted a big one on the small contraption and stuffed it into the envelope along with the rest of my goodies. Closing the drawer, my gaze snagged on the message light flashing on Evie's telephone.

No touching, I told myself. First off, I didn't want

to leave a fingerprint because if the cops fingerprinted they would know I'd been here.

Then again, they'd probably already fingerprinted and even if they hadn't, this was my place. My fingerprints were everywhere. *And,* I was pretty sure that leaving a fingerprint wasn't like getting offed and having the contents of your stomach examined for time of death. It was a fingerprint, for heaven's sake. There was no way to tell what time or date it had been left. Or was there?

I was sort of figuring this stuff out as I went along and my curiosity quickly voted N-O.

I turned the volume button down all the way so as not to alert Columbo that there was anyone inside and pressed the play button. My vamp hearing tuned in to the nonexistent sound and the words echoed through my head.

"You've reached Dead End Dating, where finding love is as easy as applying for a modest, but well worth it, home equity loan."

It wasn't the greatest slogan, but I was still working on it.

"Our offices are closed, but if you'll leave a name and number, someone will contact you on the next business day." *Beeeeeep.*

"I'm calling for Lil. This is Ayala Jacqueline De-vanti."

Aka my one and only Dead End Dating failure.

Okay, so she wasn't my only one, but the f-word was such an ugly term that I reserved it for only the most disastrous of experiences. In a nutshell, Ayala was the daughter of one of my mother's friends and the perfect female vampire. She was ultra hot. Educated. Her orgasm quotient rivaled even mine (baker's dozen, or it had been the last time I'd actually *had* sex, say, about a hundred years ago) and she desperately wanted to settle down and contribute to the vampire race.

I know, she should have been an easy match, right? I'd thought so, too, which was why, before I'd paired her up with a real candidate and added her to the Wall of Fame, I'd hooked her up with Wilson Harvey. See, Wilson had had the hots for my best friend, Nina Two (brunette, conservative, did the financials for her father's female sanitary products plant in Jersey) but he hadn't wanted to admit it. Nina had been slow on the uptake as well. So I'd paired them each up with primo potential mates and sent them to the annual midnight soirée sponsored by my mother's huntress club. They'd each been insanely jealous of the other (am I good or what?) and had come to their senses (hello Wall of Fame), but not before Ayala's werewolf lover had shown up and staked me in the shoulder.

Ouch.

He'd been aiming for Wilson, of course, but I hadn't been able to stand idly by and let some crazy wolf off my best friend's eternity mate. Not to mention, Wilson had yet to pay his hook-up fee and I wasn't eating *that*.

Anyhow, in the short time since getting staked, I'd introduced Ayala to several potential eternity mates, expecting each one to be It. Surprisingly, she hadn't clicked with any of them. She didn't like brunettes. She didn't like blonds. She didn't like doctors. She didn't like lawyers. She didn't like condescending men who only cared how many times she could scream their name during one sexual encounter.

At least none who fell into the born vamp category. I'd broached the subject with her a few times and suggested she let me fix her up with, I don't know, maybe another werewolf? I mean, she had listed *Wolf* as her all-time favorite movie. And her number one song? Big surprise. "Werewolves of London."

Forget the writing on the wall. She had it tattooed on her forehead. But, alas, she wasn't ready to come out of the closet. She wanted to settle down and make babies, and she was looking to me to make it happen.

Always up for a challenge—and a free shopping spree (her father was well-connected with Barney's)—I was still searching for Ayala's perfect someone.

"Friday was a total disaster. He wore a navy suit and I absolutely abhor navy. Did I mention that on my profile?"

Uh, no.

"It made him look even more washed out," the message continued. "Even after we had dinner, he still looked as dead as ever. But I'm not crying over a spilled martini. There's always next week, right? Provided, of course, you have someone. You do have someone else lined up, don't you?"

No.

"But of course you do," she went on. "You're the expert."

The line clicked and the second message played.

"Lilliana? This is your mother."

As if I didn't know.

"Things are chaos right now. Pure chaos."

And it was all my fault.

"I'm at my wit's end." My mother's voice actually faltered and my guilt gave way to a rush of warmth. Awww, Mom. "Both your father and I are. We haven't a clue where we went wrong."

You didn't do anything. It's my fault. I'm the one who opened the dating service. I'm the one who's on the run.

"We've failed as role models. And mentors. And parents."

No, no, no! You're both good role models. Great mentors. Kick-ass parents.

Okay, so maybe kick-ass was pushing it a bit, but they'd been good. The best a pair of ancient, snotty, aristocratic vamps could be, I supposed.

"That's the only explanation for what is happening right now. It's our fault. We must have done something horribly wrong to have our handsome son fall victim to the wiles of a mere *human*."

The only thing *horribly wrong* they'd done had been when they'd forced me to go on the family vacation to Rome rather than letting me fly off to Paris with The Ninas—wait a second. Handsome son? Mere human?

"Jack's ruining his afterlife and there seems to be nothing we can do to stop him."

Jack?

"He's fallen for a human, which brings me to the reason for the phone call. We had to move the hunt from Sunday to Saturday because we've committed to meeting the human's parents for tea on Sunday evening. Your father wants everyone here early so we can put our heads together and come up with something effective to dissuade Jack from his present course of disaster and get him to cancel the tea. An intervention, so to speak. Your father's ready to take away his 401K and his PTO, but I think that's a bit drastic. PTO maybe, but both? I mean, Jack's still young. It's only natural that he'll make *some* mistakes. Speaking of mistakes, your father and I fully expect that you've learned your lesson about all this dating nonsense. We told you it was a bad idea, just like the time you decided you wanted to become a nun."

I'd been like, *five,* and totally enamored of Sister Mary Elizabeth who'd been my *au pair* at the time. At least, I'd thought she was my *au pair.* It turns out she'd been my aunt Sophie's food source on account of Aunt Sophie had been going through a strictly Kosher phase. I know, she's a vampire, right? She had been, before she'd nuked herself in a tanning bed not so long ago.

Bye, bye Vampie!

Before then, however, she'd been an adventurous and fun-loving spirit who'd been fascinated by all things *not* vampire, including various cultures and people. She'd worn sarongs and learned how to make poi. She'd belly danced for kings, ridden camels across the desert (at night, of course), and dog-sledded through the Andes. She'd traded beauty tips with Queen Elizabeth (the first one) and made love to the real Don Juan.

I'd been told more than once that I'd taken after Aunt Sophie, but I couldn't really see the connection. Sure, I'm sort of fascinated by unvamplike stuff and I do know more than my share of beauty tips, but you wouldn't catch me doing it with a player like Don, or wearing a sarong—unless it had a Christian Dior label.

"Now that you've seen for yourself, you can forget this crazy nonsense," my mom's voice continued, "put your nose to the grindstone and get back to work at Moe's." *Click.*

Back to work?

I'd never actually reported *to* work.

But since I had a whole stack of lime green polo shirts (courtesy of my father) with my name embroidered right above STORE MANAGER, I was considered the head honcho of my father's second NYU location.

I listened to three messages from various clients and fast-forwarded through two sales calls, a couple of *I told you so's* from my mother and one more *poor Jack* before I reached the end.

I took one last, lingering look at my office. It wasn't the biggest space in Manhattan, but it was *très* chic. Even more, it was mine and I'd grown sort of attached to it. Enough that a lump worked its way up into my throat as I walked toward the back door and slipped out into the alley.

Hello? It's not like you're calling it quits and head-

*ing over to NYU. You've still got your very own busi-
ness to run. Small and floundering, particularly with
murder charges hanging over your head, but a business nonetheless.*

I clung to the hope, locked up, replanted the spare
key and morphed back into the batmobile.

My tiny wings beat a fast, furious pace as I topped
the building and headed for number one on my *Alpha
Meet Markets* list—a Knicks game.

Thirteen
❤ ❤ ❤

"**E**vie. That sure is a pretty name." The man (Knicks cap and matching shirt, and jeans) smiled and glanced up from the business card I'd just handed him. I'd purposely grabbed a stack of Evie's cards back at the office rather than my own—do I know how to lay low or what?

We stood in the Play by Play near an air hockey machine. The P by P was a sports bar located inside Madison Square Garden where fans could play video games, make jump shots, and scarf nachos.

The game had ended less than a half hour before and the place overflowed with people psyched over tonight's victory against the Orlando Heat. The two dozen TVs that lined the walls broadcast highlights and the postgame show. Nickelback blasted from the speakers. Cigarette smoke fogged the air. Beer flowed. Testosterone oozed.

I had my foam finger tucked under one arm (okay, so I'm a Knicks fan, too) and an appletini in my hand. I'd been making the rounds when this guy had flagged me down. A table full of men flanked him. Beers in hand, they eyed me and waited for me to (a) throw myself at their friend and renew their faith in womankind or (b) kick him in the nuts like the usual snotty bitch.

The guy had a twinkle in his eyes and a *come here, baby* grin. He leaned in closer and *eau de* Heineken burned my nostrils. "Listen here, sweet thing, why don't we blow this joint and go back to my place?" He winked, which looked more like a blink on account of the fact he was sloshed and both eyes were involved. "I'll let you ride the pony."

Pony? I shook my head, snatched my card back, and stuffed it into my pocket. "Sorry, but I'm in the market for a Clydesdale."

"What?" He looked confused until one of his buddies leaned forward and clapped him on the back.

"She's saying your equipment's too small, dude." A round of laughter erupted and *eau de* Heineken's face turned bright red.

"Actually, I didn't say anything." I smiled at the blinker. "You filled me in on your own." I held up my drink in salute. "Have a good evening."

"Wait a second! That was just a figure of speech." He grabbed my arm as I started to turn. Quite forcefully, I might add.

I gave him another once-over. "Cross your heart and hope to die?"

"Damn straight." He nodded fiercely and puffed out his chest. "There isn't anything small about my equipment. I'm locked and loaded, baby."

My mouth twitched. Where did men come up with this stuff?

"Come on," he begged. His gaze dropped to my chest as if to remind himself what was behind door number one. "Lemme have the card back. I'll give you a call and we can get together. I swear you won't regret it."

"Maybe." *Look into my eyes, bozo.*

He did (have I got it going on in the vamp department or what?). I met his gaze and his stats echoed through my head. Scott Martin Danvers. Played high school football and one year of college. Injured his knee during his sophomore year and felt like his world had ended. Graduated college—barely—with a degree in liberal arts. He worked construction for the city five days a week, played hockey every Saturday afternoon, and went out with his buddies every Saturday night. He liked his beer cold, his women "stacked" and his pre-sex conversation nonexistent. He had a few hang-ups about the size of his package, but what man didn't?

"Here." I tucked several cards into his shirt pocket. "Pass the rest out to your friends." I pointed to the table full of guys who were now whistling and high-fiving each other.

He glanced at the cards. A smile spread from ear-to-ear as dozens of suggestive images raced through his intoxicated brain.

I started to turn.

"Where are you going? I thought you wanted to—"

"Not me," I cut in. "I'm here on behalf of a few close friends. Hot friends," I added when disappointment killed his smile. "They're mega hot." He perked back up. "And busy. They don't have time to cruise for their own men, so I'm doing it for them. If you or your buds are interested, give me a call at my home number—it's on the back—and we'll set up an interview."

"You want to interview us for sex?"

I nodded. "Twice. The first is a preliminary where I find out your sexual likes and dislikes. The second is a little more detailed, including some health questions. If you pass, I'll pair you up with a woman and introduce you to her. You're on your own after that." My throat tightened on the last word.

When I'd thought the process out, it had struck me as very smart and meticulous. But saying it out loud made it sound so . . . smart and meticulous and completely *un*romantic.

Hello? Viola doesn't want romance. She wants sex.

Case in point. I was an advocate for lifelong commitment. A crusader for deep, meaningful relationships. A cheerleader for (gimme an) L-O-V-E. With all of my undead heart and soul, I'd rejected the idea of meaningless sex, yet here I was facilitating it.

On the other hand, if I didn't help Viola and the NUNS, they would simply go on the prowl themselves. Who knew what jerks they might end up with?

Not to mention, the survival of all paranormal species hinged on keeping a low profile.

I had a mental picture of twenty-seven ferocious werewolves humping unsuspecting men during the next Knicks tip-off. Smack-dab in the middle of the Garden. In full view of *mucho* television cameras and a gazillion reporters. Talk about in your face.

The guilt faded in a rush of conviction. I wasn't going against my principles and hooking up one-night stands. I was preserving the safety and well-being of all the Otherworldly races. For a fee, yes, but we're talking *preservation*.

Pumped, I downed the rest of my appletini and headed for a particularly rowdy group of men near the jump shot area. I was halfway across the room when someone touched my shoulder and a deep voice slid into my left ear.

"Yo baby, you give fries with that shake?"

I turned and sized up the man who'd stopped me. He was tall with broad shoulders and a trim waist. Blond hair curled down around the collar of his Knicks T-shirt. Jeans and an interested smile completed the outfit.

I met his gaze.

Jeff. Single. Personal trainer. Hadn't been laid in six months on account of having been desperately in love with his last girlfriend—Tanya—and he wasn't ready to jump into a relationship for fear of getting his heart stomped on *again*.

My nice guy-o-meter registered a big, fat ten.

"Sorry." I shook my head. "McDonald's is closed."

Viola and her girls would swallow this poor chump in one bite. I started to turn and he caught my arm.

"Look, I'm sorry. I know it was lame but I haven't done this in a while. What's your name?"

"Li—*ttle*," I finished. "Little Evie." I'm not used to being undercover, okay? Give me a break. "But my friends call me Evie, without the Little. Evie Dalton. I work for Dead End Dating, the hottest dating service in Manhattan."

"A dating service?"

"It's really more like a life-long commitment facilitator. While we do set up dates initially, we're ultimately looking to hook up each of our clients with their one true love. We're all about the future."

"What about you?" His pale green eyes sparked with hope. "Have you found that one true love?"

"Yes. I mean, no. I mean, it's a bit more complicated for me. See, there are other factors involved when I personally hook up with someone."

"So you don't do much dating yourself?"

"Actually, no." His disappointment was so profound, that the words tumbled from my lips before I could stop them. "Not anymore. I mean, I can't because one of those factors I mentioned actually involves a boyfriend. See, I have one. Yeah." I smiled. "I've got one of those, so I really can't go around dating."

"Say no more. Good luck." He let go of my arm and started to turn.

"But you can still call me." I stopped him with a card. "I mean, not me personally, but I'm sure I can find someone nice for you." When he hesitated, I added, "You have to get back in the game sometime." *Besides, you're a great guy. Forget about whatshername. She wouldn't know a good thing if it jumped up and bit her on the ass. I know dozens of clients who would kill for a guy like you.*

Okay, so maybe not *dozens*. But I had a good two or three human women who would be totally jazzed to go out with a single, successful guy who actually believed in love.

"You think?" I nodded and the doubt swimming in his gaze faded. He stood a little taller. A smile tugged at his lips as his fingers tightened around the DED card. "Thanks. Maybe I will give you a call."

"I hope so." *I really hope so*, I added silently. "I'll be waiting." The prospect of making a genuine love connection on top of preserving the races pumped my ego.

I spent the next hour and a half until last call scoping out alpha material and handing out business cards.

It was half past one a.m. when I decided to quit for the night. Not that it was late by my standards, but I hadn't slept much that day and I felt tapped out. Besides, I had every intention of getting home before Ty.

After all, the poor guy was going out of his way, putting his own career and reputation on the line just to help me out. The least I could do was limit the amount of stress I heaped on him.

In other words, what he didn't know wouldn't hurt him. Or me. Nuff said.

*   *   *

Being a hot, happening, fantastically well-dressed vampire wasn't all it was cracked up to be. When people thought of vampires, they generally pictured these extraordinary, larger-than-life beings with oodles of power and charisma and sex appeal.

Talk about a tough image to live up to.

For the most part the portrayal was pretty accurate, but we did have some flaws. Obviously minimal compared to most humans, but flaws nonetheless.

Geez, nobody's perfect.

In fact, it's really those imperfections that make us likeable. Loveable, even.

I stared at Ty's front door and barely resisted the urge to beat my head against the damned thing. Instead, I reached for his doorknob and turned. Again.

All right, so I'd locked myself out. Loveable, remember? He had said to keep the door locked, and I've always been an extremely conscientious houseguest. The delectable aroma of rich leather and hunky male drifted from the other side of the door and teased my nostrils. I had the sudden urge to kick off my boots, collapse on Ty's couch, close my eyes and drink in the scent of him that filled the place.

My grip tightened on the handle. I could get in if I really wanted to; at the same time, I didn't want to mess up Ty's door.

No problem.

I turned and put my back to the door. Sliding into a sitting position, I crossed my legs and settled in. I would simply sit here and when he arrived, I would make up some reason for being out in the hallway.

Yeah, Einstein? Like what?

I wasn't sure, but I figured I had at least twenty minutes to figure it out. I'd left the bar at one thirty and Ty's place was a five to ten minute flight—whoa!

The door jerked backward and I found myself lying flat on my back, staring up at Ty, who towered over me.

He wore the black jeans and T-shirt he'd left the house in, black biker boots, and a mad-as-hell expression.

Uh-oh.

"You're home," I blurted.

"And you're not." He plucked the foam finger from my hand and left me laying on his doorstep.

I scrambled upright—another black mark on the ultra hot vamp image. Vamps didn't scramble. We vaulted or glided or whirled, or something equally cool sounding.

I searched my brain for a believable story as I climbed to my feet and followed him over to the sofa. I had a really good one by the time I reached him, too. I'd heard a loud siren and I'd felt certain the cops were about to bust through the windows (did I mention I heard choppers, too?). Anyhow, I'd panicked and ran. But his words had stayed with me and so I'd subconsciously locked up behind me. Once I'd realized the choppers weren't real, I'd been forced to camp out on his doorstep and wait for him to return.

Sounded good to me.

I opened my mouth, but the only thing that came out was, "Give me the finger."

"Believe me, I'd like to."

"No, really." I reached for the foam contraption.

He held it just out of my reach. "The Knicks," he mused, turning the souvenier this way and that. "Can't say as I've ever seen a game in person. I've wanted to, but I'm usually too busy chasing down bad guys and helping stubborn born vampires who refuse to listen and completely undermine my efforts."

"You've helped another born vampire before?"

His frown deepened. "You're going to get us both staked."

He looked so serious that my stomach tilted and I knew then that there was more to my situation than just clearing up a little misunderstanding. "It's bad, isn't it?"

He set the finger aside, ran a hand through his hair, and nodded. "Worse than I expected."

"How much worse?"

"They have evidence. Real evidence."

"The cell phone picture, right?"

"That and a DNA sample."

"My DNA?" I smiled. "This is good news. See, there's no way they can have *my* DNA. If I go in and they test me, they'll know that. The charges will be dropped and I won't be starring on this week's *Cops*."

"And what if it does match?"

"But it can't. I didn't do anything."

"I know that."

"Then what are you trying to say?"

"That I think someone is trying to frame you for murder. Someone really smart. Someone who left absolutely no evidence behind that could incriminate them. Instead, it all points to you." His bright blue gaze collided with mine. "Someone's *framing* you."

His words sank in and panic ballooned in my stomach and floated into my chest. My throat burned. *Framed? Me?*

My brain raced with this new information. I wanted to argue with him. Who in their right mind would want to frame *me*?

I was *so* totally likeable. Just ask The Ninas. Or Evie. Or any of my clients (with the exception of Mr. Slice and Dice) who put their faith in me to find them a soul mate, for Damien's sake. I also gave change to homeless people and waited my turn at crosswalks and I'd always tipped Dirkst, my tanning specialist, rather generously (the guy had the biggest spray gun in Manhattan and knew how to use it). Sure, there was that time when the cashier at Starbucks had given me a twenty back when I'd only handed her a ten, but that had been her mistake, not mine. Overall, I rocked in the likeable person department.

No way would someone want to frame *me*. It simply wasn't possible.

At the same time, Keith and his new blue shirt were dead and I was wearing oversize sweat pants and a Hanes T-shirt.

"That's the only explanation," Ty went on. "The pieces fit together too well for this to be just a circumstantial thing. You were there, you get your picture taken minutes before the murder and just so happen to leave fingerprints everywhere, including on the murder weapon, and a few samples of your own blood."

"A blood sample?"

"I told you they had DNA evidence."

"I know, but I was thinking saliva or something."

"Did you salivate at the victim's apartment?"

"No, but . . ." I shook my head. "There's no way they could have my blood."

"I would agree with you, but this thing's been too carefully orchestrated to bet on the off chance that the murderer messed up on this one detail that solidifies the case against you. I think we have to assume it's yours and work under the assumption that someone is out to nail you for this."

"But who would do such a thing?"

He eyed me for a long moment. "You tell me." When I just shook my head, he added, "Literally. I want you to make a list of any and everyone you can think of who might want to frame you for murder."

I sank down to the sofa as the reality of the situation hit. There really was someone out there who *hated* me. So much that they wanted to have me arrested and locked up for the next hundred or so years. Surely they couldn't give me longer than that? But what if I got a life sentence? I could be locked up for *eternity*.

"You're not going to start crying again, are you?" Ty's deep voice slid into my ears and I glanced over at him.

His image swam and I blinked frantically.

Before I could respond, he said, "Don't. If there's one thing you need to do right now, it's keep your head on straight. You have to think." He pushed to his feet and retrieved some paper and a pen from one of the kitchen drawers. "Think hard and write. That'll give us a place to start looking."

I blinked furiously and (big high five for me) managed to hold back the moisture that stung my eyes. He was right. I needed to hold it together if I wanted to get out of this. *Write,* I told myself as I stared at the paper.

"I don't know anyone who hates me," I said fifteen minutes later. A sniffle punctuated the sentence.

"They don't have to hate you. They just need a motive. Think of someone you might have pissed off recently. Maybe a dissatisfied client. A disgruntled neighbor."

"So they don't have to *hate* me." I wasn't sure why this new information made me feel less icky, but it did. I sat up straighter and managed to swallow despite the tightness in my throat. "You just want someone with a motive. Maybe someone I've wronged, however inadvertently."

He nodded. "It doesn't take much to motivate a psychopath."

"I'll try, but I'm afraid it might be a little short," I warned him.

What can I say? I *was* voted Most Popular at my four hundred and eighty–year class reunion. Granted, it was just me, The Ninas, and my old tutor Jacques doing the voting (we're talking *four hundred and eighty years*), but it was the principle that counted.

Namely, I'm all that and a chocolate martini. I mean, really. Who would want to hurt *me*?

Fourteen
❤ ❤ ❤

"Can I have more paper?" I asked Ty a good half
hour later.

"Did you mess that one up?"

"No, I filled it up."

So much for a short list.

"The entire sheet?"

"You said to write down anyone I could think of.
That's what I did."

"But an entire sheet?"

"Thanks for sounding shocked. So much for telling
myself I'm not a total loser." His lips twitched and I
knew he wanted to grin.

He motioned to me. "Let me see what you've got."

He scanned the list I gave him, which started with
my neighbors, the Griffiths, who lived on the first
floor of my building. While they didn't have children,
they had meddling mothers and a cat. A big, fat Sia-

mese who absolutely detested vampires. The Griffiths themselves always waved whenever we passed near the mailboxes, but Sasha always hissed.

While I didn't think Mac and Eileen were kooky enough to let a cat dictate their friends, what did I *really* know about them (except that Mac's mother drove Eileen crazy and her mother kept him *this close* to a straitjacket)? Maybe they were psychotic killers who went after anyone, no matter how fantastically dressed, who didn't make the grade with Sasha.

Hey, it could happen.

"I doubt a cat is framing you for murder."

"The owners of the cat. The cat is just part of the selective process."

He shook his head and kept reading. A few seconds ticked by before he arched an eyebrow at me. "Maybelline Magenta at L. C.? Is that someone's name?"

"Lip color." Some people remembered names. Others faces. I rocked when it came to shades of lip gloss. "She was this lady I ran into at Liz Claiborne last week." When he didn't look any more enlightened. "During their last designer closeout." Still no lightbulbs. To think I actually lusted after this guy.

"They do them every so often—all the designers do—usually with just a last-minute notice to the public," I prodded. "This one was done after hours as a special perk for repeat customers. While I don't do Liz as often as I'd like, I'm still on a first-name basis with most of the sales staff. Particularly Kiki who handles the closeouts."

Kiki was a doll with great taste in clothes, a pixie

haircut (I *know*: so yesterday, but on her it kicked butt and looked totally retro), and flawless makeup (Kiwiberry from Sephora).

Kiki also knew my size and wasn't shy about stuffing any and everything I might like under the counter until I zoomed in. What can I say? She was bisexual and totally susceptible to my vamp charms.

"Anyhow," I went on, "Kiki called and invited me. I got there as soon as I could—I obviously had to wait for sunset—but the place was already packed. That's when I ran into Maybelline Magenta. We had a difference of opinion. She thought she should be in front of me, and I thought she shouldn't. Kiki was too busy trying to help this other woman stuff her size fourteen ass into a pair of size ten jeans to referee."

"And?"

"And I elbowed her. The woman, not Kiki."

His eyebrow kicked up a notch. "Hard enough to make her go to the trouble to kill someone and frame you for the murder?"

"I might have kicked her, too."

"*Might* have?"

"Okay, so I kicked her." I shrugged. "But I didn't mean to. I was trying to trip her. See, the elbow in her ribs made her double over, but she kept on running. She was as heterosexual as they come, so vamping was out of the question. I had to do *something*. She was headed for the last pair of black linen gauchos."

"I'm assuming the L'Oreal Wild Cranberry and the Clinique Slick Sunburst are part of the same incident."

I gave a nod. "I needed a white button-up and a scarf to go with the gauchos."

"I doubt any of these women would *kill* over an outfit."

"It was a really cute outfit."

Ty folded the list and stuffed it into his pocket. "If the extra paper was for more of the same, just keep it to yourself. I'll check out everyone you've already written down and see if anything turns up. We'll work it from there. In the meantime . . ." He handed me back my foam finger. "No more Knicks games."

"No problem." I'd already maxed out my alpha possibilities at the stadium. I was headed for Home Depot next.

He frowned. "You're not going to a Home Depot, or anywhere else, for that matter." His eyes narrowed to dangerous slits and my heart pitter-pattered. "I mean it. This is a lot more serious than some stupid misunderstanding. We're talking fucking *DNA*. You have to stay off the radar until we can give the police enough evidence and a motive that points to someone besides you." When I started to open my mouth, he added, "They've upped the reward."

"How much?"

"One hundred thousand."

I smiled. That was more like it. Then I frowned. "Which means even more people will be gunning for me."

He nodded and my stomach bottomed out. "Humans and vamps, and neither play nice when that much money is involved." He let his words sink in for a few seconds before he added, "You'll be safe here, provided you do what I say."

"And stay put."

"Exactly."

"For how long?"

"As long as it takes." He pushed to his feet. "I have to go out again for a little while—I've got to meet someone—but I'll be back in an hour." He pulled a slim silver cell phone from his pocket and handed it to me.

"What's this?" Dumb question since I already knew (see description above). What I didn't know was what it *meant*.

It means you can talk for longer than thirty seconds, provided you don't call a number that's being tapped.

I gave him my most chilling stare. "I *really* hate it when you do that."

He grinned. "I picked it up this evening. It's registered to a safe user and can't be traced back to you. Meaning, your name won't show up on anyone's call list. I've also blocked the number from caller ID. You can call anyone except Dead End Dating. The cops are tapping the phone line there and tracing all incoming calls. While they wouldn't be able to trace this particular phone to you, they're bound to have voice recognition capability, which means they'll figure it out. So no calling the office."

"But I can call Evie at home, right? And The Ninas?"

He nodded. "The judge issued a warrant to monitor DED's line only in addition to your personal cell phone. The cops pushed to get a tap on your parents, too, but Judge Ellis refused." At my surprised expression, he added, "While he can't ignore the evidence, he isn't ready to give up one of his own by being overly cooperative."

"He's a vampire?"

Ty nodded. "Lucky for you. Otherwise, you wouldn't be able to call your folks."

Lucky for me.

I ignored the depressing thought and focused on the positive. I was reconnected to the world!

Sort of.

"You can also check your voice mail. Just don't delete anything or tamper with pre-existing messages in case the police are keeping tabs on them, as well." He eyed me. "You should really connect with your parents ASAP. I'm sure they're pretty freaked with everything going on."

"I don't know if freaked is the right word to use for my folks." Freak-y maybe.

"They can't be that bad."

I frowned. "Could you not do that?"

"What?"

"Read my mind."

"I'm not reading it. You're broadcasting thoughts. If you don't want me to hear, you need to learn to keep them to yourself."

"That's a great theory and everything, but it doesn't clue me in on how to do it."

"Put up a shield."

"Much better. You know, you should really give a

few seminars on the topic. You're a natural born teacher."

"Later." He winked and my heart jumped. "Have fun."

The "fun" that rushed through my mind as the door closed behind him had nothing to do with the phone and everything to do with Ty and his wink.

And a few, er, certain body parts.

That lasted all of two minutes—not Ty, but the thoughts—before I managed to kill the fantasy and focus on the pressing matter at hand: reconnecting with the outside world. There were a dozen calls I needed to make, starting with the most pressing person on the list. The one who was surely killing herself with worry over my whereabouts and my well-being. The woman whose livelihood and contribution to the species depended solely on *moi*.

I punched in Viola Hamilton's number.

Fifteen

"**V**iola Hamilton, please," I murmured when a woman's voice murmured "Hello?"

"Just a sec." I heard a lot of crackling—or maybe that was growling. After all, it was still a few hours until sunup. Viola and the NUNS were most likely enjoying the clear, moonlit night.

More growling and lots of panting and . . .

"Was that a scream?" I asked when Viola picked up the phone.

"Practice," Viola clarified. "Marnie Jackson is here with this guy she met at the shooting range—he's a cop—and they're making a practice run before the full moon."

Several things registered in the next few moments. Namely (a) they were having their "practice" run in front of everyone, and (b) Marnie was one of the twenty-seven I needed to hook up, which meant that knocked the total down to twenty-six, and (c) they were having their "practice" run in front of *everyone*.

Of course, I focused on the point that had me the most freaked out. "Does that mean that you only need twenty-six alpha males?"

"Actually, the practice run isn't going as well as anticipated—he's the one who screamed—so Marnie's still on the list. And I need to add Emily. She and her live-in just had a terrible breakup. Of course, we'll be happy to pay the necessary late fees that might apply."

I smiled. "Of course."

"So how's the search going?" she went on.

"Great. In fact, that's why I'm calling. To touch base with you and reassure you that I'm on top of things and that there's nothing to worry about. Not that you're worried since you have nothing whatsoever to worry about. But just in case you might be inclined to worry, don't. I'm searching as we speak."

"I was talking about the search for you, dear. That was a nasty little episode at your office. No blood, unfortunately, but still nasty. Have you ever seen so much polyester in your life?"

If I were a vicious werewolf in desperate need to hump during the next full moon, I would have fallen head over Manolo heels for Viola.

"It *was* a lot of polyester, wasn't it?"

"Positively ghastly. If you're out cruising for men, I'm assuming everything is straightened out."

"I'm still wanted for murder. Temporarily. The police will soon realize they've made a mistake and turn their attention to the real killer. In the meantime, it's business as usual."

"So you're back at work in the office."

"I'm back at work, but I'm doing things from a different location. Not that it matters where I work from. It's really the legwork that counts the most in the matchmaking business, and I'm doing plenty of that. I'm functioning at full capacity and raking in the alpha males."

"Have you found any matches?"

"Well, no. Not yet. But I have found several prospective matches, and you can be certain that I'll have twenty-eight tall, dark, and dangerous alpha males ready to go in time for the full moon."

"About the dark part . . . Emily's a little quirky. She likes redheads. She's got a thing for Ron Howard."

"Who?"

"Ron Howard. He's a director and producer now—*A Beautiful Mind* and all that—but he used to act. He played Richie Cunningham in *Happy Days*. It's this old series that featured this really clean-cut kid and the perfect 1950s family. But he had a wild side. He played in a band on the show and that's when Emily fell in love with him. Needless to say, she can't shake the infatuation and it's colored every relationship she's had since. Which is why she doesn't have a suitable partner now."

In my opinion, Emily needed a therapist more than a matchmaker.

"I know it's short notice, but I'll be glad to write you a check for adding her on at the last minute and catering to her particular fetish."

I smiled. "I can do Ron Howard."

"Ron Howard with an attitude. While she likes the look, she still needs the guy to ooze testosterone to get her biologically worked up."

"So what does this Ron guy actually look like?" I so needed to watch more television. "Other than the red hair?" I crossed my fingers. "Is he rugged like the Marlboro Man?"

"Harmless. Like Howdy Doody."

"Howdy who?"

"You know. Howdy Doody and Clarabelle? The kids' show."

I'd never seen *Howdy Doody*, but the phrase *kid's show* was enough to tell me this was way over my head.

"Howdy's this puppet. He has pasty white skin and lots of freckles and he wears a plaid shirt. And a neckerchief."

O-kay.

"And he parts his hair on the side."

Just say no. You can't produce an alpha Howdy Doody. No one in the Free World could come up with one. Ever. Much less in a week and a half.

"One alpha Howdy coming right up."

Hey, we're talking *late fees.*

"Wonderful. Oh, and tell your father that he can spray as much weed killer as he likes on my bushes, but it won't work. The girls and I have been peeing on them for at least a month. They're so healthy, they're immune to any and everything short of nuclear fall-out."

I had a quick mental of Viola and the NUNS "fertilizing" the length of hedges that separated her property from my folks.

"I'll be sure to pass on the information." Just as soon as Morse code became vogue again and put Sprint out of business. "I'll contact you in a few days. And remember, there's no need to worry. I can do this."

"I can't do this," I told Evie a few minutes later when she picked up the phone. "Not by myself. I need your help."

"Lil?" A yawn punctuated the question. "I mean, Mrs. Vandergartenpitt?"

"It's *flunkin*pitt, and you can lose the alias. The police aren't tapping your line."

Another yawn. "How do you know?"

"I've got connections."

"The bounty hunter." Sheets rustled and mattress springs creaked. Her voice took on an air of excitement. "You're with the bounty hunter, aren't you? I knew it. I went over all of the possibilities in my head, and it could only be the bounty hunter. He's the only one who could actually help you get out of this mess. I mean, he's got connections and he knows how to track down killers. It only makes sense that you would go to him for help."

"I am *so* not with the bounty hunter."

"You are *so* lying."

"Am not."

"Are, too."

"Can we get back to the subject? We both have work to do."

"It's four in the morning. I'm not due into the office for another five hours. Tell me about Ty."

"Who?"

"Ty Bonner. The bounty hunter. You *are* with him."

I tried for a laugh, which came out sounding as nervous as I felt. "Says you. Listen, I really need your help."

"I already told the police that you would never chop anyone into little pieces."

"Thanks for the vote of confidence, but that's not what I'm talking about. You know our new client? Viola Hamilton?"

"The one who was in your office when the cops came?"

"That's the one. She wants me to make several matches, which is no problem except that one of them needs to be a redhead. A testosterone-oozing redhead."

"Like a young Kenneth Branagh?"

"More like Howdy Doody."

"You've got to be kidding."

"You know Howdy?"

"I don't just watch *CSI*. Listen, Lil. It's not possible. We're talking *orange* hair. You're not going to find a man with orange anything who oozes testosterone."

"Just keep your eyes open. If you see anyone on the street who fits the bill, slip him a card. Also, check out some of the online sites. Cruise profiles and see if you can spot someone—anyone—who might work. I'll be looking, too. Oh, and you know the new client—Rachel Sanchez?"

"She called yesterday."

"I'll work on her while I'm doing Viola." While I knew Evie could make a great match, herself, she wasn't privy to all Rachel's quirks—namely that she morphed into the Taco Bell spokespooch when the moon was full—and so I felt compelled to handle the were myself. Step one? Googling the mating habits of were-Chihuahuas.

"Oh, and Esther called again," Evie said. "She wants to know if you've found her anyone and I said no. You haven't, have you?"

"No." Esther, made vampire and old maid, was proving to be a much more difficult match than I'd originally expected. The problem? I didn't really know any male made vampires, except for Ty, and he totally was not her type. At first, I'd thought so, but after I'd gotten to know him (via Google—ya gotta love the Internet—a really hot and heavy kiss, and, oh yeah, drinking his blood), I'd ruled him out as a possibility.

"She sounds so . . . sad. What should I do?"

"You don't have any more uncles do you?" We had, on at least one occasion, paired up a client with one of Evie's relatives for a practice date until we could find the real thing. While it hadn't been a huge success (he'd been old and prone to falling asleep and she'd been a vivacious vampire who'd liked to dance), it hadn't been a total failure either (vivacious vamp had bought the practice date spiel and given us another chance). "Maybe one who isn't collecting social security?"

She seemed to think. "There's my uncle Darwin. He's on disability rather than social security because he lost a testicle during World War I."

In other words, the man was older than dirt.

On the other hand, Esther *had* been around during that war (she was over one hundred and she hadn't had a date in as many years) which meant they might actually have something in common.

"Set them up," I told Evie.

I called The Ninas next, but neither picked up, so I had to leave a message. I also called my brothers, and Francis and Melissa (my first vamp client and his live-in human girlfriend), and Ayala aka the pickiest born vamp in existence. The night was still young (if you were a vamp) and so the only one who actually answered was Melissa. I explained my predicament and gave her my new cell number in case she needed to contact me (not that she would since she and Francis were extremely happy despite their obvious differences). But the phone call pumped my ego enough that I actually started to think I could find a redhead who oozed testosterone. I'd matched up Francis, the geekiest vamp in the universe. Nothing could be harder than that. Right?

I left a message for Ayala, along with a "Born vamp coming right up!" and then I sat staring at the phone.

I really should call my folks. Then again, I was a businesswoman (not a chicken). I had priorities.

Punching in the number, I spent the next minute navigating through my voice mailbox until I reached my messages.

"Hi, Lil. It's Ayala. You still haven't called me back and I'm wondering about this weekend. I think we should try something different. Maybe a blond again. But taller this time. With very little facial hair because I really don't like a lot of facial hair. And loyal. This last guy had the number for Marc's Speedy Supper programmed into his cell phone. I absolutely won't abide by an eternity mate who's constantly sinking his fangs into someone else. I want a bottle man." A beep signaled the end of the message.

While I wasn't much for blonds, the bottle part I could relate to.

"Message two," an automated female voice said. Followed by a familiar "Lil?"

It was Nina One. Blond, beautiful, and totally superficial. "I need to talk to you right away." Anxiety filled her voice. "It's an emergency. I can't decide between the Dolce and Gabbana snakeskin clutch or the new pink Louis Vuitton. The first will totally go with these divine shoes I just bought, but the pink Louis is absolutely the cutest thing you've ever seen. Call me." *Beep*.

"Message three . . . Lilliana, this is your mother. We're hunting tomorrow night rather than Sunday. Your father and I have a pressing commitment on our usual night which is why we have to reschedule for Saturday. Make sure you're on time. Oh, and your father needs you to stop off at Golftown on West Thirty-second and pick up a box of Ben Hogans. Make sure you get the Tour Deep balls and not the Hawk Twelve. Your father absolutely detests the Hawks. He says they shorten his putt. I'm inclined to think that it's his swing that shortens his putt, but you know your father." *Beep*.

"End of messages."

I hit the off button and stared at the phone.

Golftown? Sure, it was a pretty cool store if you were into golf, but I wasn't. Even more, I was on the run from the cops. Polyester-wearing cops. A place like Golftown would surely be crawling with police. With all those loud, obnoxious pants, it was like church.

My mother, of course, hadn't given one thought to the fact that she was sending me into the lion's den. No, she only cared about golf balls. And being on time to the precious hunt.

I was a fugitive, for Damien's sake! On the run. Fighting to get my afterlife back. I didn't have time to go to Golftown, let alone the hunt. Sure, we'd been doing it for over three hundred years and in all that time, the only person who'd ever missed had been Max. But he'd gotten held over at Moe's doing inventory and so he'd been quickly forgiven by my parents. Otherwise, all children had been present (albeit grudgingly) and accounted for. End of story.

I wasn't counting highlighters and Liquid Paper, but I was doing something equally important—laying low. I wasn't going to risk getting caught by traipsing all the way out to Connecticut.

No way. No how. Nuh-uh.

That's what I told myself as I crawled into Ty's bed and closed my eyes just before daybreak.

Done deal. No hunt. Not this vampire.

Sixteen
❤ ❤ ❤

"I forgot Dad's balls," I blurted when my mother opened the back door at a quarter past nine on Saturday night.

While I did have *some* backbone (I'd purposely bypassed Golftown on my way over), it went all soft and Jell-O-ey when faced with the prospect of breaking three hundred years of Marchette tradition.

"I meant to stop off and pick them up," I rushed on, "but I couldn't get away and—"

"It's about time," my mother declared.

Jacqueline Marchette wore a chocolate-colored silk wrap dress, a diamond Tiffany choker and matching bracelet, and a disapproving frown. Her long, dark brown hair had been slicked back into a chic ponytail that accented her high cheekbones and sculpted nose. Thick eyelashes fringed her rich brown eyes. Chanel's Chocolate Mousse slicked her full lips. She smelled of

French perfume, cherries jubilee, and *lots* of money (what born vampire didn't?).

I'd been fortunate enough to snag my favorite Diane von Furstenberg wrap dress—black and white with cap sleeves—before fleeing from the cops and a fab pair of black leather Vivia's, so I didn't feel under-dressed.

"Your brothers have been here for over an hour," my mother informed me.

Geez, Mom, It's great to hear you're doing so well. Me? Well, I'm wanted for murder, which means every cop between here and Manhattan is looking for me. I've got an overprotective bounty hunter for a baby-sitter. And my hair—damn its traitorous soul—refused to cooperate. In a nutshell, I'm peachy. Just peachy.

"Your father and I count on these nights, Lilliana," she went on, "and we fully expect our children to hold them in the same regard."

"I do." I smiled. It was that or bust into tears, and my mom isn't really the type you can cry in front of. (Plunder small villages? Yes. Cry? No friggin' way.) "The next time I resist arrest and go on the lam, I'll be sure to ask for hunt nights off in advance."

"It's the very least you can do, dear."

I know she gave birth to me and we share the same bloodline and I should be eternally thankful and all. I wouldn't be here in all my vamp glory if it weren't for the sixteen hours of extremely painful labor valiantly endured by the woman standing in front of me. I *know* (namely because she reminded me on all major holidays and my birthday) and I appreciate it. Really. It's just that sometimes (i.e., now) I felt like smacking her.

"Don't just stand there." She motioned me inside. "Everyone is waiting."

While she was as uptight and pretentious as ever, I knew something was off when, instead of gliding toward the living room in her totally fab pair of strappy leather Jimmy Choos, she reached for a bottle of Scotch that sat on a nearby counter and downed a swig.

It wasn't the alcohol that clued me in, but the fact that she didn't bother pouring it into a glass. My mom was the walking poster girl for born vampire decorum. She dressed her best, minded her manners, and never played with her food (except that time she'd played a few sets with Martina Navratilova).

"*Everyone.*" She took another swig and swiped the edge of her mouth with the back of one perfectly manicured hand. "Including Jack's human."

My brother had been bringing his human flavor of the week for as long as I could remember. While my folks didn't like it, they usually dismissed it with a "Male vampires will be male dicks, er, that is vampires" mentality. But this was different. This was . . .

Realization hit and I perked up. "Dr. Mandy's here?"

My mother cut me a startled stare. "You know her?"

"Um, no. Not really." Sure, she'd loaded me into a morgue drawer, but that didn't mean we were friends for afterlife, right? "I know she's a doctor and her name is Mandy." When Mom arched one perfectly sculpted eyebrow, I added, "Jack told me."

"Since when do you and Jack talk?"

Since I've been on the run for murder and he loaned me an obscene amount of money that I fully intend to pay back just as soon as my life gets back to normal and the planets align.

She seemed to have forgotten that all-important tidbit—me being on the run—in her desperation for Scotch and I wasn't about to remind her. Besides, she looked upset. Shaken, even.

I know, right? *My* mother.

I couldn't help but respond to her desperate need for empathy (and my desperate need to stay off the chopping block) and lie. "Did I say Jack? I meant Max."

I expected the usual long, thoughtful, suspicious look.

She waved a hand. "I can't believe he brought her tonight." She shook her head. "Your father and I agreed to meet her and *those* people tomorrow evening. Not that we fully expected to actually meet them. Your father and I felt certain we could reason with him after the hunt. *Tonight.* It's obvious he and this Mandy human are completely wrong for each other. But then he showed up with her. Now she's here and he's . . ." She shook her head again. "I simply cannot believe this. You should see him. He's completely beside himself." She shook her head. "He's just so *different.*"

"He's in love."

She looked at me as if I'd sprouted a halo before waving her hand again. "There's obviously some powerful magic at work. She *has* to be a witch. That's the only explanation for this drastic behavioral change. He's like a different vampire since he met her."

"That's actually a good thing." On account of Jack's usually a shit and all.

Okay, now I'd sprouted a halo *and* angel wings. "Are you *insane*? How in the world is he supposed to spend forever with a *human*?" Before I could point out what was obvious to everyone except for my mother (who would sooner drive a stake into her own heart than do the unthinkable and *make* a vampire) she added, "I need another drink." She downed a long swig.

I stepped forward (to smack her, of course) and found myself patting her back and mumbling, "It'll be all right."

Crazy, right? But I'd been freaked out myself when I'd seen Jack with Mandy. I could only imagine how my mom felt what with him being the fruit of her womb (my mother's words, not mine).

She took several more drinks before setting the bottle on the counter and straightening her shoulders. "I'm ready," she said. "The sooner we get in there, the sooner we can send Mandy back to the city and talk some sense into Jack."

"Sounds like a plan."

I followed my mother into the living room and braced myself for my father's reaction when she announced, "Lil forgot your balls." Followed by the inevitable, "Lil, we'd like you to meet . . ." where she introduced me to this week's fix-up. Aka the latest prime specimen of born male vampness wealthy and fertile enough to be her future son-in-law and the sire of her grandchildren.

"Lil's here," she said. "Rob's *it*." She clapped her hands. "Come on, vampires. Let's get this show on the road!"

Wait a second.

I glanced around. My father. Max. Rob. Jack. Dr. Mandy. Mom. My father. Max. Rob. Jack. Dr. Mandy . . .

Holy shit.

"Are you okay?" Jack asked as he came up next to me.

"I love you, bro." I planted a big, wet one on his cheek. "I *really* love you." I headed for the back veranda before I broke down and wept with gratitude.

No awkward fix-up. No Mom on my back, pointing out my flaws, berating me for not doing the expected thing and squeezing out a grandchild for her like so-and-so's daughter. No dad giving me the "eye" and wondering if I'm a lesbian. Not that I have anything against same-sex relationships, but I wouldn't want people thinking I'm a Sephora girl when I do all my shopping at MAC. Same principle.

The point? This moment . . . What can I say? It was my fondest dream come true (okay, so maybe it wasn't *the* fondest, but it ranked right up there with finding my eternity mate and rolling around naked on the beach with Ty). We're talking *heaven*.

Not that I did much talking or thinking about the big H. I rarely gave any thought to the "What happens next?" concept. After all, I'm immortal.

But every once in a great while when I did imagine the "What if I were human—not that I want to be—but what if I *were*?" thing, when I did, H-E-A-V-E-N always consisted of an accepting, supportive family that didn't think of me as the black sheep.

Black is so *not* my color.

Seventeen

❤ ❤ ❤

The next few moments passed in a frantic blur as my mother herded everyone outside, toward the veranda steps.

Rob got the usual head start and raced down the steps, across the lawn, and into the trees. The *it* person takes the lead and whoever catches him first and gets close enough to blow the whistle around his neck wins.

My father had his usual stopwatch, but before the hand could tick off a full minute, my mom gave the "Go" signal to the rest of us.

My mother and Max took off after Rob. My father was slow on the start, but once he realized what was happening, he hit the forest at warp speed, an enraged look on his face, a competitive gleam in his eyes.

I lagged behind as usual, ready to circle back

around just as soon as everyone was out of sight. Mandy was slowing Jack down, however, and so the three of us practically crawled toward the cluster of trees that loomed just beyond the lawn.

Eventually my bro and his sweetie came to a dead stop for a long, lingering kiss (totally cute or what?), and I took advantage of the distraction. I cut to the right and headed for my usual spot—the pool house.

I'd barely settled into a lounge chair to go over my Alpha Meet Market list when I heard the shrill sound of the whistle that signaled the end of the hunt. I glanced at the clock on the portable fridge.

Three minutes?

Not that I was complaining. I was just surprised.

Even more when my mother emerged from the woods a few minutes later dragging a startled Rob by the whistle wrapped around his neck.

"You have to be kidding me," Max said as she hauled him up the veranda steps. "She hasn't won the hunt in, like, two hundred years."

Not since the time she'd beaten my father and he'd pouted for three decades. While she always participated, she usually held back and let someone else walk away with the coveted Moe's vacation days.

Usually.

Then again, she was desperate to speed things along and get Jack away from Mandy.

Obviously, mothers didn't just lift cars to save their children. They also tackled other vampires (even the fruit of their womb) and beat the shit out of them when necessary.

"You didn't have to hit me." Rob followed her as she led him past us and into the house.

"Stop being such a *bébé*," she snapped and tugged him even faster.

Inside, he collapsed on the sofa in the living room and leaned his head back against the cushions. His left eye was black and swollen and he looked as if he'd just tangled with a pack of werewolves rather than his own *maman*.

My mother shrugged and walked over to the bar to pour him a glass of blood. "It's a hunt, dear. One must do what is necessary to capture one's prey."

"You kicked me, too." He touched his thigh and his face went visibly pale.

"Only once." She handed him the glass and studied him for a nanosecond. "You're fine."

"I hurt like hell and it wasn't just once. It was two and a half times."

"How do you kick someone a half time?" Max asked.

"She tried to kick, but I ducked and rolled and so she barely grazed me," Rob explained.

"That was ducking and rolling? It looked more like crying and begging to me." My mother shrugged. "I had to subdue you and prevent you from running."

"The chase is half the fun." My father sank into an armchair, a glass of his favorite AB-negative in his hand and a sullen look on his face. "But you killed that, Jacqueline. As usual."

"Oh, hush. I've let you have your fun for two centuries. On top of that, I say nothing when you and

Viola go at it every other week when it's time to trim those blasted hedges."

"Those are *my* hedges and I can trim them when and if I damn well feel like it. Of course, I won't have to once the weed killer really sets in."

I opened my mouth to tell him about Viola and the pee fest, but then thought better of it. I mean, really, who was I to interrupt when they were so totally engrossed in a conversation with each other? No need to distract them.

"The man at the nursery said it should take a few weeks and then *bam,* no more azalea bushes." His mouth crooked in a devilish smile.

"See?" my mother told him. "You're having fun. You always have fun. The least you can do is lose gracefully this one time."

My father's expression faded back to sullen. "I did not lose. You can't lose if you don't get the chance to even try. I would have beat you hands down if you hadn't broken the rule about no contact in the first ten minutes."

"Since when is there a rule about no contact in the first ten minutes?"

Since my father had made it up.

"There's always been a ten minute rule," Dad went on. "Why do you think the hunt always takes so long?"

"Because our children have become victims of modern civilization and we aren't as fast as we used to be."

"For your information, I'm as fast and as vicious as I ever was." He bared his fangs and flashed my mother a *See this?* look. "My guard was down tonight because I didn't expect you to break the rules. If I had known, I would have put my best foot forward a hell of a lot sooner, I'll tell you that much. A hell of a lot sooner."

"Certainly, dear." My mom retreated into her usual appeasing self—when it came to my father, that is. I guess after six hundred years of commitment, it's easier to just go with the flow sometimes. "It's my fault. It won't happen again."

"I thought you were spectacular," Mandy chimed in. "You won one for us girls." She waved a hand in the air. "Way to go, Jackie!"

While Jacqueline Marchette considered herself many things—devoted mother, supportive wife, heartless bitch (at least when it came to fighting for a parking space at the monthly meeting of the Connecticut Huntress Club)—a "girl" wasn't one of them. And no one ever—*ever*—called her Jackie. Her gaze grew dangerously dark.

"Why, thank you, dear," she said with tight lips. "What an interesting way to phrase something." She shoved a drink in my hand and turned to fill another glass. Her knuckles were white on the bottle and I waited for the explosion of crimson.

Surprisingly, she managed to hold her temper and play the proper hostess. She passed out glass after glass as quickly as possible—blood for us vamps and a watermelon martini for Mandy.

We'd just settled onto the sofa to enjoy our refreshments when my mother plucked the glass out of my hand.

"But I wasn't—" I started, but she cut me off.

"Would you look at the time?" She reached for the next glass . . . *Pluck*. "We'd better wrap this up." *Pluck. Pluck.* "I have a huntress club meeting in less than fifteen minutes."

"But you met last week," Rob protested, staring longingly after the drink she carted away from him.

"We're meeting again this week." She set the glasses down and recorked the bottle.

"But you only meet once a month." Rob wasn't giving up. I didn't blame him. I could feel the pain radiating from him. He needed sustenance.

"It's an emergency," she told him.

"It's a social club."

"It's a social emergency." She cut him a glare. "Marge Ellen Weisenbocker's daughter is getting engaged. To a werewolf. Marge is beside herself." She stared pointedly at Jack, who gazed adoringly at Mandy. "She knows that a mixed commitment can never work."

"I wouldn't say never." Did I just say that? "Francis and Melissa are making things work." Oh, no, that *was* me. I clamped my lips shut. I was *not* saying another word. My mother had already shifted her full attention from Jack to yours truly. "It's not easy, but it *is* possible. He hasn't bitten and made her yet, but they've already decided they're perfect for each other. I'm sure the rest is inevitable."

"Time to go," she ground out. "*Now.*" Her gaze lingered on me. "I'll speak with you later, Lilliana."

Black, here I come.

She herded everyone toward the front door. Just as Jack was about to escort Mandy out onto the front step, my mother clamped a hand around his arm. "Dear, I need you to drive me over."

"I'll drive you over," my father said, coming up behind her.

"I need Jack." She tugged my brother away from Mandy. "He can drive me in the Hummer. He loves the Hummer," she told Mandy. "Don't you, dear?"

"I guess—"

"Jacqueline," my father cut off Jack's response, "I may not be as young as I used to be, but I'm perfectly capable of driving you over to your meeting in a timely manner."

"I'm sure you are, dear," her gaze drilled into Dad, "but I would really like Jack to drive me. I never get the chance to spend any time with him. We need to talk more. To connect."

The moment my mother said the last word, understanding lit my father's expression. FYI—in addition to never winning, my mother never used the word *connect*. Not when it came to emotional stuff.

"Oh, right." Dad did his best imitation of a fanged bobblehead. "Jack should drive you." He clapped my brother on the back. "He handles the Hummer like a real champ. Don't you, son?"

"Well, I—"

"Your friend," my mother cut in, referring to a startled Mandy, "can catch a ride back to the city with Lil."

I opened my mouth to point out the fact that I was wanted for a felony.

Playing escort to my brother's latest squeeze and making myself even more visible by crawling into the back of a cab might not be the smartest thing to do.

I snapped it back shut. Hey, why ruin a good thing?

"I've already called," my mother added. "There's a car waiting."

"Thanks, Mom." I grabbed Mandy's arm, hauled her outside and down the front walk. "Later."

Eighteen

❤ ❤ ❤

"They like me," Mandy declared once we'd climbed into the cab and given the driver our destination. "They *really* like me."

"How many watermelon martinis did you have?"

"Just one. Well, a quarter of one. Your mother sort of rushed us out of there. Not that I don't understand. I totally do. She's a busy woman and extremely conscientious." She smiled. "That's two for me."

"What are you talking about?"

"Two things we have in common. Being conscientious and reliable. I'm both." She smiled. "We're going to be like two peas in a pod."

Maybe an alien pod.

"I can't believe I was so worried," she went on. "Jack and I both were, but I think everything went really well. I mean, except for your brother getting hit and kicked. But otherwise, I think it was probably typical of your usual family get-together."

Okay. I don't like to be the bearer of bad news, but I felt it my responsibility to clue this girl in on what she was up against. I mean, *I* would want to know if the love of my life's mother completely and totally hated my guts.

"Mandy."

"To think I actually bit off an entire manicure worrying over this meeting."

"Mandy."

"And I ate an entire box of Oreo cookies."

"Code blue!"

She snapped to attention. Her gaze collided with mine. "What? What is it?" Worry flashed in her eyes and my chest hitched. "What's wrong?"

"I . . . That's a really cool shade of lipstick." I know, I know. I shouldn't be perpetuating the lie. But she would find out the truth soon enough, particularly when my parents showed up for tea tomorrow. If they showed up. In the meantime, what was wrong with a little hope? "So what is it? Sephora's Natural Wonder? MAC's Earth Works?"

"Mandy's Natural Lip Color."

Oh.

She smiled. "I don't wear much makeup. I don't usually have time for it." She glanced at her watch. "I took tomorrow off for the tea. It's my first day off in four years. Jack suggested I just take a half day, but I want us to have plenty of time to celebrate once the parents meet and we tell them that we're getting married."

"WHAT?"

Her face lit up. "I wasn't supposed to spill the news, but I'm so excited I just can't help myself. I have to tell *someone*." Her gaze collided with mine and I saw Jack poised on one knee, an engagement ring the size of a third world country in his right hand.

"*Engaged*? No way!" She nodded and I couldn't help my own smile even though I knew this was the worst possible thing that could happen as far as my mother was concerned.

Then again.

My smile widened.

"This is the best thing that's ever happened to me," she rushed on, as she rummaged in her purse and pulled out the Third World country. She slid the ring onto her finger and held up her hand. "You won't tell him I told you, will you? We agreed to tell our parents first. Together." She clasped her hand to her chest and gave me a pleading look.

"My lips are sealed."

Not to mention that Jack and I haven't had an actual conversation since . . . I don't think we'd ever had an actual conversation. Name-calling, yes. But nothing that qualified as an actual exchange of relevant information.

"I can't wait for tomorrow." She fanned her fingers and the ring glittered in the darkness. "It's going to be the most thrilling day of my life. I mean, other than the day I got engaged. And the day Jack rolled into the morgue. And last Thursday when he and I rented this suite at the Waldorf. We took a champagne bath together and rolled around on a bed full of rose petals and read poetry to each other."

"That's, um, sweet." In a gross way. The guy *was* my brother.

"My parents are going to be ecstatic," she rushed on. "And I'm sure your parents will be thrilled, too. Who wouldn't want their five-hundred-and-thirty-five-year-old son to finally settle down?"

When I started to open my mouth, she held up a hand. "I know I'm not a born vampire and I'm not exactly French, but I'm a nice girl. I'm from a good family. An old family. We've been around *forever*, so it's kind of like we're immortal. We've played crucial roles in several key events in history and have even been mentioned in several history books."

"You don't say?"

She nodded. "My great, great, great, great grandfather came over on the *Mayflower* and my great, great, great, great uncle Radcliffe rode with Paul Revere, and my great, great, great aunt Millicent was burned at the stake during the Salem witch trials and—"

"Whoa, back it up. What did you just say?"

"My family can be traced all the way back to the *Mayflower*." She radiated pride.

"Not that part. The other part."

"Uncle Radcliffe?"

"Fast forward."

"Aunt Millicent?"

"Bingo."

"I was saving that surprise for tomorrow." Her smile widened and a sick feeling settled in the pit of my stomach. "It turns out I'm not so human after all. They say my aunt Millicent was one of the most powerful witches of her time and since I'm her direct descendant, that means I have Other DNA flowing through my veins. Not that I know how to cast a spell or anything like that. The closest I've ever come is watching reruns of *Charmed*. But still, it's something, right?" She beamed. "I can't wait to tell your folks. They're going to flip!"

"They're going to flip, all right." I had the sudden vision of my mother, fangs bared, going for Mandy's silken white throat, and panic rushed through me.

Not your business, a voice whispered.

The same voice that said *better you than me* when it came to my mother's wrath.

Still. We're talking *fangs,* and just because of a little DNA glitch.

"You know, Mandy, you might want to keep that little piece of information to yourself. You're a terrific girl. Smart. Attractive."

"Really attractive," the cabbie added from the front seat. He flashed a smile in the mirror. "Sorry, it's just that you're really pretty. And so are you." His gaze shifted to me.

"Uh, thanks." Not. "Anyhow, where was I? Oh, yeah. Attractive. And outgoing. And fun loving."

"And an award winner," she added. "I've been Neighbor of the Month for six months in a row. I'm never home and so it's impossible for me to disturb anyone."

"A multiple award winner," I added. "And smart."

"You already said that."

"Did I?" I shook my head. "My point is, you've got it going on. You know it. Everyone knows it. So what's the use of bragging?"

Excitement faded into worry. "You really think it would sound like bragging?"

I nodded. "And who needs it? I mean, my folks already love you, right?" It's not like I was *saying* they loved her, or even implying it. I was posing a question.

I slid my hand down next to me and crossed my fingers anyway.

"You really think they *love* me? I know they like me. But love?" Hope filled her gaze as it met mine and my chest hitched again.

My mouth opened on its own. "Sure, they do." I gave her a reassuring smile. "As for tomorrow, don't worry about a thing. They'll be thrilled."

I was *so* going to hell for this if I ever got staked.

Or jail.

A strobe of red and blue lights cracked open the blackness just up ahead. A uniformed police officer appeared in the blaze of headlights and motioned for us to stop.

Uh-oh.

Nineteen
♥ ♥ ♥

It's okay, I told myself, my heart pounding, my gaze transfixed by the dizzying mix of red and blue that swirled atop the squad car that sat off to the side of the road.

Okay, okay, *okay*.

It's just the police.

On the corner of my parents' street. In the middle of the night. While I'm on the run for murder.

This was so *not* okay.

My heart jumped into my throat and my nerves started to buzz.

No need to panic. Just stay calm and cool. You're a vampire, remember? It's like having a Get out of Jail Free card. They walk up and you vamp them. Simple.

Unless, of course, it was a female cop.

My gaze sliced through the darkness. Oh, man.

Female cop equals major complication. I couldn't

vamp her unless she happened to like women instead of men.

Or both.

I held tight to the possibility and braced myself as the female officer walked to the driver's window and tapped the edge of a flashlight against the glass. She wore the typical cop's attire, her blond hair tucked up beneath her cap. A subtle swipe of Maybelline's Cotton Candy on her full lips was the only thing that hinted she was a female. Well, that and her sizeable boobs.

Not that I normally notice the size of another woman's chest, but they were right there and they were big. Her buttons tugged, threatening to break free every time she took a breath.

"Roll it down," she told the cabbie.

He punched the button and the glass hummed its way down. The officer trained a flashlight on the driver, who promptly handed over his license and registration, along with a frantic explanation.

"It wasn't me," he blurted. "I didn't lay a hand on her. She hit her face on the door all by herself. Granted, we were arguing and I should have just turned and walked away just like they said to do in anger management, but then she started talking about my mother and I couldn't actually walk on account of my legs were shaking. She really hates my mother and the woman is practically a saint who raised me all by herself and worked two jobs. She doesn't mean to call ten times a day. She's just concerned. I'm all she has.

"But Jeanine doesn't get that," the cabbie rushed

on. "She's jealous. Crazy jealous. But I held it together this time and I didn't hit her. I swear. I hit the
door, but not her, and then I slammed the door and
she was on the other side and it sort of hit her face,
but it wasn't like I did it directly. I haven't laid one
hand on her since the last time and—"

"Calm down, Mister . . . Wiley," the officer read
the name on the ID, "this is just a routine stop."

"In that case, you're one beautiful woman." He
stared directly at her chest. "And I do mean *beautiful*."

"Can it, Romeo. Who's with you?" The beam
shifted to Mandy, who sat directly behind the driver.

Mandy pulled out her hospital badge and held it
out to the officer. "I'm a doctor."

"Is that right?"

"Well, a resident. But it's still a doctor. I work at
the ME's office in the city. I was just having a nightcap with my future in-laws and my future sister-in-
law." She spared me a smile before flashing her left
hand. The massive diamond caught the glare of the
flashlight and sparkle of light streaked across the
cab's interior. "I'm getting married."

"Congratulations." The beam shifted to me and I
stiffened.

Lights, camera, action!

"Hi." My lips tilted in a sexy, inviting smile. Sexy
was the key. And sultry. And seductive. This woman
was going to fall hook, line, and sinker for me.

And if not?

I inched my right hand toward the door handle.

"Name?" she snapped as my fingers tightened around the slim handle and pulled.

Nothing. My gaze shifted to the lock button.

"Miss?"

My attention swiveled back. "Yes?"

"Your name?" the officer prodded.

"Vanderflunkinpitt," I blurted. *Sexy, you idiot!* "But you can call me Bambi." Bambi? Hey, I'm a vampire, not an actress. Besides, I was nervous and disappointed and desperate, and so I wasn't thinking clearly. "But enough about me. What about you, Officer . . ." My gaze dropped to the nametag on her uniform. "Morris?"

My memory stirred and I recognized her as the rookie who'd been with Remy Tremaine a few nights ago on my parents' doorstep. Not a good thing to recall since I also remembered that Remy had vamped her. Which meant she was straight. Which meant I was F-U-C-K-E-D.

I forced a smile. "What's *your* first name?"

"I don't think that's relevant right now," Officer Morris told me, wagging her free hand at me. "Hand over some identification."

"I didn't know your middle name was Bambi." Mandy nudged me as I reached into my purse. "Jack said it was some French thing."

"Bambi's French." I rummaged in my bag.

"Bambi is not French," she said beneath her breath.

"Sure, it is. It comes from the word *bambino.*"

"That's Italian."

"It sounds French." I pulled out my ID and reached over the seat to hand it to Officer Morris. Her gaze collided with mine and I smiled again—*ultra* sexy this time. "Here you go."

"This doesn't say Bambi," she said after shining her light on the laminated card.

"Bambi is my, um, stage name. I'm a dancer. Yeah, that's what I am. A female dancer. That is, I dance for females. Males, too, but they tend to get much too loud and rowdy, and most of them couldn't spot a pair of Kenneth Coles if their life depended on it . . ." Yikes, I was sinking fast. "But I bet you would. I bet you have excellent taste in clothes."

Here goes nothing . . .

And I bet you like dancers, too, I added mentally. *In fact, you love them. You think they're hot, particularly me. I'm the hottest you've ever seen—especially wearing my new lip gloss—and you can't wait to see me peel off my clothes one piece at a time. You're picturing it right now because you want me. You want me B-A-D.*

"I need you to step out of the car . . ." she started, but then her words faded. A bright gleam lit her eyes and a look of pure rapture slid across her face.

I reached across and plucked my ID from her hands. She didn't budge. She simply stood there, frozen. Enamored.

What can I say? I totally rock.

"Actually, I'm the one who rocks." The deep, familiar voice slid into my ears as I stuffed my ID back into my purse. My head swiveled and I found myself staring through the glass at Remy Tremaine.

Relief swept through me, followed by a mega dose of "Oh, no!" when he motioned for me to step out of the car.

My fingers went to the unlock button, but I couldn't make myself press it.

"Come on, Lil."

"No." What if Remy had changed his mind about me? What if he now believed the mounting evidence? What if he'd gambled away all of his earnings and desperately needed my bounty to bail his own ass out of a difficult situation?

"I don't gamble and my ass is perfectly fine, and I don't just think you're innocent. I know it."

My gaze snapped up and collided with his. He grinned. "You were thinking out loud. Now open up."

I stabbed the button, opened the door and climbed from the car.

"Give us a sec," he said to Mandy as he closed the door behind me.

I followed him up onto the sidewalk. The nearest house sat a half mile up the winding, shrub-lined street. Moonlight spilled down around us and lit up the darkness.

Remy wore a white dress shirt, his tie undone, his collar unbuttoned. He had on navy slacks and inexpensive shoes. His badge hung on his belt near a very dangerous looking gun.

He crossed his arms and eyed me for several long

moments before I finally broke the uncomfortable silence.

"So how's it going?" I tried to sound nonchalant.

"It would be better if I didn't have wanted felons prancing around Fairfield's most affluent neighborhood in the middle of the night."

"I'm not prancing. I'm riding. Back to the city with Jack's fiancée."

His gaze slid past me to Mandy, who leaned forward in her seat and passed a hand in front of Officer Morris's transfixed stare. "A human?"

I shrugged. "They're in love." I braced myself for the expected "Vampires don't believe in love" speech so popular with most of my kind.

"I bet your parents are really upset."

"They don't actually know, not about the fiancée part. They think Mandy's a phase."

"What do you think?"

"I think it's none of our business. What's up with the roadblock?"

"It's not a roadblock. It's a checkpoint. To monitor activity in and out of the area. See, if I don't keep an eye on things here, NYPD will move in and do it for me, and I'm not going to let that happen. They've been back and forth, stepping on toes as it is. They're determined to find you." He eyed me. "And they intend to be first in line."

"I guess you heard about the bounty."

"Fifty thousand dollars is a lot of money."

"It's one hundred thousand," I clarified. "They just raised it on account of some really incriminating evidence that makes me look extremely dangerous." He didn't look the least bit impressed. Rather, he looked worried.

Remy *was* a family friend. It only stood to reason that he would be worried about a huge bounty. That would mean more people looking for me. Questioning my parents. Disrupting his town.

"Don't worry, they won't find me. I'm keeping a low profile."

"By showing up at your parents' on a Saturday night?"

"The hunt was tonight." 'Nuff said.

Remy nodded. "Still, you shouldn't be riding around in a cab. It's too risky. There are too many people looking for you."

"Not for long."

"You're not planning on turning yourself in, are you? Because that wouldn't be a good idea. This case is really stacked against you and unless you know something that we don't—"

"Not yet," I cut in. "But I'm working on it. That's what I meant. I plan on putting a stop to all of this myself. Soon."

"How's that?"

"I've got a plan. I'm going to find the real murderer—the person framing me—and expose them."

"You and what team of investigators?"

"Not a team. Just one, and he's not an investigator. Not officially, anyway. He's an independent fugitive apprehension agent."

"A bounty hunter?"

I nodded. "Ty's been really great. He let me crash at his place and he's helping me figure all of this out."

"Ty? Ty Bonner?"

"You know him?"

"I know of him. Colors outside the lines, but then most of his kind do."

"He's a really decent guy. And extremely smart."

He nodded. "Obviously. He knows a good investment when he sees one."

"What's that supposed to mean?"

"That you're the key to whoever did it. If you are being framed for murder, it's because someone's out to get you. Meaning they're not likely to sit by while you evade the cops. They'll go after you again, and when they do, Ty will be right there. He gets the real murderer and the bounty. And you get to clear your name. Sounds like a mutually beneficial arrangement."

I'd never really thought about it like that. Instead, I'd been thinking of Ty as this white knight, believing in me, rescuing me, sacrificing for me. When all he was really doing was making an investment in his own future.

Still. He *had* believed me *and* rescued me and he *was* sacrificing his own bed for my comfort.

"Nice work." I killed the subject and pointed to the female officer, who stood transfixed by the driver's window. "But I thought she was married."

"What can I say? She's got an active imagination starring yours truly."

"Just her imagination?"

"We might have spent a little time together before

she tied the knot, but we're just friends now. I've given up humans for a while. After so many, they all start to blend together. I figured I'd hold out for something that might last a little longer."

As in eternity.

I eyed Remy. Blond. With definite loyalty potential since he'd given up humans. "Are you serious? Because if you are, I've got a hot, sexy, mega-orgasmic born female who would be perfect for you."

He grinned. "I thought I wasn't your type."

"I wasn't talking about me." Even if my heart did skip its next beat. What could I say? I was wired from my near brush with incarceration and obviously not thinking clearly. Me and Remy? No way. "Her name is Ayala. If you're game, I could hook the two of you up." I handed him a card.

He slid the number into his pocket. "I'll call you." He motioned to the cab driver who seemed mesmerized by the steady rise and fall of the female officer's chest. "Make sure he thinks this is all just a really great dream when he gets back to the city."

"I'm on it."

His grin faded into a stern look. "And don't give him one of your cards. The less evidence there is that you're moving around, the better."

"Who? Me? I would never do such a thing."

I would, however, jot Evie's name and number down on a piece of paper and slip it onto the cabbie's dash. Just in case, you know, he got lonely.

Not that I mentioned as much to Remy. Instead, I spent the next few minutes talking about my dating service and filling him in on more Ayala facts. In the back of my mind, I pictured Ayala and Remy tying the knot and naming their firstborn after me. I also pictured Ty.

For his own personal gain.

The notion followed me back into the cab after I said good-bye to Remy. *After* a full five minutes of him lecturing me: Stay inside, don't go out, don't do this, don't do that, don't let Ty get too close—okay, so what was that about? It's not like Remy should be jealous. Sure, we'd been on dates, but I didn't like him and he didn't like me.

Did he?

Nah. Otherwise, he wouldn't have practically agreed a date with Ayala. One that I was certain would be extremely successful. How could she *not* like Remy?

I tried to dwell on that question rather than the personal gain thing, but number two eventually won out.

What can I say? I was extremely hurt. And angry. And ready for a confrontation.

Twenty

❤ ❤ ❤

By the time I reached Ty's loft, I'd abandoned the idea of a confrontation and glommed on to the notion of delving.

Confrontation was such an ugly word and hinted at wrongdoing, and Ty really hadn't done anything *wrong*. The guy was helping me—for whatever reason—and so there was nothing to call him out on.

But *delving* . . . That I could do subtly, carefully, without appearing ungrateful and mega bitchlike. I would just kick back, keep the conversation going, and ease into the subject slowly. Very slowly. And sort of feel him out.

Can you say paranoid? I wasn't trying to be, I just couldn't help myself. I wanted to know why. Even more, I needed to know. Then, if Ty really wanted the money more than he wanted to help me, I could classify him as a good-looking shit and maybe, just maybe, I wouldn't be so in lust with him.

But if he really was trying to help me with no thought for his own personal gain . . . My heart fluttered at the prospect and my determination grew.

"Where the hell have you been?" he demanded when he hauled open the door before I'd so much as turned the knob. He wore the usual black jeans, but he'd traded the black T-shirt for a black leather vest that made his shoulders look even more broad and muscular. He looked as sexy as ever, and royally pissed. "Didn't I tell you to stay put?"

"Are you just after the reward, or are you helping me because you want to?" So much for *delving*.

He blinked. "What?"

"You heard me." I moved past him into the apartment and turned. Our gazes collided. "Why are you helping me?"

"Because you asked me to." He slammed the door closed and threw the deadbolt. "Not that I'll have to do it for much longer because you're *this close* to landing your sweet ass in jail."

That wasn't really the answer I was looking for.

"I know I asked, but *why* did you agree? *Just* because I asked or because I'm sitting here with one hundred thousand dollars stamped on my sweet ass and you know if you help me, you'll find the real killer and collect the bounty?"

He eyed me. "What the hell difference does it make?"

"I know it seems irrelevant because, bottom line,

I've got a safe place to stay and zero reason to bitch, and I'm not bitching. Not really. And I wasn't even remotely concerned about it until Remy said that you—"

"Remy?" he cut in.

"Remy Tremaine. He's the police chief in Fairfield where my folks live. He said that you—"

"Wait a second. You've been with the Fairfield police chief for the past three hours?"

"Not exactly. I was at my parents' most of the time, but then I ran into Remy when I left—he had this roadblock set up—and we talked and he said—"

"You talked to the chief of fuckin' police?"

"It's okay. He's a good guy. Although in this situation, I suppose we could call him a bad guy since I'm considered the bad guy and he's on my side, but he's totally cool and he said you were a really smart guy." There. That should ease the frown drawing his face tight.

The face got tighter. "You mentioned me to the chief of *fuckin'* police?" He raked a hand through his hair. "Did you write down my address and invite him over for dinner, too?"

"Well, no. He likes to eat alone, but—you're being sarcastic, aren't you?"

"Shit." He went a little red around the cheeks. "Why don't you just advertise your whereabouts in Times Square? Better yet, put it on CNN. A late-breaking story. Stop killing yourselves, guys. She's right fucking *here*."

"What? You're really worried about *Remy*?"

Even as the question left my mouth, I remembered my own initial panic in the cab when I'd seen the Fairfield police chief. Friend or foe, I'd wondered— for, like, five seconds.

However briefly, the point is, I *had* wondered.

Still. We're talking Remy.

"He's a very good friend of the family's and completely devoted to my folks, as well as all of the extremely wealthy members of his community. The real killer could torture him and he wouldn't spill his guts." At least, I didn't think so.

"And if he's the real killer?"

What? "You've got to be kidding." I couldn't help but smile.

Just as the expression slid across my face, Ty's look grew even more thunderous. His eyes narrowed to dangerous slits and I felt a tingle down south.

Wrong time, wrong place, wrong man, I know. What can I say? I was desperately horny and a total sucker for dark, dangerous, delicious-looking bounty hunters.

I forced my lustful thoughts aside and shook my head. "Remy's a nice guy."

"He's a vampire."

"A nice vampire." Okay. That sounded ridiculous even to me, and I'm the one who said it. "Sure, we're all vicious bloodsuckers, but some of us aren't as vicious as others. We have a civilized layer beneath the hunger. And the greed. And the narcissism." I was definitely digging my hole deeper. "You just have to peel all the other stuff back to get to the real character beneath. Besides"—I shrugged—"he likes me."

"He likes you? So you spilled your guts and compromised our position because he *likes* you?"

"I didn't tell him where you lived."

"He can find out."

"If he wanted to find out, which he doesn't."

"Because he's a nice guy and he *likes* you?"

"Exactly."

He shook his head. "You're going to get us both staked."

"The cops don't want to stake me. They want to arrest me."

"I'm not talking about the cops. There's a murderer out there."

"And there are two extremely powerful vampires in here."

"More like stupid." His eyes blazed. "You should've stayed put."

"But—"

"Dammit, Lil, can't you just own up to it? You've made a mistake. The least you can do is admit it and apologize."

He shook his head again and looked as if he wanted to wring my neck. Or kiss me.

I voted for number two. I lost.

"What the hell am I saying?" He threw up his hands. "I don't need your apology." He glared at me. "You don't set foot out of this apartment."

"I—"

"Or float out."

"I—"

"Or fly out."

"But I—"

"*Nothing.* You got that?"

"I really think you're blowing this out of proportion. Even if he had it, Remy wouldn't disclose our location to anyone. He's not like that."

"Says you."

"What's that supposed to mean?"

"That you're not exactly the best judge of character."

"For your information, I'm an excellent judge of character. I can see right through anyone."

"Except other vampires," he pointed out.

I gave him a pointed stare. "Oh, yeah? I can see right through you."

"Is that so?" He stepped toward me.

While I've never been one to cower in front of any male—vamp or otherwise—I found myself stepping back.

Not out of, you know, fear or anything. We're talking pure, unadulterated, just call me "Old Faithful" lust.

My nerves hummed and my pulse quickened. The sound thundered through my ears. He stepped even closer and my gaze anchored on the small scar just shy of his eyebrow. I wanted to reach out and touch the flesh, feel it beneath the pad of my finger, imagine what sort of man he'd been when he'd been wounded. Just a man.

My nostrils flared, drinking in the delicious aroma of worn leather and soap and fierce male. Talk about yum.

"Then why did you ask me about helping you? If you're so insightful, then *you* tell *me* why."

"Because I asked." I tossed his words back at him and he grinned.

His bright blue eyes sparked, blazing with a sudden feral intensity that made me take another step back, and another, until I came up against the wall. Sheetrock pressed into my backside, while Ty plastered himself to my front.

He leaned into me, his erection hard and thick against my leg. Catching my elbows with his hands, he slid his fingertips up my bare flesh, until his palms rested on my shoulders. His thumbs played at the edges of my clavicle.

Electricity sizzled through me from my head to my toes, and damned if it didn't pause at several choice spots in between.

Duh. He's questioning your judgment of character—the jackass. Of course, your heart is pounding and your body is tingling. You're thoroughly pissed.

My head knew that, but my arms . . . They weren't as quick to agree. But they were quick to snake around his neck. I pressed my lips to his.

He stiffened at first (the rest of him, that is) but then his resistance seemed to crumble. His mouth opened and his tongue darted out to tangle with mine.

Where I'd initiated, he quickly took the lead, pressing me up against the wall and devouring me. His mouth was hot and wet and *hot*. It was the best kiss of my life.

Even better than the first time he'd kissed me while hovering outside an eighth floor window, watching a human couple have S and M sex.

"You like me," I murmured when we both finally came up for air. I leaned my head back against the wall, a smile playing at my lips, and closed my eyes. "I knew it."

"So what if I do?" He nibbled my neck. "It doesn't change who I am."

"A nice guy," I breathed, all the while my conscience whispered, "A *made* guy."

But we're talking *nibbling*.

"You bought me bottled blood," I added to emphasize my point—and drown out the whole *made* thing.

"Maybe I'm just protecting my investment."

"Maybe. Then again, we're talking my *favorite* blood type."

His grip on my shoulders tightened until it bordered on painful and killed my smile. My eyes snapped open to find that he'd abandoned the nibbling. He stared back at me, his look fierce, his eyes the brightest blue I'd ever seen them.

"You don't know anything about me, Lil. You don't know who I am. What I'm capable of doing. What I've done."

The thing was, I did. I knew him. I know it sounds ludicrous, but I felt . . . safe with him. Even now with his gaze drilling into me and his fingers biting into my skin.

Because I knew it wouldn't go beyond that. My body was completely and totally safe with him. As for my heart . . . That was a different matter altogether.

I ignored the last thought (for obvious reasons, including the whole made vampire issue) and blurted out the first thing that came to mind. "You helped me after I got staked in the shoulder."

"For my own pleasure." His grip softened just enough to ease the pressure. He feathered his lips over mine before grazing a path across my cheek. "Not yours," he murmured in my ear. "I liked having you draw on my vein. It felt good."

"So you only agreed to help me because of the bounty on my head? If that's true, then say it. Look me in the eyes and say it."

Please look me in the eyes. Because with your mouth so close to my neck, all I can think about is you taking a bite and then me taking a bite, and then you. And then me. You. Me. You. Me. Me. Me . . .

His lips trailed from my ear, down my throat, tracing my jugular. His body stiffened and a growl tickled my skin, followed by the sharp prickle as he unsheathed his fangs.

A sliver of fear worked its way up my spine and I stiffened.

Crazy, I know. Biting was a totally erotic experience, and not the least bit scary.

But this . . . This went beyond the two of us and the desire that drew us together so tightly it felt almost suffocating at times.

This was all about Ty and the emotion tearing him up inside.

"Pain and agony and self-loathing."

As soon as the deep voice sounded in my head, he jerked away from me. His image was little more than a blur before I heard the door slam, and then I was alone.

I leaned against the wall, my heart pounding and my lips tingling.

What was *that* about?

I wasn't sure, but I had the gut feeling that it had something to do with his past before becoming a vampire. Maybe he'd been a terrible, awful human and his horrible, criminal actions had led him to becoming a vampire.

So that he could right his wrong?

Or spend forever agonizing over it?

I really don't do pain and agony all that well, let alone self-loathing, so I ignored the questions and focused on the one thing I could deal with at the moment—being majorly ticked off.

My mind reversed back through the past few delicious moments, through the like and the lust and the *awww, poor thing,* and latched onto the actual conversation we'd had.

I blew out an exasperated breath and tried to process his words. What was it he'd said? Something about me compromising our position and getting us staked and apologizing—

Apologize? As if I'd done anything wrong.

I'd merely been following his advice.

Connect with your parents, he'd said. Let them know you're okay.

Sure, I'd connected via an actual face-to-face rather than the suggested phone call, but it was the principle of the thing that mattered.

If you looked at it that way, I'd done exactly what he'd said. Not that he should be giving me orders in the first place. I mean, hel—*lo?* We'd evolved to the twenty-first century. I was a mature, rather attractive born vampire fully capable of making my own decision.

I didn't need some overbearing *made* vampire dictating to me. I hadn't lived five hundred years (and holding) by being stupid.

Spoiled maybe, but not stupid.

If anyone should apologize, it should be Ty.

You said it, sister. Talk about balls. All he's done is give you a safe place to stay (regardless of his motivation) and a helping hand to untie the noose tightening around your neck while you've (a) risked getting yourself caught by flying around in full view of New York to round up alpha males and (b) dragged him in for aiding and abetting by mentioning his name to the chief of the Fairfield Police Department. Yep, he owes you big time.

Okay. Maybe I could kind of see his point.

I headed for the front door.

When I reached the street, I did a visual search for his familiar muscular bod, and came up with *nada*. It was late by human standards—well after three in the morning—and the street was empty. He was probably long gone, but I drank in the scents surrounding me anyway.

The overwhelming aroma of oregano and garlic drifted from the Italian restaurant near the corner. The sharp scent of newsprint wafted from the newsstand locked up tight across the street. The smell of coffee grounds and old tuna fish carried from a nearby Dumpster.

I scrunched up my nose and turned in the opposite direction.

A breeze wafted, bringing with it the faintest hint of leather and hunky male and something else . . . something sticky and sweet and . . . blood.

The realization should have clued me in to what was going on, but I was wound too tight. I hadn't gotten laid in as long as I could remember (the multispeed Rabbit The Ninas had bought me didn't count) and I hadn't had more than a few sips of dinner at my parents. I *so* wasn't thinking with my head.

I moved swiftly, letting the scent lure me until I found myself more than a block away, standing in front of what had once been a giant warehouse. The building had been renovated and now housed an upscale home décor shop and an art gallery that featured local artists.

But it wasn't the jeweled Christian Dior frame surrounding the abstract featured in the front display that stopped me cold (although it *was* choice).

It was the sound.

Ka-thunk. Ka-thunk. Ka-thunk.

The pulse beat echoed in my head and drew me around the side of the massive building, toward a small alley that separated it from a sports bar and grill.

My gaze sliced through the darkness to the couple who stood at the end of the alley near a mountain of empty beer crates and several trash cans.

The woman was a tall and leggy brunette. She stood pinned to the wall by the man in front of her who was feasting on her neck.

Ty.

My stomach hollowed out and my chest hitched. Crazy, I know. I'd seen vamps drink before. Hell, I *was* a vamp and I'd certainly drank before. The sight shouldn't freak me out.

Still. We're talking Ty. Drinking. From someone who's name didn't start with *L* and end with *il.*

Not that I wanted him to drink from me, mind you. I had enough problems. I'd quickly dismissed the little exchange back at his apartment as *mucho* stress syndrome. I had, after all, compromised our position. Talk about anxiety, which equaled frantic, which equaled zero common sense. No more.

At the same time, we were sort of living together. We were *connected.* Even more, he liked me. And I liked him.

Yet here he was drinking from someone else.
Cheating bastard.

The thought rushed from my mind before I could stop it and Ty's head snapped up. Blood gushed from his mouth and splattered the woman's white tank top. His fierce blue gaze sliced through the darkness and collided with mine.

My first instinct was to turn the other way. A lot of people might think it was because I have a weak stomach. That's what I thought. Until Ty looked at me and I realized in a startling instant the real reason I avoided blood (other than the bottled sort) and, especially, the whole biting issue.

He was as beautiful as he was fierce. A primitive male completely at ease to take what he wanted, to overpower and consume.

My nipples tingled and my stomach growled. A hunger as old as time and just as fierce welled inside. It was as painful as it was sweet, and as all-consuming.

I'd felt it before (in my earlier, wilder, totally temporary days) and my body remembered. My nerves latched onto the sensation, welcoming it until it gripped me tightly, completely, and urged me to step forward.

To take what I so desperately wanted, with no thought to the consequence. Be it Ty. Or the sweet crimson heat. Or both.

I braced myself against the need and clung to the one and only thought I should have had at that moment—besides *cheating bastard*, that is.

Namely *yuck*.

The woman gasped, the sound like an explosion in

my head, disrupting the hypnotic lure of her pulse. I tore my gaze from Ty's.

And then, because *yuck* wasn't working and I was *this close* to giving in to my inner vampire, I turned and started walking.

Twenty-one
❤ ❤ ❤

I ended up back at Ty's loft. But not right away (I walked at least an hour) and not because I didn't have anyplace else to go at four in the morning.

I went back because of my two suitcases, one of which held my newest acquisition—this great little Dolce & Gabbana number that had been a steal. I couldn't skip out on my buddy Dolce.

"Lil." Ty's voice carried from the doorway.

"I'll be out of here as soon as I get my stuff." I shoved the nightshirt I'd worn the day before into the opening.

"You're not going anywhere." He stood directly behind me now, but I didn't turn around.

I wasn't going to look at him.

"Yes, I am. I'm so outta here."

He shook his head. "Why?"

Good question. Because he'd . . . and I'd . . . and I was afraid we'd . . .

Are you, like, five or five hundred years old? The man's a vampire. He bites women for sustenance. That's what he does.

Okay, I knew that. I understood it (being that I had my own inner vampire). But knowing it and seeing it . . . Therein lies the monumental difference.

"She was really pretty." The words were out before I could stop them.

"Excuse me?"

"Nice body. The hair wasn't very impressive. A bottled job if I've ever seen one. But otherwise, she was sort of hot."

"She was dinner."

"An attractive dinner."

"Is that what this is about? You're mad because I bit someone?"

"No." I kept stuffing my case to avoid looking at him.

"You are. You're mad because—"

"I am not mad. I just don't think it's a good idea for me to be here."

"Why?"

"Because." I ran out of my own stuff and reached for one of his discarded T-shirts. I shoved it in with my own things.

"Because why?"

"Because I like you, all right?" My hands trembled. "I like you and I shouldn't like you. Other than being exceptionally hot, there's really nothing remotely attractive about you. You're bossy and overbearing and all wrong for someone like me." I worked at the clasp of my suitcase.

"I'm not helping you because of the bounty." His words drew my attention and I glanced up. Our gazes collided. "I've collected more bounties than I know what to do with. I'm helping you because—"

The words died on his lips and his head swiveled toward the street. Red and blue lights lit up the darkness. Tires screeched. Engines sputtered. Doors slammed.

"*Shit.*" In the blink of an eye, Ty stood at the windows and peered down at the street below. "They're here."

My heart thundered. "They can't be here." My gaze darted from the windows to the door and back. "They don't know where *here* is."

He turned toward me. "They do now."

Hinges creaked. Wood splintered. Footsteps clamored up the back stairs. The freight elevator kicked into gear, creaking toward Ty's loft.

"I don't suppose you have a trap door?"

"Under the bed." He moved at the speed of light and gripped one of the bedposts. A flick of his wrist and the thick wood slid across the floor like a hockey puck gliding across ice. Flipping back a rug, he revealed a square hatch.

"I was joking."

"I wasn't." He eased his fingers into the two small holes cut into the wood and lifted. Metal groaned and popped as the hinges twisted. "This place used to be an old slaughterhouse around the turn of the century."

They didn't call it the meatpacking district for nothing.

"We're standing in the kill area. The carcasses were then tossed down a chute that led to the first floor where they were stored for disposal." He motioned me over. "The people who renovated the place put in a staircase to connect the bottom levels and make the building one huge living space. The folks who bought *them* out wanted more bang for their buck so they converted one massive apartment into three and got rid of the staircase. They were too cheap to redo the flooring. They locked the hatch and tossed a rug over it. It wasn't a deal breaker when I was looking for a place, but it did help sell me."

"You do a lot of running from the cops?"

He shook his head. "He's not a cop."

He?

Before I could voice the question, he grabbed me by the arm.

"I can't just leave my stuff."

"You've got five seconds to get basic necessities."

In a flash, I reached for my cosmetics bag, purse, and cell phone. I was just about to grab a suitcase when Ty's voice exploded in my head.

"Move!"

His hand closed over my arm, and I found myself pulled toward the trap door. He shoved me through the opening.

I landed on a tapestry rug (I know, right? nobody

does tapestry anymore) that covered the floor in the apartment below Ty's.

The floor plan was basically the same except that Ty's neighbor had set up the living room where Ty had put his bedroom, and the bedroom in the living room spot. Luckily, or we would have pounced on some poor schmoe and his girlfriend during their early morning quickie.

They stopped humping and their heads swiveled in our direction.

"Don't mind us," I mumbled as Ty flung back the rug and yanked at the next hatch. "Just passing through." Hinges creaked and groaned. We dropped through the opening to the first floor.

The loudest snore I'd ever heard bounced off the walls and surrounded us. I gazed toward the man who slept in the full-size bed just a few feet away. He wore an eye mask and a facial mask (I'm guessing Clinique Cucumber Madness). His nostrils flapped. His chest lifted. A loud "Ugggggggg" filled the room.

I started for the door while Ty kicked aside yet another rug.

"We're on the first floor, dumbass." I sent him the silent message as I reached for the doorknob.

"I know, dipstick." His gaze met mine. *"This place was owned by a large company that held title to the whole block. There's an underground level where the meat was cured and stored. It connects all four buildings on this street. I don't think it's been used for quite a while, but I know it's still there."*

I knew it, too. I could hear the scurry of a rat somewhere below. The scent of old cedar mingled with smoke made me wrinkle up my nose.

I abandoned the front door and joined Ty at the entrance to the pitch-black tunnel. My gaze sliced into the darkness and I saw said rat scurry toward a cluster of his buddies.

"Go."

I hooked the strap of my cosmetics bag over my head, my clutch purse under my arm, and dropped into the darkness. The smell swallowed me up. Ty followed and we fled through a narrow tunnel that soon opened up into a larger area surrounded by several cold, lifeless fire pits.

"This is where they smoked some of the meat."

"Ya think?" My nose was burning now and I grimaced.

A few seconds later, we cracked open the hatch that led into a nearby building—now the production headquarters for a fledgling sportswear designer. The place wasn't very impressive (hey, the guy was just starting out) with its unfinished ceilings and concrete floors, but what it lacked in style, it made up in size. We're talking *big*, with dozens of cutting tables and sewing machines. Air conditioning ducts crisscrossed above us. Fluorescent lights dangled from fifty-foot chains. Another huge plus—it didn't smell like cedar or smoke.

We wound our way through a maze of headless mannequins and I paused to eye a silk tank dusted with rhinestones. "This guy's pretty good." I glanced toward a nearby rack. "I wonder if he has this in my size."

"Come on!" He tugged me forward, only to bring us to a staggering halt.

I didn't have to ask why. My ears picked up everything from the rustle of rats digging through the garbage out back, to the footfalls that rounded the rear of the building and the frantic, "Signal when you're in position." The walls seemed to tremble. The chains that held the light fixtures swayed ever so slightly.

"*Surrounded.*" Ty's voice echoed in my head as he gripped my hand and tugged me toward the one spot that wasn't about to be crawling with cops—the ceiling.

My feet left the ground and suddenly I was weightless. Just as my back met the ceiling, I heard a frantic "Now!"

Both the front and back doors crashed open. I caught my bottom lip and stared down as cops rushed into the building, guns in one hand, flashlights in the other. Several crawled up through the open hatch we'd just come through. Lights sliced through the darkness as dozens of men combed through the warehouse, searching . . .

"*It's okay.*" The deep, husky voice slid into my head and Ty's fingers tightened around mine. I shifted my attention to the vamp who levitated next to me and remembered his words.

"*I'm helping you because . . .*"

Because . . . He'd fallen madly, passionately in love

with me and couldn't stand the thought of me rotting in jail?

Suddenly I was even more desperate not to know.

Loopy, huh? I'd been hounding the guy, eager to know the truth. Yet here I was ready to avoid the subject entirely.

Because . . . I already knew the truth. The answer had been there when he'd had me pinned to the wall back at his place. When he'd stared down at me, into me. When he'd kissed me. When he'd nibbled at me.

Yep, the nibbling had been a truly defining moment.

Hearing the words would only complicate matters.

"What's wrong with you? You just went white."

"Dizzy," I mentally blurted. It wasn't like I could tell him I was freaked out because I liked him and I knew he liked me and that hearing it would make me like him that much more. A shitty realization since we were completely doomed, relationship-wise.

I hiked my cosmetics bag onto the back of my shoulder and glanced down at the chaos below us. *"We're pretty high up."*

"Since when have you been afraid of heights?"

"Since I don't usually hover on the ceiling during a raid. All the movement . . ." I made a big show of swallowing. *"It's really unsettling."*

Before my heart could give its next beat, Ty slid in front of me and killed the scene unfolding below. I found myself staring at the back of his head. He floated up flush against me, pinning my body between his back and the ceiling.

His butt nestled into the cradle of my thighs and his shoulder blades pressed into my breasts.

"Just relax. They'll make their sweep and then it'll be over."

Relax? Was he nuts? He was much too close and his body was much too hard and my body was much too needy. We're talking a recipe for extreme stress. No way was I going to chill in this situation.

Unless, of course, it went on for *forty-five* minutes.

I know, right?

Even a sexually super-charged vamp like myself had her limits. I gave up the notion of ripping Ty's clothes off and having my way with him and let my guard down enough to relax against him. There. As stimulating as it was being close to him, it was also sort of nice. Comfy even.

I rested my cheek against his back and listened to the steady sound of his heart. It was slow, just like every other vampire I knew.

But he wasn't like other vamps. He was *made*. Different.

I gave myself the mental nudge to keep from getting so cozy stretched out atop him, but damned if it didn't lull me even more until I closed my eyes and started to think. To wonder.

"What's it like?" I projected the mental thought before I could stop myself.

"What's what like?"

"The sun. I've watched it set many times in my mirror, and I've even crept close to the window a time or two. But I've never really felt it."

"Honest." His deep voice echoed in my head after a long, silent moment. *"It feels honest."*

Okay, so maybe made vampires didn't have access to the same quality education we born vamps obviously took for granted. Otherwise, Ty would have had a much more abundant store of adjectives. Like fiery. Blistering. Exhausting. Blinding—

"That's the thing," his own thoughts cut into mine. *"It's just the opposite. There's no darkness to cover up the flaws. No shadows to hide the monsters. Just this bright, warm light that keeps everything real. What you see is what you get. Honest."*

I so wasn't getting this. *"You're a veritable artist with words."*

A silent chuckle vibrated his hard body. *"Just close your eyes and try to feel it."*

"I need more description."

"You haven't even given it a shot."

"Are the cops finished yet?"

"Almost. Stop trying to change the subject."

"It's a boring subject."

"You're the one who brought it up."

"And now I'm trying to drop it."

Another chuckle vibrated his strong physique. *"Too late. Come on. Give it a shot."*

"Here goes nothing." I closed my eyes and conjured my second most favorite beach fantasy—the one with me chilling à la carte on a chaise loungue, drink in hand. *"I don't feel anything."* Except the condensation on my glass. And the fabric of the chaise loungue at my back.

But I'd felt those things before and so they were easy to imagine.

"First you have to look."

"I want to feel the sun. Not see it."

"You will. Now look around you."

I shifted my attention from the yellow ball of fire glowing above and stared at a nearby palm tree. The rich green leaves trembled with the slightest breeze. I noticed the criss-cross pattern on the foliage. A fly buzzed nearby, the tiny wings beating at the speed of light. The water lapped at the shore. I noted the fine grains of sand that floated back out as the water slithered toward the sea. It was both fascinating and oddly soothing. Peaceful, even.

"Honest," came the rumble of Ty's deep voice.

A smile curved my lips.

Twenty-two
❤ ❤ ❤

We took off via bat as soon as the cops fled the designer warehouse. The three-quarter-inch moon lit up the night sky as I followed Ty north. At least, I'd thought that was the direction we were heading. But from the looks of things now, I'd obviously been mistaken.

We'd headed south. Straight to hell.

The Animal Planet version, that is.

I stared around at the inside of the large cabin. Lifeless eyes stared back at me from the faces of the numerous deer, elk, and boar mounted on the walls. A massive bear stood in the far corner on his hind legs, lips drawn back, teeth bared and claws poised.

While I'm as primitive and animalistic as the next vamp (sort of), I've never really understood the sport of hunting. Hunting for survival? Yes. But purely for tasteless décor? Do *not* get it.

The dead animal motif extended beyond the walls to every nook and cranny of the spacious cabin. A stuffed raccoon clock ticked away from atop an unfinished pine end table. A bear skin rug covered the worn hardwood floor. The sofa and chair had been upholstered in camouflage print. A matching print comforter draped the four-poster bed that sat off to the side. The loft area held a small twin bed with a mini-size version of the same comforter. Camo print cushions covered two kitchen chairs. A small stuffed squirrel sat center stage on the pine table and gnawed a fake nut. A stuffed fox graced the mantel above a floor-to-ceiling rock fireplace. A chandelier made entirely of antlers gleamed overhead.

"I think I've seen this place."

Ty slid the chain lock into place on the cabin door and drew the curtains on the window beside it. "You've been upstate before?"

I shook my head as I set my cosmetics bag on the unfinished pine coffee table—smack-dab between an antler candle holder and a rawhide leather-bound photo album. "The Travel Channel's *Ten Places Not to Stay When Vacationing in the Free World*." My gaze swept the interior a second time. "Wasn't this number one?"

He pulled the curtains—what else, camouflage—on each window before retrieving the one and only bag he'd snagged before we'd fled his apartment. "This is the nicest cabin in the area," he said as he walked toward the sofa. "It belongs to this guy I know."

"See there." I settled in a chair. Comfy even if it did

sort of give me the creeps. "You *do* have friends." Ty avoided the F pool, while I constantly fished for potential clients.

"We're not friends." He retrieved his laptop and wedged it onto the coffee table. "We've worked a few cases together. He's with NYPD."

"He's letting you borrow his private space. That smacks of friendship to me." I reached forward and retrieved my cosmetics bag to give him more room. "This guy. He wouldn't happen to be a made vampire, would he? Because if he is, I really think you should let me introduce him to my client, Esther. The one I mentioned to you?"

"This wouldn't be the one you tried to set me up with a while back?"

"That's her, although she really isn't your type. Sure, she's made, but the common traits end there. Even though she wouldn't make a good match for you," *because she's not me*, "she *is* really sweet." He shot me a glance as he opened his computer and a fierce light gleamed in his eyes. My mouth went dry. "Not literally, of course. I mean, she might be, but I wouldn't know because I've never actually tasted her." I averted my gaze and busied myself digging in my cosmetics bag for my lip gloss. "I was speaking figuratively." I punctuated the sentence with a few dabs of Shimmering Heaven and rubbed my lips together.

Ty's gaze hooked on my mouth and he watched as I dabbed again and rubbed, as if mesmerized.

My tummy tingled and I fought to clear my suddenly dry throat. "So, um, how about it?" I capped the gloss and slid it into my bag.

He tore his gaze away and shook his head. "He's not a made vampire."

"Born vampire? Because I have quite a few clients—"

"Nope."

"Were-Chihuahua?"

A grin tugged at the corner of his mouth "You don't give up, do you?"

"I'm a professional. No job is too small or too large." Except maybe Rachel the were-Chihuahua. I ignored the depressing thought and gave Ty a hopeful glance. "He wouldn't be an alpha human only interested in mindless, gratifying sex? Because I've got several female werewolves who would be extremely happy to make his acquaintance."

The grin turned into a full-blown smile and my heart skipped its next beat. "I seriously doubt you have a client who could match up with this guy. He's in a league all by himself."

You couldn't fault a girl for trying.

I pushed to my feet and went around to sit on the sofa next to Ty. Not because he'd smiled at me or because I felt all warm and tingly inside. It was strictly a matter of survival.

Okay. So maybe the tingling was a factor. But it was survival, too. My livelihood had been compromised tonight. On top of that, Ty's livelihood had been compromised, as well, because now there was no doubt about a connection between us. Someone was framing me for murder and whoever it was knew that Ty was helping me. Which meant they would more than likely be out to get him as well.

"I'm sorry I dragged you into this."

"Maybe next time you'll listen to me and stay put."

I'd expected a "Don't worry your pretty little head. I thrive on danger."

Or a "Helping a beautiful vampire is all in a day's work."

Or even an "Are you kidding? You're my ultimate fantasy. I can't let you face off with your enemies all by yourself."

What can I say? I've got an active imagination.

"If you had listened," he went on, "we wouldn't be here right now."

And that was so bad?

The question echoed through my head and I reminded myself about the dead animal motif. Unfortunately, the intoxicating scent of fresh air and freedom and hunky male teased my nostrils and distracted me from everything except the vamp sitting nearby.

"So what are you doing?"

"I'm about to go over our suspect list for the hundredth time."

"That's good." I nodded and ignored the insane urge to press myself against Ty and beg for another kiss. Crazy, I know. I had things to *worry* about. I didn't have time to spend the adrenaline pumping through my body and ease my anxiety with hot, wild, life-affirming sex.

Really, I didn't.

I licked my suddenly dry lips. "We definitely should figure out who could have tipped off the cops."

"I think we already know who tipped off the cops."

"Maybelline Magenta?"

He shook his head. "Chief Fairfield."

"I don't know anyone named Fair—wait a sec. You think *Remy* blew the whistle on us?"

"You don't?"

"Well, no. I mean, he wouldn't . . ." My words faded as I remembered the *he likes me* exchange we'd had back at Ty's apartment, followed by the kiss and the nibbling. "Never mind."

Not that I thought Remy had done it.

I just wasn't one hundred percent positive that he *hadn't*.

What I was positive about was that he'd taken an oath to serve and protect (my folks had been at the ceremony when he'd been sworn in), which certainly included blowing the whistle on suspected felons who ran the streets of his small, exclusive, upscale Connecticut community.

Even if said suspected felon was only running the streets out of obligation to said suspected felon's overbearing, conservative, crazy family.

He punched buttons for a few moments, sent an e-mail to his "guy in a league all by himself" friend and then snapped the lid closed. "I've got to go out and get supplies."

"But it'll be daybreak soon."

"That's why I have to go now. It's been a long

night. You should relax and turn in. I'll be back in a little while." He pinned me with a stare. "I mean it. Stay inside. We've got a safe place now, but we won't if you start flying around and socializing again."

"Who needs to fly?" I held up the cell phone he'd given me. "I can still use this, can't I?"

He nodded. Then he moved so swiftly that I saw just a black blur. The door closed and I was all by my lonesome once again.

Alone. Not lonely, I reminded myself. Big difference. I was (a) used to living alone and being independent and (b) not the least bit dependent on Ty's presence to make me feel complete.

Sure, I'd just had a close brush with the cops and whoever was out to get me had dragged my fantasy man into it. My nerves were on edge, but I could deal. It wasn't like I was really and truly *scared*.

Get real. I was a *vampire,* for Damien's sake. The baddest of the bad. The fiendiest of the fiends. The most wicked of the . . . well, you get the idea.

I ignored the urge to check the lock on the door, picked up my cosmetics bag, and headed for the bathroom. After I washed up—while humming "Dontcha" by the Pussycat Dolls to kill the oppressive silence—I climbed up into the loft and slid beneath the camouflage comforter.

Considering my mood, it wasn't nearly as creepy as I'd anticipated. What can I say? I'm a sucker for a pillow-top mattress. I closed my eyes and focused on the exhaustion that tugged at my muscles.

Exhaustion was good.

It meant sleep rather than tossing and turning and feeling like a beta in a fishbowl thanks to the stuffed bobcat who sat in the loft corner and eyed me.

Then again, I *did* have an entire thirty-three minutes until sunrise. I'd never been much for turning in early. I sat up in bed and reached for the cell phone that sat on the nightstand.

Twenty-three
❤ ❤ ❤

I had a total of five messages waiting in my voice mail. Not a huge number, but enough to pass the time until Ty returned and distracted me from the bobcat.

"It didn't work," my mother announced as the first message played. "Your father and I spent two hours with him after you left with that woman. Two useless hours. Jack is completely bewitched."

"That's *whipped*," my father added in the background.

"Whatever, dear. The point is he's not listening to reason." Aka my mother. "He's going through with this madness and actually pursuing a relationship with a *human*. I swear I'm this close to throwing myself on the nearest butter knife."

The Wedding March played in my head. Wait until she heard the real scoop.

"He insisted that we show up tomorrow," my

mother went on, "and while my first instinct is to decline, I can't *not* show up when my son is being so obviously manipulated. What kind of mother would I be?"

The non-interfering kind who let their children grow up and make their own mistakes. In other words, *not* my mother.

"That woman won't hurt Jack. I simply will not allow it. I have every intention of saving him by whatever means necessary. If that includes destroying a few pesky humans, then so be it. I've already notified your brothers that we have a family crisis and I'll need all of you at tea tomorrow."

Code for "I'm butting my nose into his business and I expect the fruit of my loins to show their support and join in."

"Eight o'clock sharp," my mother added. "Do not be late again." *Beep*.

The *again* lingered in my head and I remembered my mother's first message when she'd switched hunt night.

If the police had been monitoring my voice mail— and Ty had assured me they were—then they had known about the hunt. Which meant they'd had my parents staked out on the off chance that I would show. I did and so they'd followed my from my folks' house, back to the city, to Ty's place. Hence, the raid.

Then again, if they *had* been following me, why hadn't they nabbed me when they'd first spotted me in Connecticut? Why tail me all the way back to the city and risk losing me along the way?

Because no one had been watching.

Except Remy.

I thought again of Ty's accusation. The dead certainty in his gaze. The conviction in his voice.

But we're talking *Remy.* We'd been fixed up dozens of times. We'd talked. He *liked* me.

Duh.

He's head over heels for you, pining away every night, plotting various ways to make you fall in love with him.

Meanwhile, you're hiding out, playing kissy-nibble with a megalicious made vampire.

On top of that, you're trying to set the poor schlub up with someone else. Of course he freaked and tipped off the cops. He's jealous. You're the one and only as far as he's concerned and he can't stand the thought of facing eternity without you.

It made sense.

Message two played and a familiar male voice slid into my ear. "Hey. It's Remy. I know I told you to call me, but I figured why wait? So here I am. I know you're not picking up, but I'm really psyched. I can't wait another minute."

What'd I tell ya?

"I know it's short notice, but I have a city council reception on Friday night and I need an escort. I usually go solo, but I'm getting sick of being named Fairfield's Most Eligible Bachelor. It's time I took myself off the auction block and settled down. You mentioned Ayala and she sounded so perfect that I figured there's no better time than the present to bite the bullet."

Wait a sec. Ayala?

"Set it up and send the bill to my office." *Beep*.

So much for jealous. Unless he was just a really skilled actor.

My pride went with number two and I made a mental note to call Evie and have her set up the Friday night date. Come on, if the guy had it bad for me, I didn't want to return his call and put him through even more agony with the sweet sound of my voice.

And, of course, I didn't want to have the cops after me again. While Ty had said the cell was untraceable, Remy Tremaine was very well connected. And a born vampire. I wasn't taking any chances that he might be able to sniff me out at my new location.

The third message was from Evie.

"Ayala called again and said she absolutely can't sit home this weekend. At least, that's what I think she said. I hadn't had any coffee since noon and she called really late. I think I might have missed something. But then I realized that I wrote it down so it seems I'm not so brain dead after all. The woman's a ball buster. Help!"

Woman being the key word. Evie was still clueless when it came to my Other clients. She thought Ayala was simply a snotty, spoiled, pampered princess instead of a snotty, spoiled, pampered princess of darkness.

I smiled. Evie was going to be majorly psyched when she heard about Remy.

Message four? Nina One.

"I went for the pink, and I absolutely love it! At least, I think I love it. I won't know for sure until I see it with a pair of shoes. The problem is I can't decide between the ones I mentioned, or a pair of pussycat slides I saw at Gucci. I know, I know. Gucci and Vuitton? Arrest me now. But these slides are really the bomb and they look totally phat with the bag. But maybe not. Call me." *Beep*.

Message five . . .

"Would you please call Nina?" It was Nina Two, the brunette half of The Ninas who'd recently committed to her soul mate—a born vamp accountant named Wilson—thanks to *moi* and my fantabulous matchmaking instincts. They were now living eternally ever after in Hoboken and desperately trying to populate the race.

Which meant a phone call from her these days was pretty rare, on account of her being so busy populating and all. Being mindful of my own responsibilities as a born vampire, I was totally understanding. Being mindful of my own sucky love life, I was also insanely jealous.

"She's driving me nuts with this purse thing," she went on. "She called right when Wilson and I were about to have sex during *The O'Reilly Factor*, and totally killed the mood."

Okay, so maybe I wasn't *that* jealous.

"Not to mention, she's turned into a point of contention between us. She blurted out the whole thing to Wilson and sucked him in. He's voting for Gucci since their corporate stock is on the rise, while I think she should abandon the entire idea, return the Louis Vuitton, and invest her money in a nice CD. It's safe."

Did I mention that Nina Two is the practical one?

"Of course, she refused to listen," Nina added. "The girl wouldn't know a sound investment if it jumped up and bit her on the ass. Call her. *Please*. I have to go. CNN is running a special on the national deficit and Wilson gets really excited when they flash the coming year predictions." *Beep*.

I ignored the visual that rushed at me courtesy of Nina Two's parting statement and glanced at the front door. Still no sign of Ty. Not that I was counting the minutes or anything like that. Sure, I knew he'd been gone a total of twenty-six minutes because I'm an extremely conscientious person who keeps track of such things. But it wasn't like I *cared*.

"Go for the pink pussycats," I told Nina One after I pressed my speed dial to distract myself from the clock ticking away on the nightstand. Her answering machine picked up. "It's totally retro," I added. "Oh, and I'm fine. No bullet holes from my near brush with the authorities. Thanks for asking."

I was feeling a little put out. I mean, geez, I'm wanted for murder and all my two best friends can talk about is shoes? Sure, we're talking totally hot shoes, but still just footwear. Am I evolving or what?

I debated whether to call Nina Two, but a quick glance at the clock confirmed the start of the early morning news—complete with the latest market statistics—and I changed my mind. I was feeling bad enough. The last thing I needed was to interrupt someone having mad, passionate sex. Particularly since I wasn't having any and Ty still wasn't back.

Twenty-nine minutes . . .

I called my brother, Max, next and told him I couldn't make the intervention/tea.

"I didn't call Mom because she's probably still up. I don't want to talk to her because she'll make me feel guilty and I can't buckle this time. I'm already in enough trouble."

"You worry too much."

Uh, yeah.

"I'm a *murder* suspect, Max. I might go to prison."

I knew I was being a bit melodramatic. I'm a vampire, after all, and so the possibility of me actually rotting away in prison was really slim to none. I had the resources to skip the country and live out my days in some exotic place with servants at my beck and call. Courtesy of my parents, of course. Which meant I could live out my days in some exotic country surrounded by servants and guilt.

But my life as I knew it—the life I'd come to actually like—would be over.

Bye-bye Dead End Dating. *Au revoir* Ty. *Hasta la vista* Neiman's.

"What am I supposed to tell her?"

"Tell her the truth."

"She'll still expect you there."

"Tell her I met someone—a born vampire—and

we're too busy having wild, crazy monkey sex to come up for air, let alone tea."

"Vampires don't need air."

"The point is, we're busy. Making grandbabies."

"And what's the name of this baby-making vampire?"

Sheesh, did I have to make up *everything*? "I'm wanted for murder. I'm working the biggest client of my career. I'm barely keeping my hands off the guy who's helping me out of this mess. Can you say mega stress? The least you can do as my oldest, and most protective, brother is come up with a really great name."

"Okay, okay. I'll tell her, but you owe me."

"Put it on my tab." I hit the off button and dialed Evie to tell her about Ayala.

"I love you," she said groggily. "You're the best boss *ever*. I'll set it up as soon as I get to the office."

"Any luck on the alpha hunt?"

She yawned. "I've got five candidates I spotted on-line. A construction worker, an extreme sports nut, owner of a local Harley dealership, a fireman, and a bond enforcement agent." Another yawn. "Actually, the bond guy has a twin which means I might have six. Except the twin is shy and that really isn't an alpha trait." *Yawn.*

"We can deal with shy."

"Also, I've had seven phone calls from guys claiming to have met me at a Knicks game. I'm assuming it was you."

"Play along, call them back, and ask them the first screening questions."

"What screening questions?"

"The ones I'm going to e-mail you this afternoon. It's just an interview to weed out the serial killers and make sure we don't have any closet betas in the mix."

"Oh, I forgot. The super in my building is really bad ass with a power tool. He's not much in the looks department because he had his nose broken back when he played high school football, but he's got a great physique. On top of that, he's single."

"Does he have red hair?"

"Are you kidding? Anyway, he's in his late twenties, single, and looking strictly for a little enthusiastic female companionship. Or to quote him, 'A broad that really puts out.' Tell me again why we're remotely interested in players like this?"

"Because our clients want players."

"For sex." *Yawwwwn.* "So we're like a sex service instead of a dating service."

Actually, we were more like a procreation service, but I wasn't going to tell Evie that. I ignored my own twinge of conscience. Survival of the species, I reminded myself. Higher purpose. Yada yada.

"Because if that's what we are," Evie went on, "we'll have to lose the 'happily ever after' part of our ad. Maybe we could go with temporarily ever after?"

"You haven't had your morning coffee, have you?"

"It's five-thirty. I haven't even opened my eyes yet."

"We're not setting up sex sessions. We're a matchmaking service, i.e., we provide the initial match. What happens after they meet, be it sex, or falling in love, or both, is totally up to the individuals."

"True. Besides we're talking a whopper of a retainer fee."

Have I mentioned that Evie and I were sisters in a past life? "And a bonus when we provide an Alpha Doody."

"*If* we provide one."

Okay, so maybe we were more like cousins. Second cousins. "Think optimistic."

"It's *five-thirty*. The only thing I'm thinking about right now is how many more minutes I can squeeze in before the alarm goes off. And speaking of squeezing, how goes it with the bounty hunter?"

"For the last time, I'm not with the bounty hunter. I'm flying solo. No accomplices. *Nada.*"

"You're not getting any, are you?"

Not yet.

I squelched the thought. "Go back to sleep. I'll call you later."

"When it does happen, I want details," she mumbled. "Lots of details." *Click.*

When.

Yeah, right.

Not my type, I reminded myself. I needed a born vampire.

Even more, I needed fifteen alpha males (in addition to the thirteen Evie had come up with), one of which had to be a redhead. And I needed them in less than five days (it was now Sunday and the full moon rolled around on Friday). Otherwise Viola and the NUNS were going to miss their one shot to grow the species.

Which meant they would be pissed.

Which meant they would demand their money back.

That, or my head on a stick so they could plant it right next to the controversial azalea bushes. A little birdseed in my mouth and I'd be doubling as a feeder for the rest of eternity.

The realization was enough to distract me from any lustful thoughts I may have had when Ty arrived back at the cabin with several bags of supplies. He had everything from bottled gourmet blood to a three-pack of plain white Hanes T-shirts and a few pairs of blue jeans.

"Connections," he told me when I arched an eyebrow at him.

After he put everything away, he stripped down to a pair of white BVDs, and stretched out on the full-size bed below.

All right, already. Maybe I wasn't *completely* distracted, but I only looked for a few heart-pounding moments before I managed to tear my gaze away.

I rolled onto my back and shifted my attention to the ceiling, and the real problem—a backup plan to grow my alpha list.

One that didn't have me visiting every sports store in New York. Or every shooting range. Or every biker bar. I needed a plan that wouldn't require me to leave the cabin, and risk capture, and piss off Ty.

The possibilities didn't exactly rush at me, but I wasn't going to be discouraged. I wasn't afraid of hard work. Or of getting creative and thinking outside the box.

I *lived* outside the friggin' box.

I could totally do this.

Twenty-four
❤ ❤ ❤

"I can't do this," I told Ty.

It was Tuesday evening (yes, *Tuesday*) and I'd spent the past two days racking my brain for a viable method of rounding up alpha males without leaving the cabin, and I'd actually hit pay dirt.

Sort of.

I'd cruised every matchmaking site on the Internet and had come up with five more possibilities. Evie, bless her, had found an additional two, which gave us seven. Seven and thirteen made twenty. We were still eight shy, one of which had to have bright red hair.

Eight.

And the moon grew full in exactly three days.

"I mean it." I paced toward the kitchen where Ty sat at the table, laptop in front of him. "I'm desperate."

His gaze stayed riveted on the screen. "If you want

out of this mess, you'll have to be patient. This sort of thing takes time."

"I'm not talking about the murder rap." Ty's quest for the real killer was going about as well as my search for an Alpha Doody.

Thanks to the cabin guy, we'd learned that the tip about my whereabouts had been made by an anonymous caller. What we didn't know was whether or not the caller had been Remy Tremaine.

I waved a hand between him and the computer screen and he finally glanced up. "I'm talking about the Viola situation."

She'd called to check my progress twice already.

Well, once to check my progress and the second time to inform me that she was taking out an official contract on my father and that she hoped his imminent death would in no way put a strain on our business arrangement. Apparently my dad had abandoned the weed killer idea and gone back to hacking away at the bushes himself. His choice of gardening tool? A chain saw.

Hey, his chain saw, his problem.

Anyhow, the point is, she'd *called*.

"I've got exactly seventy-two hours to fulfill her requests," I told Ty. Short of it starting to rain men—I had to admit I'd actually resorted to praying (*do not* tell my mother)—I'd come to the painful conclusion that it wasn't going to happen.

I was going to fail Viola and Dead End Dating would be royally screwed.

"Would you just calm down? Everything's going to be all right."

"Easy for you to say. You don't have an ovulating werewolf breathing down your neck."

He grinned. "That's true."

I frowned. "I'm glad you find this funny."

"It *is* funny."

"Because it's not your ass on the line." I eyed him. "Do you know how hard it is to sit idly by while everything you've worked so hard for just gets pushed aside and your life gets put on hold?"

He glanced around. Half-empty bottles of blood sat here and there (yep, he'd been bottling it since the "other" woman incident). A stack of paperwork overflowed one cabinet and kept growing thanks to the portable printer/fax he'd set up in place of the squirrel centerpiece to keep in touch with the outside world while he was on hiatus helping me. "I sure as hell wouldn't know about that."

"Okay, fine. But do you know what it's like to have your ultimate dream dangled right in front of you, so close you could touch it? But the thing is, you can't because your hands are tied?"

He eyed me and something dark and dangerous and sensual flashed in his gaze. "Nope." His voice was deep and husky and I swallowed. "Wouldn't know about that one, either."

"Forget that." My brain raced, desperate to trade *deep* and *husky* for *clear* and *to the point.* "I bet you don't know what it's like to have an employee depending on you for every mocha latte and TiVo and her ultimate *survival*."

"Wouldn't know what that's like, either. I've got three depending on me."

"Three employees?" My brain stopped racing and tried to process. "But you don't even have a real office. Do you?"

"I don't need a real office. I just need a cell phone and a computer. My guys do what needs to be done, wherever it needs to be done, whenever I tell them it needs to be done. I direct deposit the funds in return for their help."

"You offer health insurance?" Evie had been bugging me for the past month and I'd promised to look around at a few different options for small businesses.

He shook his head. "I doubt they need it. They're not exactly human."

"Vamp?" When he shook his head again and opened his mouth, I waved a hand at him. "This is going to be another one of those 'in a league all by himself' things, right?"

"More like a legion."

I *so* wasn't going to ask, no matter how much I suddenly wanted to.

"Okay, so maybe you have an inkling of what I'm going through, but I bet you don't have a stack of credit card bills waiting for you in your underwear drawer?"

"You got me there." He shrugged. "I keep mine in the cookie jar."

I frowned. "You're a real comedian."

"Come on." He arched an eyebrow at me. "Your underwear drawer?"

"It's the one place that I don't go very often." When he arched an eyebrow at me, I shook my head. "It's not like that. I do wear underwear." When it didn't compromise the integrity of my outfit, that is. "I just don't keep it in the drawer. I hand wash most everything and so it ends up hanging on the shower rod in the bathroom until I need it." I shrugged. "I'm not much for laundry."

"You're not much for housework, either." He glanced around at the chaos that surrounded us.

"And I'm not about to acquire a taste for it."

He grinned. "I won't get my hopes up, then." He shifted his attention back to the computer and I went back to pacing.

I lasted all of ten minutes during which I turned on the television, tried my hand at several crossword puzzles, and even righted an empty bottle of blood that had tipped onto its side. Not that I was cleaning, mind you. I was straightening. Big difference.

"Ty." I sank onto the camo-cushioned chair directly across the kitchen table from him and waited for him to look up.

That's what I needed. His full attention. Then he would see how serious I was, and how miserable. And if he didn't notice that, he was bound to notice how sexy and sultry I looked, particularly when I batted my eyelashes and flashed some cleavage. Then he would surely do anything I asked.

Made or born, he was still male.

He kept tapping away at his computer.

"Earth to Ty."

Tap. Tap. Tap.

I abandoned the cleavage idea and gave him a great big mental kick in the ass. *"I'm naked!"*

His head snapped up. "What?"

Case in point.

His gaze narrowed as it roved over me. "Very funny."

"I'm not being funny. I'm being serious. I have to stop wasting time and get back to work. I can't lose this client."

"So get back to work. You've got a computer and a cell phone. What more do you need?"

"A Home Depot."

"This isn't Home Depot." I glanced around at the cluttered store, the shelves overflowing with everything from female sanitary products to deer corn. I spotted a stack of prepackaged Hanes and a folded mountain of Wrangler jeans, and I knew this had been one of Ty's stops when he'd gone out for supplies our first night upstate. A hand painted placard that read *Morty's Commissary* hung behind the cashier's counter, along with a faded *Nixon for President* sign and an autographed picture of Babe Ruth.

"It's the best I can do. Besides, there's a hardware section." Ty motioned to the right and I turned to see a small shelf filled with hammers, screwdrivers, and several coffee cans full of nails.

I glared at him. "You said you were taking me to a hardware store."

"I said a store. You assumed it was a hardware store because I said it was the next best thing to Home Depot."

"Another lie."

"Hey, around these parts this is Home Depot."

"This is a retirement home." I pointed toward the two men sitting on either side of a checkerboard near the front entrance. "I need alpha men. Not old men."

"We can go back to the cabin."

Then again, I've never been one to discriminate. I glared at Ty, turned toward the two men, and stepped forward.

Sure, they were old. But older meant wiser. They probably knew everything that went on in their town, and everyone.

"I'm looking for alpha men."

"Don't know no Alfred Mann," one of them replied. He wore glasses and had a head as shiny as the gold nickel sitting on the table near his checkers.

"She said alpha men, Ernest," the other man said, his voice raised to an ear-splitting level. "Not Alfred Mann."

"Don't know no Alphie Lynn, either." Ernest shook his head. "You know good and goddamned well there ain't no Alphie Lynn around these parts, Morty. Why, you been here even longer than me." Ernest waved a crooked finger at me. "Born and raised right up the road."

"That's nice."

Ernest frowned. "We don't play no dice around here, little lady. We're strictly checker men."

"He's hard of hearing," Morty told me. The old man had a head full of snow white hair and a bushy mustache. The mustache wagged as he took a puff on his pipe before adjusting his glasses to get a good look at me.

I smiled and he frowned.

Here's the deal. Vamp magnetism works on the opposite sex provided they still have a little oomph left. Obviously, Morty was oomphed out.

When his gaze collided with mine, I realized why. He'd not only won several battles in World War II, but recently a knock-down drag-out with prostate cancer. He was healthy as a horse now and proud of it, and a little lonely, too. While he didn't need a woman to replace his dear, departed Rosie, he did appreciate some company when he watched his nightly game shows. And a few soap operas, though he wasn't admitting that to anyone, least of all the guys down at the local VFW hall.

Likewise, Ernest had fought in the same war. He was a widower, too, and the proud grandfather of fourteen grandchildren and three great-grandchildren. Unfortunately, none of them lived nearby and so he spent most of his time playing checkers and making birdhouses and helping his brother-in-law, Morty, with the store.

I shifted my attention back to Morty. "Nice store you boys have here."

"Thank you, little lady. What can I help you with? You in the market for fresh fruits? We got the finest."

I eyed the huge crates overflowing with apples and peaches that sat against the far wall.

"That sounds really delectable, but I was actually wondering if you could help me with more of a tourist dilemma."

"We don't carry them fancy schmancy drinks around these parts," Ernest said as he slid his king into place on the checkerboard. "You got to drive down to the highway to Mitchell's Texaco if you want that."

"It ain't a drink," Morty called out, raising his voice. "She's talking about a dilemma. A problem. On account of she's a tourist."

"I don't care if she's Italian. We don't carry nothing fancy like that."

"Deaf old goat." Morty waved a hand. "What sort of dilemma you in, little gal?"

"I was wondering if there was a club around here or someplace where a lot of men might congregate. Single men, that is."

He puffed and seemed to think. "There's the VFW hall," he finally said, waving his pipe toward the right. "Just up the road, there. They're having a spaghetti dinner tomorrow night. Should be lots of fellas at that and a danged many single ones to boot. Know for a fact that Howard Eisenbacher'll be there. Damn good catch, that one. Lost his missus about twenty years ago and has been living off the life insurance ever since. Been banking his social security since then, too, which means he's got one hell of a nest egg."

"He sounds really great, but I'm really looking for someone a few years younger."

He shook his head. "Can't help you there. Most of the folks around here are retired, and so's all the VFW members. Except my nephew, that is. Lloyd's a damned sight younger than the rest of us."

"Really?" I smiled. "How is he with a hammer?"

"The boy was born with one. There ain't a car he can't fix, or a tree he can't chop. Why, me and Ernest, here, would be lost without him. Helps us right here at the store."

"Today?"

"As a matter of fact, he's out back right now." He grinned. "Would you like to meet him?"

"Are you kidding? I'd love to meet him." One down and seven more to go. "He wouldn't by any chance have red hair?"

"As a matter of fact, he does."

My livelihood might not be totally screwed after all.

I smiled and waited as Ernest went to fetch Lloyd.

Twenty-five

♥ ♥ ♥

I stared at the man who walked from the back of the old-fashioned general store.

He stood well over six feet, with massive shoulders and legs like tree trunks. He wore a red flannel button-down shirt, jeans, and hiking boots. He carried an ax in one hand and a bundle of firewood in the other. He smelled of freshly cut timber and pine cones. A real man's man.

A hairy man's man.

I stared at the mass of bright red hair that spilled over the V of his button-down shirt. More hair sprinkled the backs of his meaty hands. A thick mustache and beard surrounded his mouth and obliterated most of his face. Bright red fuzz peeked from the insides of his ears.

He had hair *everywhere,* except where it should have been.

His head gleamed as shiny as a cue ball and my heart gave a disappointed thump.

I was *so* screwed.

"This here's my nephew, Lloyd," Morty said. "Lloyd, this little lady's eager to make your acquaintance. She's looking for a single man who ain't an old geezer like us."

"Really?" Hope fired in Lloyd's pale green eyes. Nice eyes, actually, once you got past the whole Sasquatch meets Mr. Clean thing.

My gaze met his and his stats flashed in my head.

Lloyd Herbert Price. Forty-four. Only child. Parents deceased. Never been married. Addicted to the Discovery Channel. Never been married. Liked to fish and hunt and had his own dead animal motif going back at his cabin. Never been married. Worked for his uncle during the day and did taxidermy work at night.

And did I mention *never been married*?

Not for lack of trying, of course. He simply hadn't found the right woman who shared his interests and didn't mind that he had as much hair on his back as he did on his chest.

Ugh. Too much information.

I focused on the hope in his gaze and gave him a dazzling smile.

"I'm Lil Marchette—that is—" I cleared my throat as my frantic brain reminded me of a few key points—*on the run, wanted for murder, low profile.* "That is, I, um, *work* for Lil Marchette. A wonderful woman. A goddess among the fashionably well-dressed. Anyhow, my name is Evie and I'm with Dead End Dating, a fantabulous new hook-up service in the city." My smile widened. "And it would be my honor to help you out."

"Already got a towing service around these parts," Morty chimed in.

"Rowing service?" Ernest frowned. "We ain't got any rowing services 'round these parts. Everybody I know with a boat uses at least a fifty horsepower. Then again, there's Stuart Jenkins. He's got that piss-ant bass boat with the trolling motor."

"That's TOWING," Morty said. "A *TOWING* service."

"Don't need a towing service," Lloyd told me, his voice deep and gruff.

Okay, so maybe he was a pretty decent alpha specimen. Totally rough and tough. But attractive?

Mentally, I did some cutting and pasting to rearrange the body hair. A little more here, a lot less there . . . Maybe.

"Don't have a car for you to hook up. Had a pickup a few years back, but I traded it in. I don't get down to the city too often."

Imagine that.

"I meant hook-up service, as in personal hook-ups, not vehicular ones. We're a *dating* service. I'm afraid I don't have any business cards on me." I'd left them back at Ty's loft when fleeing from the cops. "But I'm staying just up the road. I'd love to talk to you about your options as a single, brawny male."

"Come again?"

"Well, a young, virile man like yourself has various choices when it comes to the opposite sex. There's the obvious—meet a woman, settle down, sink up to your neck in mortgage payments." The comment produced the expected narrowing of the eyes. "Or you can maintain your own space. No one to tell you what to do or make you cart out the trash and gripe about the seat being up. You can stay loose and un-attached and just have some fun. Sort of test the waters. As a professional, I thoroughly recommend testing the waters."

Lloyd simply stared at me a few silent seconds be-fore shaking his head. "Thanks, but no thanks. My well's pumping one hundred percent spring water. Had it tested just last year."

"Not that water, you dummy," Morty chimed in. "She's talking about the deed."

One bushy red eyebrow inched higher. "Don't have no deed for my well. Got one for my cabin, though. Clear and free as of last year."

"Not that deed." Morty shook his head. "*The* deed. You know. Cleaning the old shotgun." When Lloyd didn't look the least bit enlightened, Morty added, "Sex, you moron. The lady, here, is talking about S-E-X."

His gaze zigzagged from Morty to me. "You want to have sex with me?" It was pure lust that fired his eyes this time.

Not that I could blame him. Sure, I didn't look all that impressive in a no-name T-shirt and stiff, off-the-shelf jeans, but beneath the brandless clothes, I was a vampire. I oozed magnetism.

"Not me," I clarified. "Not that I wouldn't love to have sex with you. It's just that I never mix business and pleasure. And this is purely business. See, I have a beautiful, vivacious, extremely wealthy client who's eager to find a brawny specimen like yourself for some, er, companionship."

"That's sex," Morty clarified for his nephew. "Ain't that what you mean by that there *companionship*?"

"Maybe. While I'll make the introduction between you and my client, after that it's up to Mother Nature."

"So you can't actually guarantee he'll get lucky?" Morty asked.

"No. Not exactly."

"Well"—Morty waved his pipe—"you can just forget it. He ain't saying yes unless there's a guarantee what comes with it. Ain't that right, Lloyd?"

When Lloyd simply stood there, Morty nudged him. "Ain't that right?" he prompted again.

"Uh, yeah. If you can't give me a guarantee, I'm not interested. I got better stuff to do than waste my time on a blind date."

Yeah, like stuffing poor, defenseless bunnies.

"I can't *promise* sex."

"*And why not?*" Ty's deep voice slid into my head and I turned to see him standing across the room, his back to me as he examined a row of fishing lures.

I'd heard his voice in my head too many times over the past few days and it had always unnerved me. As if he were intruding on my private space. But standing in the middle of the store, I felt this odd sense of camaraderie.

"Isn't that the goal?" he went on. *"To give Viola and the girls a wild night of cleaning the shotgun?"*

I was *not* going to smile.

This was serious. I was down to the wire. Viola wanted results and I had to give them to her, even if they weren't exactly what she'd asked for.

Lloyd was close enough.

Or he would be by the time I finished with him.

"My goal is to give her possible candidates for a wild night of cleaning the shotgun." I sent Ty the silent response. *"The actual 'cleaning' is none of my business. Besides, I already told you, I don't clean."*

He turned then and his gaze collided with mine. Humor sparked in the dark blue depths of his eyes and my stomach hollowed out. *"That's not the kind I'm talking about and you know it."*

I did. The thing was, I didn't *want* to know it. I wanted my life to get back to normal.

"I know, but I don't do guns, either."

Okay, so I wanted to jump Ty first and then have my life get back to normal. But I was exercising some self-discipline and controlling that want. Having him teasing and flirting in my head, however, chipped away at my resolve.

I licked my suddenly dry lips and forced my attention back to Lloyd. "I can't guarantee that the two of you will get *that* familiar with each other." I could only hope and—don't tell my mom—pray. "It's really a matter of chemistry once you meet. But I can promise that she'll be exceptionally beautiful and very amorous."

Lloyd's eyebrows kicked up a notch. "Amorwhat?"

"Amorous," I said again.

"Horny," Morty quipped before taking a quick puff on his pipe.

Understanding lit Lloyd's pale green eyes, but he didn't so much as blush.

I couldn't decide if that was a good or bad thing. Good if I were judging his alphaness. Alpha males obviously didn't go around blushing. That particular quality fell to the full-blooded betas.

On the other hand, Richie Cunningham had probably blushed up a storm during each and every *Happy Days* episode, which screamed *beta*, which screamed *you are so screwed*.

"If you're through pimping, we really need to get back," Ty said as he came up next to me.

I shot him a glare before giving Lloyd a brilliant smile. "So what do you say? You interested in a date?" I focused my most intense vamp stare on the brawny man. *Yes*, I sent him the silent message. *You'll say yes to anything I want because I'm so hot and you simply can't resist my inner sexuality.*

His eyes glazed over and he stood dumbfounded for several long seconds before Morty elbowed him in the ribs.

"Speak up, boy."

Yes, yes, yes, I echoed silently.

Lloyd's gaze seemed to clear and he nodded. "I guess so."

Bingo.

I think.

I watched as he shoved a finger into one hairy ear and scratched. I tried to ignore the rush of dread in the pit of my stomach and focused on being as positive and as enthusiastic as possible. "Great! The date is Friday night. I'll pick you up here and you can drive in with us."

Drive? Ty asked silently. *Sugar, we flew.*

"Maybe you could drive," I told Lloyd. "Women love a man who drives." He nodded and I smiled. "It's such a macho thing to sit behind the wheel and have all that power right at your fingertips."

"I guess I could borrow Uncle Morty's station wagon."

"Then again, maybe we could rent a car. What do you say, dear?" I turned my most charming smile on Ty.

"Are you nuts? We're laying low, remember? Laying low does not include handing over proof of insurance and a driver's license to rent a car."

"But it's a station wagon. He can't show up at Viola's in that. He needs something big and macho. A Hummer maybe. Or a Dualie."

Ty shifted his attention to Lloyd. "Borrow the station wagon." Before I could protest, he slid his arm around me and squeezed tight enough to make me wince. "We'll give you directions to Connecticut and you can go it alone, buddy. Later."

"Thursday," I called out over my shoulder as Ty

steered me around. I was this close to breaking a rib with my elbow, except that I couldn't manage to get my arm high enough to give him a powerful jab.

For a made vampire, he was surprisingly strong. That, coupled with the fact that I'd been drinking as little as possible around him to avoid stirring the hunger that lived and breathed inside of me. My senses had dulled. I couldn't see as clearly or notice every little detail the way I usually did. Likewise, my hearing wasn't as fine-tuned. Not that I still didn't have it going on in the vamp department. I hadn't lost my abilities. I just wasn't functioning at full capacity.

I stayed glued to Ty's side as he ushered me toward the door.

"Wait a second," Lloyd's voice followed. "I thought you said the date was Friday?"

"Thursday is the predate prep. I'll meet you here."

"You're a jerk," I told Ty when we reached the front porch of the store.

"And you're going to get us caught again. A Hummer? Please."

"Or a Dualie. Can't you just try to see what I'm up against."

"A murder rap."

"I meant professionally."

"A murder rap."

"You have a one-track brain. Do you mind?" I glanced at the hand that clamped around my shoulder.

Ty's grip loosened and he winked. "All you had to do was ask."

"Lloyd can't drive a station wagon to Viola's."

"He'll have to."

"Okay, let me make myself clear. Lloyd can't drive a station wagon to the full moon powwow at Viola's because it's totally un-alpha, not to mention I don't do station wagons."

"Then you don't have to worry because you're not going. You're staying right here."

I opened my mouth only to clamp it back shut.

I *know*. Me? Who would've thought?

But from the stern set of his jaw and the intense glare in his neon blue eyes, I knew he wasn't about to change his mind at the moment. Besides, I was tired. I didn't have my usual energy and what I did have I needed to preserve. I had much bigger problems to deal with between now and Friday.

Hairier problems.

"Fine," I huffed. "Can we get out of here?"

"That's my girl."

I ignored the warmth that spread through me at the comment and followed Ty around the side of the store and into the woods. In a matter of seconds, we'd covered the few miles to the cabin.

Inside, Ty headed back to his computer and I made a beeline for my cell phone to tackle problem number one.

Twenty-six

❤ ❤ ❤

"I need you to overnight me a few things," I told Evie when she finally picked up her phone after several rings. I sank down onto the sofa and propped my feet between the photo album and the antler candleholder. Yikes, I needed a pedicure.

"Business cards?" she asked.

"A waxing kit." I conjured a mental image of Lloyd. "Make that five waxing kits." We're talking *Lloyd.*

I gave Evie the lowdown on my Alpha Doody progress and the mini-makeover I had planned.

"Still," she said when I finally came up for air. "He's bald. Richie Cunningham was *not* bald."

"Maybe Viola's friend won't notice."

"Wouldn't you notice?"

"Maybe she'll be too busy." While I hadn't actually seen a pure werewolf up close during the full moon,

I'd had a few long-distance peeks through a pair of binoculars at my folks' house. "Viola's parties can get a little wild."

"We're talking *bald*. Sure, it's ultra sexy to some women, but to others it's a complete turn-off. Total blah. More effective than a cold shower."

"You don't like bald men, do you?"

"Can't stand 'em. My ex was bald and he was the lowest form of life. Just the sight of a smooth head makes my stomach turn."

"Maybe you're the exception."

"I say we don't risk it. Let's just send twenty-eight regular alphas and hope for the best. How mad can she get? I'm sure she doesn't really expect us to send her a redheaded one. That's probably just her ideal. The icing on the cake, so to speak. And who likes icing anyway?"

While I'd never tasted icing, I knew for a fact that it was the best part. A must-have for any decent dessert.

"We'll stick a wig on Lloyd," I told her.

"Wig, check. Anything else?"

My memory stirred and I remembered a glimpse of a very aggressive female werewolf tugging and pulling at her mate's fur. A wig would *never* work. "Throw in a few bottles of superglue." Never say never.

"Superglue, check, check. If I get this stuff out first thing in the morning, you should have it on Thursday. Where do you want me to send everything?"

I gave her the address for Morty's Commissary

printed on one of the bags Ty had brought home our first night at the cabin.

"You're upstate?" she asked after she'd written the information down.

"Yeah, right. Like I would even consider going upstate when there's sun and sand and cute Jamaican guys just a plane ride away." Guilt niggled at me because I (a) had never ridden a plane in my life and (b) would go up in flames at the first ray of direct sunshine. But Evie didn't know either of those things, along with the biggie—I was a vamp—and I didn't want to drag her any further into my mess. Besides, the less I acknowledged my desperate situation, the better. Denial was sometimes a beautiful thing. "I am *not* upstate."

"Just like you're not with the bounty hunter, right?"

My gaze slid to Ty, who sat at the kitchen table once again, laptop open in front of him, a bottle of blood in his hand. He took a long swig. His Adam's apple bobbed. I felt an ache in the pit of my stomach.

"Exactly," I managed, despite my suddenly dry throat. "Other than the alpha search, how goes it?" I asked Evie. When denial failed, go for a distraction.

"Well, Esther went out with my uncle."

"And?"

"They went bowling. He had a ball. He threw ten strikes."

"And Esther?"

"She didn't throw any."

"But did she have fun?"

"At first."

"What does that mean?"

"That my uncle can't see very well and he didn't notice she was standing in the middle of the lane when he went to take his turn. He sort of hit her with the ball."

"Sort of?"

"Actually, he knocked her down with it and then he stepped on her. She didn't need stitches or anything, just a case of napkins from the concession stand. There was a lot of blood."

Duh.

"But she's okay now. I talked to her myself just this evening. She said she's ready to try again. But no bowling this time. And no one with cataracts. Otherwise, she's up for anything. Talk about a real trooper."

"Send her some flowers and tell her we've got something extra special planned for date number two."

"What do we have planned?"

"I don't know yet, but I promise it'll be extra special. Right now, just do the flowers and stall her until . . ."

Until I successfully matched up Viola and her werewolf sisters and found the person trying to frame me and made it through another night in the same room with Ty Bonner.

I cleared my throat. "Until things get back to normal."

"I could call another one of my uncles."

"No uncles, but if you've got a few aunts we just might be in business."

"They're all dead. But I do have a widow lady who lives down the hall from me."

"Does she have a friend?"

"She's got a twin sister. They just celebrated their eightieth birthdays. Why? You thinking about a *ménage à trois* for the *something special*?"

"Not for Esther. For Morty and Ernest." I gave her the details on the two old men.

"They're interested in our services?"

"Well, no. Not yet." But once I talked to them when I went to pick up the care package Evie was going to send, I was certain they would want to add their names to the ever growing list of Dead End Dating clients.

At least that's what I was hoping.

With both Evie and me so focused on fulfilling Viola's request, we'd sort of forgotten about any continued advertising efforts. Sure, we had clients now, but when all was said and done?

I wasn't going to worry over that now. I couldn't. As far as I was concerned, my world didn't extend beyond Friday and the numerous things I had to do to get ready for Viola and the NUNS.

I went over the alpha list with Evie and instructed her to double-check with each of the men to make sure they knew when and where to go on Friday.

I was this close to hanging up and avoiding any and all distractions when I heard myself blurt, "Did my mother call?"

Oy, what the hell was wrong with me?

Guilt, that's what. I hadn't checked my voice mail

since I'd called Max and asked him to make my excuses for missing the tea/intervention.

"Eight times," Evie informed me.

"That's not too bad." I'd expected at least a dozen.

"That's eight times today. She called fifteen times yesterday. She said you can't be having that much sex and that you should call her." I could hear the smile in Evie's voice. "Did you tell her about the bounty hunter?"

"I'm not with the bounty hunter. I had to miss a family function for obvious reasons and I told her I had a new boyfriend so that she would forgive the absence."

"She didn't sound forgiving. Then again, she didn't sound mad, either. Just upset. She kept going on and on about someone named Mandy who was ruining your brother's life."

Obviously the intervention hadn't worked and Jack and Mandy had announced the news about the wedding.

"That was yesterday," Evie went on. "Today she sounded more medicated."

"She drinks when she's upset."

"That explains why she kept mumbling something about burning Mandy at the stake."

Obviously, the wedding hadn't been the only news.

"Either that, or she was hungry for a steak and she wanted to take Mandy along."

I voted for the first one.

"Anyway, she wants you to call her. I told her you

might not be able to because of being wanted by the police."

"What did she say to that?"

"That she's sacrificed years of her life to nurture and raise you. The least you can do is spare her a measly five minutes."

Jacqueline Marchette hadn't been named the CEO of Guilt for nothing.

I finished my call with Evie and then turned my attention to the pen and paper in front of me to outline a makeover plan for Lloyd.

I'd barely managed to write my mission statement when I felt Ty's gaze.

I glanced up and met his neon blue stare. "What?"

"I've finished checking out the suspects on your list."

"And?"

"And other than a half dozen fellow shoppers who'd like to see you tarred and feathered and hanging from the Empire State building, I've got zilch."

"A half dozen doesn't sound like zilch."

"They all have solid alibis, sugar. Which means we're back to square one. We need someone with a real motive." He pushed to his feet and paced toward the window. "Whoever's doing this has it in for you in the worst way. We're talking intense hatred. On top of that, they obviously know you well enough to know just how to get to you." His gaze zeroed in on me again. "To hurt you." A light fired his eyes a bright blue. "You have to think, Lil. I need someone else. Otherwise . . ."

Otherwise I wasn't going to get out of this mess.

I would be on the run for the rest of my life. Forget Viola and the NUNS. I wouldn't need them because I wouldn't be a matchmaker. I would be a fugitive.

I swallowed as the truth weighed down on me. My gaze fell to the outline I'd just started and I read the first sentence: *Make Lloyd as attractive as possible to the werewolf with the Alpha Doody fetish.*

My gaze lingered on the *werewolf.*

"There has to be someone."

Or something.

"The jealous werewolf," I blurted, my mind racing back to the night of the annual Midnight Soirée sponsored by my mother's huntress club. "Remember the night I unveiled the new Francis to the rest of born vamp society? That was the night I ran the little experiment with Wilson and Nina to see if they liked each other. Namely, I set them each up with someone else to make the other jealous. And it worked. Not that that's the point. The point is, the setup also made someone else jealous. Ayala's ex-werewolf lover. He showed up ready to take Wilson out. That's when I got staked." That would explain the DNA evidence. I bled all over the place.

It wasn't like I'd been able to stand idly by and let a crazed Other stake my best friend's intended. I'd intervened, of course, and I'd gotten it in the shoulder.

"My brothers took him out," I told Ty. "After I fainted, they attacked him."

"Which means he can't be out to get you."

"No, but his family might be. I know that if some-

hing happened to me, my family would be really
pissed." Then again, at the rate I was going . . .
"Maybe they're mad enough to want to punish me."

"Did he have any family?"

"I'm sure he does. Everybody has family." Except
made vampires.

I saw the strange look that passed over his face and
I had the sudden urge to reach out. Thankfully, the
look passed as quickly as it had come, and I stayed
rooted to the couch.

He seemed to think. "It's possible."

"It's more than possible. That's it. It has to be it." I
smiled. "It's his family. They have it in for me. That
explains everything."

"Maybe" was all he said as he walked back to his
laptop.

"A little enthusiasm wouldn't hurt, you know?
Maybe a 'Gee, Lil, that's totally Einstein of you.' "

"You should have mentioned it in the first place."

"I didn't remember." In fact, I did my best not to
remember getting staked. Not only had it hurt, but
now I was forever linked to a made vampire who was
so *not* my type.

I watched as he punched in some information and
sent a few e-mails before pushing to his feet.

"I've got some things to do. I'll be back."

I ignored the strange emptiness that settled around
me whenever he walked out the door. Namely because I was *not* empty. And I *wanted* him to walk out
the door.

It made working and falling asleep easier when he wasn't a strip and a pounce away.

Much easier, I told myself, basking in the newfound information and turning my attention back to my makeover outline.

One problem down, one to go.

"It feels really warm," Lloyd said on Thursday night as I spread the warm wax onto his right shoulder.

I'd set up a chair in the storeroom of Morty's Commissary when I'd arrived just after sunset. After clearing some space on one of the wall-to-wall shelves, between the Pringles and the Cheez Whiz, I'd unpacked the care package from Evie which had included not only the requested items, but a pair of latex gloves.

Yep, Evie and I were soul sisters, all right.

"It's sort of soothing," Lloyd said as I smoothed.

"Glad to hear you say that." I scooped more of the wax I'd just nuked in the small microwave that sat next to a Mr. Coffee on one of the shelves, and slathered it onto Lloyd's skin. "It's always best to focus on the positive in these kinds of situations."

As if the thought had just struck, he stiffened. "It's not going to hurt, is it?"

"Maybe a little."

"How little?"

"Relax. Women do it all the time. It can't be that bad, right?"

"True."

I rubbed a piece of cloth over the wax, gripped the edge and *rrrrrrip!*

Lloyd screamed.

Then again, women gave birth all the time, too, and it was common knowledge that that hurt like a sonofabitch.

"There, there." I patted his opposite shoulder with my gloved hand. "It can't be that bad."

"You . . ." He panted. "It . . ." More panting. "I can't . . ." Inandoutandinandout.

"Easy, big guy. The first time is always the worst."

"R-really?" he finally managed after more panting interspersed with a little wheezing.

"Sure. From here on out, it's smooth sailing. See, your body is buzzing with intense pain which keeps it from noticing less intense pain." I smoothed more wax onto the next hairy patch and rubbed the cloth strip on top. "Just count to five, brace yourself, and I'll pull. Okay?"

His head bobbed and he rasped, "One, two, three— *ffffuck!*"

"I guess that one hurt, too?" He called me several choice names. "So much for the element of surprise." I smoothed more wax onto his ultra hairy skin. "If it's any consolation, you're starting to look mega hunky."

"R-really?"

I eyed the pink patches of raw skin and tried not to wince. "Sure."

"In that case, I g-guess it's w-worth it. You say this woman is really h-hot?"

"The hottest." At least, I was pretty sure, even though I hadn't actually met the Alpha Doody lover. Viola was attractive and weren't all werewolves just hairier, fangless versions of vampires? Since we were all real lookers, I was assuming the same could be said for our fellow weres.

At least, I was hoping.

More smoothing, another *rrrrrrip*! and Lloyd burst into tears.

"There, there, Lloyd. It's just a little harmless wax. If you carry on like this, what's going to happen when I pull out the superglue?"

Twenty-seven
❤ ❤ ❤

I stared into the small bathroom mirror early Friday evening and eyed my reflection. I wore my black and white Diane von Furstenberg wrap dress with the cap sleeves and my python and leather Vivia sandals—the same outfit I'd been wearing when Ty and I had fled from the cops.

While it wasn't my first choice—which would be my black Dolce & Gabbana suit with the Francesco Biasia bag—for meeting my most important client to date, it would have to do.

At least I hadn't been snuggled in Ty's bed wearing boxers and a ratty old tee when the cops had shown up. Talk about deep shit.

I drew in a full, easy breath in an effort to ease the frantic pounding of my heart.

No luck.

I killed the whole breathing effort, gathered my

courage, and reached for the doorknob. My heart beat a Metallica drum solo as I walked out of the bathroom and headed for the kitchen, where Ty sat hunched over his laptop.

He wore faded jeans and nothing else. His back was broad and muscular, his arms well defined. His long, dark hair rested against his neck and I had the sudden urge to run my fingers through it.

Or I would've had the sudden urge, except that I was a committed professional with one thing on her mind: satisfying Viola and raking in the rest of my cash. Okay, so that qualified as two things. The point was—work, not play.

Got that?

Ty obviously shared my dedication because he didn't so much as glance up as I walked around the table and slid into the seat opposite him.

Since I'd thought of the pissed off were-family angle, he'd been neck deep running background checks on the jealous werewolf's mother, father, sisters, brothers, cousins, second cousins, third cousins, fourth cousins, aunts, uncles, grandfathers, grandmothers, great grandfathers, great grandmothers (what'd I tell ya?).

Out of two hundred sixty-two relatives, Ty had found at least two leads worth pursuing. One of the wolf's brothers had done time for assault, while a female cousin recently had a restraining order put against her by an ex-boyfriend. Both situations confirmed one thing—crazy ass relatives capable of violence.

I cleared my throat. "Nice night."

He merely grunted.

Distracted. That was good. It meant that he wasn't really listening. So when I announced, very matter-of-factly, that I was leaving to meet Lloyd, there was a microscopic chance that he might not even hear me.

I'd never been one to worry over odds, so I opened my mouth. "I'm—"

"No."

"You don't even know what I'm going to say."

"You're not going."

"I have to go."

He punched a final button and closed the lid of the laptop. He leaned back in his chair and crossed his arms. Muscles bulged and my stomach hollowed out. His gaze roved over me.

"Why didn't you just go out the bathroom window?" he finally asked.

I motioned to the Vivias. "In these shoes?"

"You could have morphed," he pointed out. "Bats don't wear shoes."

"What are you trying to say?"

"That you could have, but you didn't."

"Surely you're not implying that I have a conscience?" That I might possibly feel some obligation to the one person actually going out of his way to help me? "Yeah, right."

"Then why didn't you?"

"My night vision is acting up." There. That was the truth. Part of it, anyway.

He stared at me long and hard before he seemed to come to a conclusion. Then he reached for a half-empty bottle of blood he'd been nursing and slid it across the table toward me.

The sweet, intoxicating scent teased my nostrils and I felt the sharp edge of my fangs against my tongue. My fingers itched to reach out.

Just one taste and all my worries would be over.

No more wanting and aching and fantasizing.

About the blood, I mean.

As for Ty, I had the feeling I could gorge myself for hours on end and never get enough.

Which was why I kept my fangs to myself and balled my hands in my lap. "No, thanks."

"Come on. You'll feel better."

If only. "I drank earlier."

"I didn't see you."

"You don't see everything."

"Don't kid yourself."

My mind raced back to the previous day when he'd stripped down to his BVDs and I'd eyed him from the loft. Unknowingly, or so I'd thought. Judging from the sudden light in his eyes, I had a feeling he'd been all too aware. Of my stares and what I'd been doing with my . . .

Easy, girl.

"You're a vampire. You have to drink."

"Look who's telling who. I've been around for five hundred years. I think I know that."

"So what's up?"

"I already told you. I had a few sips here and there. Listen, I have to go tonight. I swear I'll be careful. I'll keep a very low profile and I won't talk to anyone except Viola. And Lloyd. And the other men. And, of course, the NUNS. I'll have to talk to them. And if Viola has any guests, then I'll be obliged to say hello and be at least civil, but that's it. Once midnight strikes, I'm outa there."

"Send Evie."

"Are you kidding? She doesn't know about Viola, or me, or the mating orgy—I should be so lucky—about to commence in less than four hours." When the clock struck midnight and the moon was at its fullest, the werewolves were at their horniest. "And I intend to make sure that my secret stays safe."

"You should have hired a vampire instead of a human." I arched an eyebrow and waited for his own words to sink in. "Forget I said that. You're the only vampire who actually believes that people need to date in order to mate."

I frowned. "I'm not the only one." I was pretty sure that I'd made believers out of Wilson and Nina Two. They had found each other because of me. And then there were Francis and Melissa.

Then again he was a vampire and she was still a human, and so they weren't really mating. Humping on a regular basis, yes. Mating? That implied commitment, which implied living out eternity and making baby vamps together, and it just wasn't going to happen for them. Ever.

Even so, they seemed happy, which made me think again of Ty and his fabulous pecs and how much I'd really like to run my hands over his hard muscles and . . .

I shook away the seductive image that pushed its way into my head. Okay, so where was I?

Orgy. Midnight. Must go.

"Give me ten minutes to make the introductions, collect the rest of my fee, and ease the situation with Lloyd. I have to at least make sure he isn't going to be eaten in a fit of anger. Then I'll hang back until things get into full swing and leave. Cross my heart." I made the motion and Ty shook his head.

"You're the damndest vampire I've ever met."

"Does that mean yes?"

"No."

I stiffened. "Okay, fine. I didn't want to have to pull rank on you, but you give me no choice."

"Pull *what*?"

"Rank. I'm the born vamp here lest we forget. I'm the one in control." I plopped an elbow on the table and motioned to him. "So come. Let's get this over with. Winner chooses whether I go or stay."

A smile tugged at his lips. "You want to arm wrestle?"

I shrugged. "I figure it will be easier on your ego than a full-blown ass whipping."

The smile faded and his gaze darkened. "You're serious?"

"As serious as you are scared."

He braced his elbow on the table and gripped my hand. "You're on, sugar."

I should have drank the blood, I decided several minutes later as I intertwined my finger's with Ty's and did my damndest to hold my own.

I knew I was stronger. At least, I'd thought so. I'm a born vampire, after all, and five hundred years of training and conditioning wasn't going to disappear in a matter of seconds.

Was it?

Ty *was* pretty strong. The muscles of his arm bulged with his effort. The neon glow of his eyes held mine and refused to let go. He looked determined and relaxed at the same time. The only clue that maybe, just maybe, I was putting it to him in a major way was the frantic beat of his pulse where the inside of his wrist met mine.

I gathered my determination and focused on a mental picture of Viola handing me another check, complete with a big, fat bonus for Lloyd. Then me going to the bank. Me paying my bills. Me heading off to Barney's for that divine Hermès scarf I'd seen a couple of weeks ago—

"You're good." His deep voice echoed in my head and shattered the illusion.

"Thanks." I sent the silent reply and gave him a small smile.

"But not good enough." He forced me down a fraction of an inch and wiped the smile off my face.

"Psyching me out won't work," I tossed back at him. *"I want this too much."*

"It could be a trap. Viola is a werewolf. She was in your office when the police showed up the first time. Don't you think it's too much of a coincidence?"

"She's lived next to my family for decades. She wouldn't do that."

"How do you know?"

"I'm a vampire."

"Vampires read humans. Not Others."

"Maybe I'm different."

"You're telling me you can read Others?"

"I'm telling you that I can sense things about them. If they're creepy, then I get a creepy feeling. If they're honest, then I get an honest feeling from them. If they're perverted, then I get a perverted feeling, followed by the urge to wash my hands." I thought of Rachel the were-Chihuahua. "If they eat dog biscuits and play fetch when the moon is full, then I get the urge to scratch them behind the ears." I clamped my fingers tighter around his and held on. "I know Viola and I know she isn't a part of this."

At least I was ninety-five percent sure. The other five percent? Undecided. She might, indeed, have something to do with what was happening. At the same time, I'd never been one to play it safe, especially with such slim odds.

Besides, Hermès was calling . . .

"Please." I sent the silent plea.

He stared at me long and hard, a determined look in his eyes. His grip tightened and he started to push—

"Shit." He released my hand and shook his head. "Shit." He eyed me. "Fine. We'll go. But we're going straight there and straight back. No bullshit. Got it?"

"Straight there. Straight back." I bolted to my feet and grabbed my purse before he changed his mind.

"And I'm not riding in a station wagon. We'll fly and Lloyd can fend for himself."

"He's nervous. He needs me. Besides, he borrowed a minivan from a friend of his."

"That's as bad as the station wagon."

I thought so, too, but I was trying to look on the bright side. "At least it's blue."

"And?"

"And blue says male."

"Black says male."

"It's dark blue. That's sort of male."

"If you say so."

"I really could use some positive affirmation right now."

"They're werewolves. Once they change, they won't care if they're humping a water buffalo."

"Never mind. So, you know when you said straight there and straight back?" I asked as I opened the front door, Ty on my heels. "I'm sure you didn't mean *straight* straight. Because there's straight there. And then there's *straight* there. I'm sure you were just talking about the regular old straight, which implies a minimum number of mandatory stops at low-risk locations."

"How minimum?" He followed me out onto the front porch.

"Two. One at my parents and—"

"Goddammit, Lil." He shook his head and slammed the door behind us. "You're killing me, you know that?"

"You're immortal."

He glared. "Just my rotten luck. Where else?"

I gave him my most charming smile. "The nearest Blockbuster."

It was eleven o'clock when I hauled Lloyd up the front steps to Viola's gigantic house and pressed the doorbell. Behind me, the minivan sat idling at the curb. Ty had offered to drop us off down the street to preserve Lloyd's image, but I figured if the bald head didn't hurt—he'd turned out to be allergic to the superglue—nothing would.

High heels clicked across the marble floor and the door swung open. Viola looked as fantabulous as ever with her long dark hair, crimson lipstick, and a matching crimson dress that clung to her curvaceous body. A strange light glittered in her eyes and she seemed much more breathless than usual.

"You're here," she declared. "I've been worried. We have twenty-seven men inside, but we're still missing number twenty-eight."

"Here you go." I motioned to Lloyd. "Meet your alpha redhead."

Disbelief lit her dark eyes and a smile curved her full lips. "Dear, I hate to break this to you, but he has no hair." The smile faded as she studied him even closer. She shook her head. "I'm afraid he just won't do."

"What?" Lloyd asked. "Does that mean I don't get to have sex?"

"Hush," I muttered before turning a brilliant smile

on Viola. "Of course he won't do. Not like this. But with a little help."

"I'm afraid I don't understand."

I held up a boxed DVD set of *Happy Days*. "The most popular episodes. Your friend can watch these, get a really good fantasy going, and then live out the real thing with Lloyd."

"One glance will kill the fantasy, dear."

"That's why I brought this." I held up a red hand-kerchief I'd picked up at Morty's before climbing into the minivan. "It's a blindfold." I handed it to her. "He feels the part, smells the part, and acts the part. What more can you ask for?"

She seemed to weigh my words before she shook her head. "You've done a great job, Lil. Truly. The men are superb and you've more than earned your initial fee. But this . . ."

"I almost forgot. Wait here."

I hightailed it back to the minivan and retrieved the power tool I'd swiped from my father's garage on the way to Viola's. "Here," I told her when I reached the front door again.

She eyed the yellow metal. "What's this?"

"My father's new chain saw."

Her interest sparked. "The one he's been using on my azalea bushes?" When I nodded, she added, "He'll just buy another one when he finds this missing."

"Maybe. Unless he knows you have it. Then he'll be determined to get it back because, of course, he can't let you keep it. It's the principle of the thing, after all."

"And yet another point of contention."

"Not if you use it to negotiate something in writing as far as the bushes are concerned. Something that says they lie on your side of the property line."

"Clever." She smiled. "I think you may have earned that bonus, after all."

Twenty-eight

♥ ♥ ♥

I glanced down at the check Viola had given me. Oddly enough, it didn't fill me with the expected euphoria. I looked across the surrounding treetops toward the scene unfolding in Viola's backyard.

Ty had disappeared under the pretense of "checking things out," while I'd been talking to Viola. When he didn't resurface right away, I'd retreated to the minivan to give the NUNS some privacy and let nature take its course.

After ten minutes of flipping through radio stations, my curiosity, along with a great deal of howling, had lured me up into a tree at the far edge of Viola's estate. I stood poised on a very slim branch that wouldn't have supported a cat, much less a full grown woman.

But a vampire . . . Being fanged and fantabulous definitely had its perks.

A restlessness stirred deep inside and I trembled.

Pathetic. I mean, geez, I should be feeling on top of the world. *Fulfilled*. I'd aced the job for Viola. Ayala was out with Remy at the moment and no doubt loving it since he was a primo catch. Esther wasn't upset over being trampled. I actually had some solid leads that would surely lead to the real killer and get my head off the chopping block. And I was *this* close to my parents—their estate loomed behind me—and I hadn't once contemplated impaling myself on the nearest sharp object.

Talk about a moment of triumph.

The moon hung full and ripe in the black velvet sky. The air sizzled with electricity. There was an energy that wafted on the breeze. Awareness washed over me, drenching every nerve as I stared at the scene unfolding.

It was as wild as I'd imagined it would be, as loud, as primitive. I was far enough away that I couldn't see specifics—although a glare flashed every once in a while like Morse code. I knew Lloyd was alive and well and—if the orgasmic wails that echoed in my ears were any indication—having the time of his life.

Bodies writhed and sweated. Men panted and groaned. Women moaned and howled. My stomach hollowed out. An ache started between my legs (you try watching something like this and not get turned on) and spread north, working its way up. A fullness tugged at my breasts. My nipples went on high alert.

"What's wrong?" Ty's deep voice drew my attention.

I turned just as he leapt and landed at the end of my

branch. The motion was smooth and easy and he didn't so much as stir a leaf.

He stepped toward me. "You look sad."

"I'm not sad." I glanced back toward the scene and the words spilled out before I could stop them. "It's called horny." Why oh why had I said *that*? "There are dozens of people having phenomenal sex and I'm not one of them."

His warm chuckle slid over my skin and into my ears. My skin tingled and my nerves hummed.

"That's no one's fault but yours." His voice was rich and deep and oh so stirring. "You could be right there with them."

"With a human male?" I shook my head. "Not my thing. Not that I haven't tried it, of course. Many times." Okay, I was exaggerating a little, but I didn't want Ty to think I wasn't all that. "But after five hundred years, it gets old."

"I'm not talking about the alpha males down there."

My gaze collided with his. "Then what are you talking about?"

You. Me. Us.

The possibilities floated through my head, but he didn't say anything. He simply stared at me, into me, for a long moment before he asked. "What is it you want, Lil?"

The question stirred a ton of responses, none of which I wanted to acknowledge much less say out loud. I grinned. "Another retainer fee like the one I just collected."

"I'm not talking about professionally. I'm talking

about your personal life. What is it you're looking for?"

I shrugged. "What every born vampire looks for—an eternity mate."

"Another born vampire then."

I nodded. "That's usually the way it works. Born vamp plus born vamp equals baby vamps." Which equals a happy, noninterfering mother.

Okay, so we're talking *my* mother. I'd settle for one out of two.

"And is that so important? Right here? Right now? Is that what you want more than anything else? At *this* moment?"

Ty. That's what I wanted more than anything else. What I shouldn't want for a dozen reasons I'd already gone over time and time again, none of which I could actually recall with him standing so close and the air ripe with the sounds of sex.

"We really should go." Now. Before I stopped thinking about what I should do and simply did what I wanted to do.

I was close. Much too close.

He eyed me for a long moment before his mouth crooked into a grin. An expression that didn't quite touch the dark, unreadable depths of his bluer-than-blue eyes. "The minivan awaits."

I couldn't do the minivan.

Not because it wasn't macho enough or sporty enough or cool beyond words. The thought of sitting *this* close to Ty for a two-hour drive upstate was more than I could handle at the moment. Besides, Lloyd needed a ride in the morning.

We left the van, morphed into a couple of speedy bats, and made the trip in less than twenty minutes.

Back at the cabin, Ty went to check his e-mail and see if there was anything else on the female werewolf with the restraining order. He was waiting for a last known address and, with any luck, one of his sources had come up with the information. As for me, I glided into the bathroom, straight into an ice cold shower.

I needed to calm down. Then I could face the rest of the evening with him.

But first . . . I reached for a bottle of Tail and Mane shampoo. Had I sunk to the bottomless pit of hormonal apathy or what? The kicker was, I didn't so much as shudder as I filled my hand with the white liquid and started lathering it through my hair. It wasn't my favorite José Eber, but it smelled decent enough and it was all that had been available at *Morty's*. Even more, it kept me busy and distracted for the next two hours.

After I lathered, I had to rinse. And then I had to condition. And then I had to blow dry. And style. And, well, a really good style didn't just happen overnight.

By the time I emerged from the bathroom, it was four in the morning. Ty had closed up his computer, killed the lights, and climbed into bed. Moonlight filtered through a break in the curtains and spilled over the bed, illuminating his sleeping form.

Relief washed through me. I so didn't need him looking at me right now, asking more questions, looking at me, taking up all my space, looking at me.

I bypassed the bed and, to my credit, managed not to stare as I headed for the loft. I crawled into bed, buried myself beneath the sheets and clamped my eyes shut. Now all I had to do was forget about the primitive scene I'd witnessed tonight. You know, the one that kept playing in my head, stirring my body, making my toes curl and my nipples ache?

Yeah, that one.

After about five minutes, I gave up. Sleep just wasn't happening right now. I got out of bed and walked to the railing that overlooked the first floor of the cabin and Ty.

He lay stretched out on the full-size bed, one arm over his head, the other resting on his chest. A white sheet dotted with navy blue bass fish covered his dark, masculine physique from midchest down. I couldn't help but wonder if he'd shed the BVDs tonight.

Nah. He had the skivvies intact. Hell, maybe he'd even left on the jeans.

My gaze riveted on where the soft denim lay draped over a nearby chair. Uh-oh. I glanced around but I didn't see anything white. Whew. Talk about a close call.

He definitely had them on.

Probably.

Okay, so there was really only one way to find out. Then I could forget the *Does he, does he not?* dilemma, go back to bed, and get some much needed sleep.

I focused on the edge of the sheet and willed it to move. The cotton tugged downward just a fraction.

More.

It slithered slowly, revealing an impressive six-pack bisected by a line of soft, dark hair. The sheet inched down. The hair whorled south.

Oh, boy.

The dark silk circled his belly button and funneled toward his—

"If you're going to undress me, cut the bullshit and grow some balls." Ty's deep voice slid into my ears and I stiffened. The sheet halted and my gaze swiveled to his face. Neon blue eyes stared back at me and my mouth went dry.

"Excuse me?"

"Stop playing and touch me." He moved then and in the blink of an eye, his naked body had me pinned to a nearby wall. His gaze burned into me. *Touch me.*

I wasn't sure why, but I did.

Okay, so I knew why—it had been so long and I was so horny and Ty was so naked and it just felt . . . right.

I didn't give myself time to consider that last thought. Instead, I focused every ounce of energy on leaning into him, pressing my lips to his and kissing him.

He met me lick for lick, stroke for stroke, his tongue delving and dancing with mine. The kiss was fierce and urgent, but it wasn't enough.

"You're still not touching me." His deep voice stirred inside my head and I pulled away.

Lips parted, I stared up at him for a long second before dropping my gaze, sliding it along his skin, tracing a visual path from his jugular, over his massive chest, to a very impressive erection.

His penis was dark and thick and so incredibly hard. I reached out and wrapped my fingers around him. He growled low and deep, a raw sound that stirred the primitive hunger I did my damndest to control.

I wanted him and suddenly, it didn't seem like such a big deal. I mean, really, it was just sex. It wasn't like I was going to go all the way and sink my fangs into him.

Done that.

Okay, fine. But it wasn't like I was going to let him sink his fangs into me.

Just sex, I vowed to myself and then I kissed him again.

Twenty-nine

❤ ❤ ❤

All right, already.

It was more than just sex.

It was phenomenal sex.

Particularly when Ty slid his arms around me, turned and glided us back down to the full-size bed. He pressed me down onto the mattress, pinning me with his hard body. There was nothing artful or perfect about the way he touched me. A primal heat filled his gaze, along with an uncertainty that I'd never seen in a vampire's eyes before.

But Ty wasn't just any vampire.

At one time, he'd been just a man and when he touched me, it was with a man's urgency. As if he couldn't wait. As if I were the best woman he'd ever been with.

The only woman.

Wait a second. Where had that come from?

I didn't know. Even more, I didn't want to know. I just wanted Ty inside of me.

Right.

Now.

As if he read the desperate thoughts, he slid his hands, so rough and stirring, down the length of my body, parted my thighs and thrust into me.

He kissed me then, his tongue pushing into my mouth as fiercely and as urgently as his body pumped into mine. Over and over, until I felt my muscles contract. My orgasm hit me hard and fast, turning me inside out and upside down and filling me with a pleasure so intense that I couldn't breathe.

Luckily, I didn't need to breathe.

I just needed to feel . . . the sharp ache between my legs, followed by the dull throbbing and the slow spread of pleasure through every inch of my body.

The feeling lasted several minutes until finally two important things registered. One, Ty was still hard inside me and two, his lips—make that his *fangs*—were on my neck.

I felt the steely sharpness rasp over my pulse beat and my eyes popped open. My heart paused.

He wasn't . . . He wouldn't . . .

He didn't.

Instead, he moved on, fangs grazing, tongue stroking. His hot mouth closed over one nipple and he suckled me. But he didn't sink his teeth in. Not yet.

Not ever, I told myself. No way. No how.

No matter how much I suddenly wanted him to.

I grasped his shoulders, flipped him onto his back and straddled him.

He arched one eyebrow at me. "Pulling rank, are we?"

"You know it, baby." And then I slid down onto his hard length, leaned back—far, far away from that delectable mouth of his and those razor-sharp fangs— and had the wildest ride of my life.

An hour later, I snuggled into the pillow, suddenly so tired that I couldn't keep my eyes open. The exhaustion that came with daybreak tugged at my muscles, along with the satisfaction of really hot sex.

I felt the bed dip as Ty swung his legs over the side.

"Where are you going?"

"To get something to eat." Because as gratifying as the sex had been, there hadn't been the ultimate fulfillment that came with drinking from each other. I knew it and so did he, but neither of us said anything.

I mean, really. Why kill the moment? Biting aside, we're talking *phenomenal* sex.

My eyes drifted closed. In the far distance I heard the gasp as he uncorked a new bottle. The *glug, glug, glug* as he fed his hunger. He climbed back into bed soon after that and pulled me close.

And then everything faded into the steady sound of my own heartbeat and I slept the best sleep I'd had in months.

I was starving.

I stumbled into the kitchen later that afternoon,

just after sunset, and reached for the nearly empty bottle Ty had consumed early that morning. Just one sip and I would be good to go.

I took three sips.

Okay, so they were gulps, but I had a naked vampire in my bed. I needed my strength.

I was just about to take a fourth, when the feeling hit me. A presence. Someone was watching me.

The hair on the back of my neck stood up and every nerve in my body went on high alert. My insides tightened and my stomach jumped.

I turned and stared into the bedroom, but Ty didn't move. He lay on his side, his back to me, the sheet pulled up to his waist. A distinct scent tickled my nostrils—like toffee mixed with peanuts.

"He's pretty hot." The familiar voice slid into my ears and drew me around.

I glanced up toward the loft and saw Ayala peering down at me.

Hold on. Ayala?

My stomach convulsed again and I closed my eyes. "It didn't go so well, did it?"

"What are you talking about?"

"Remy. That's why you're here. What was it this time? He wasn't blond enough? Tall enough? Short enough?"

"Actually, he was too much. Of a vampire, that is." She gave me a peculiar stare. "Haven't you figured it out yet?"

That you're a picky bitch? Got it.

"Listen, Ayala, I know you're feeling anxious. Desperate even. I've been there. Heck, I'm there right now. The parents are riding you. Society is killing you with all the baby hype. I totally understand."

"You don't understand shit."

"Of course I do. Your clock is ticking."

"Actually, it's your clock that's ticking." In the blink of an eye, she stood before me in the kitchen. She stepped around the table and plucked the nearly empty bottle of blood from my hands. "You still don't get it, do you?"

Actually, I was starting to.

My mind raced and the pieces started to fit together. The jealous werewolf had been Ayala's ex-lover. She'd been the reason I'd gotten staked.

Okay, so I'd gotten staked because I'd rushed in to protect Wilson, but you get the point.

I'd bled all over the tablecloth that night at the soirée, and she'd been right there (DNA evidence, check). She'd also been right there the night the reporter had gotten chopped to pieces, but no one had seen her because she was a vampire who'd been able to slip in and out, completely undetected. And if she had been detected, she'd have been able to easily influence any poor schmuck who happened to get a glimpse of her. She'd have been able to slip in and out right on my heels, completely undetected and without leaving a trace of fingerprints.

"It was actually much easier than I thought it would be," she said as if reading my thoughts. "I hadn't planned on you showing up at his apartment that night. I was just going to go there, dispose of him and plant the DNA evidence, and a vivid description in the mind of the doorman and anyone else who happened by in the lobby that night. But then you arrived and even let him take your picture with the camera phone." She smiled. "Talk about luck."

I stiffened and my hands trembled. My stomach jumped again. A pain this time, but I paid it little attention. Instead, I was focused on the rage that boiled inside my body and the red haze clouding my vision.

I was so going to kick her ass.

But not yet. Not until she answered the one question screaming in my head.

"Why?"

"He's dead now. Because of you."

"Actually, he's dead because of *you*. You broke it off. You went out with someone else. You drove him to pick up that stake and go after Wilson."

She shrugged and traced the label on the bottle. "I was doing what I had to do. There was no way we could have had a real relationship. I couldn't have disgraced my family like that." She shook her head. "I had to break things off and find someone appropriate." Her gaze met mine. "The thing is, I've been trying and it just isn't possible."

I saw the anguish in her bright hazel eyes and where I'd been ready to rip her to pieces—or at least hurt her *extremely* badly—I couldn't help but feel sorry for her now. It was yet another vampiric version of

Romeo and Juliet. Lovers drawn together by a fierce love, yet torn apart by forces beyond their control.

I swallowed the sudden lump in my throat.

"My father threatened to cut me off," she went on. "I had no choice but to break things off with Brian. I couldn't lose my inheritance. I told him we could still see each other as long as we kept things quiet and kept up appearances. That was the obvious solution, of course, but he wouldn't hear of it. He wanted me to actually marry him." She laughed. "Can you imagine that? Born vampires don't get *married*. Much less to werewolves."

Bye-bye, Juliet.

Hello, cold, callous, snotty, money-hungry bee-yotch.

"We have to choose someone more to our standard," she went on. "Someone like Remy." Her gaze lifted to mine. "He wasn't bad. He's no Brian, but he'll do for lack of anything better."

"Remy's too good for you. Stay away from him."

She laughed then. "But you're the one who set us up." Her smiled faded. "You like him, don't you?"

"We're friends." We were, I realized, even if he had blown the whistle on me the other night.

If he'd blown the whistle.

I remembered the strange sense of awareness I'd felt at Ty's place. The same thing I'd felt earlier when I'd turned to find Ayala watching me from the loft. "How did you find Ty's address?"

"That was easy, too. He's got a lot of connections with the New York Police Department. Once I knew you were with him, it was a piece of cake getting those guys to talk. Most of them, anyway, except for a few stuck-up vampires."

"And how did you know I was with him in the first place?"

She shrugged. "That dumb assistant of yours."

"Evie?"

She nodded. "She was such a pushover. One look into her eyes and she started talking. Of course, after I found out what I wanted to know, I had her forget all about it."

Realization dawned. "Evie isn't a lesbian."

"Says you. All I know is that I had zero trouble vamping her. Smacks lesbian to me."

Me, too.

The thought bothered me even more than Ayala and her attempt to ruin my life. Not because I'm homophobic or anything like that. But Evie and I are friends. We talk. I should have *known*.

"Dipping into the Other world can be fun, but they're just not like us," Ayala went on. "But then I'm sure you know that." Her gaze slid past me to Ty. "Made vampires just don't have the same iron-hard constitution that we do. Sure, they're strong. But they tend to be slaves to their baser urges." She made a *tsk, tsk* sound. "They simply have no self-control when it comes to controlling their hunger. He's sleeping rather soundly, wouldn't you say? Then again, he's probably not sleeping at all. He's probably paralyzed right now. Just this side of death."

I followed her gaze and noted the unnerving still-ess of his body, despite the fact that it was early vening. Time to rise and shine.

Time to die.

Cold, hard fear knotted inside me. "What did you o to him?" A gasp punctuated the question as my tomach contracted again, the reflex sharper this time. 'ainful.

She smiled and held up the bottle. "The same thing 'm going to do to you."

I stared through the clear glass at the half inch of ed liquid. For the first time, I noted the tiny particles hat swam around inside.

"Garlic," she added. "While we're not susceptible o the stuff when it's worn around someone's neck— alk about an old wives' tale—it's hell on the in- estines."

My gut clenched again and I grasped the edge of he table to keep from doubling over. "I thought the ;oal was to punish me, not kill me," I ground out, my eeth clenched as I fought against another wave of)ain.

"It's a woman's prerogative to change her mind. It nurts now, doesn't it?" she asked as she leaned into ne. Her lips grazed my ear. "That's your own fault. If /ou had drunk more instead of denying what you are, t wouldn't be so painful now. Instead, you would ;imply shut down like that delicious-looking bounty nunter of yours. Now that man can drink. Later, love. 'll give Remy your best."

Through the pain deafening me, I heard the door :lose and I knew she'd left. I tried to see past the

white dots dancing in front of my eyes. I had to get up
and check on Ty. I had to . . .

The thought faded in another rush of pain so intense that I sank to the floor this time. Another
squeeze of my insides and everything went black.

Thirty

"Lil? You in there?"

The name echoed in my ears, followed by a loud pounding that made my head hurt that much more.

Go away, I silently pleaded. *Just go away.*

Another frantic *bam, bam, bam* and the noise stopped.

There. That was better—

BAM!

The loud crash thundered through my head a split second before large hands gripped my shoulders.

My body screamed, pain exploding in my stomach, so fierce and consuming that my eyes started to water and I doubled over.

"Lil?"

"Stop," I groaned. "Don't move me." The grip eased and the pain subsided enough for me to open my eyes.

Lloyd's blurry shape loomed above me.

I blinked until his image came into focus.

He wore the same shirt he'd worn to Viola's. A massive hickey purpled his neck. Worry creased his brow and a frown drew his mouth tight.

"Lloyd?" My lips felt thick. Too thick to talk even, but I tried anyway. "What are you doing here? Shouldn't you be making werewolf babies?"

"What? I can't hear you. Your voice is cracking."

Thankfully. Werewolf babies? Where was my head?

Being bludgeoned to death by tiny little construction workers bent on sending me straight to hell.

My eyelids fluttered and Lloyd gave me another quick shake.

My eyes popped open. "Shit," I ground out, my voice louder this time. "What are you doing? Trying to kill me?"

"I came by to thank you for last night, but then you didn't answer the door and I heard you moan and—"

The words stumbled to a halt when I held up my hand. "Whisper. Please."

"What the hell happened?"

The question stuck in my head, pushing back all the pain and clearing the way for the rush of memories.

Ayala and the garlic-tainted blood and—

"Ty." I grasped at Lloyd's arms. "I . . . He's . . . Oh no."

"Just calm down." Lloyd tried to push me back down. "Don't move. He's sleeping."

"He isn't." I struggled to my feet, despite his large hands which tried to push me back down. "He's hurt. He's . . ."

I refused to finish the thought and struggled to my feet instead. In a blur of pain, I stumbled toward the bed where he still lay on his side, his back to me.

I grasped his shoulder and tugged. He rolled over, his face as passive as if he were in a deep, dark sleep.

Or finally, really, and truly dead.

No!

I leaned over and touched my hand to his chest, and felt a faint thud against my palm. Relief swamped me. His heart was still beating.

For now.

"We have to get him to a hospital," Lloyd said, coming up behind me. "I'll get the minivan."

"We don't have time." I grappled for the cell phone that sat on the nightstand and punched in a familiar number. "We have to bring the hospital to him."

"Thanks for coming," I told Jack less than an hour later. I sat on the sofa and watched as Mandy checked the bright red bag of blood that fed an IV tube inserted in Ty's left arm.

"It sounds like his blood's been poisoned. If so, the red cells are fighting in a no-win situation with the white ones. They're destroying each other," she'd told me when I'd described the situation to her in my frantic phone call. "That means we have to pump in as much new, healthy blood as possible in order to replenish the supply."

She'd come with several bags from a local blood bank and had arrived in record time thanks to Jack, who'd done his Superman imitation and given Mandy a quick ride rather than driving his Beamer.

I glanced at the IV tube in my own arm. My blood had been poisoned, as well, but not to the same degree because I'd had only a few swallows compared to Ty's nearly full bottle. Once the blood had started to flow, I'd felt better almost immediately.

Ty wasn't progressing as well.

"He'll be all right," Jack told me as if reading my worried thoughts. "Mandy said it's just going to take time."

"Thanks for coming."

"I almost didn't." When I raised a questioning brow, he added, "I was counting on you to be there at the tea and take some of the heat off me."

"Thanks a lot."

"Instead, I had mom's full attention." He shook his head. "It wasn't a pretty sight."

"I'm assuming she's not half as excited about the wedding as you and Mandy are."

"Are you kidding? She's ready to hire one of those cult guys to kidnap and deprogram me. The only thing keeping her in check is Mandy. When Mom blew, Mandy threatened to put a hex on her."

"Mandy's not a witch."

"You know that and I know that. Mom, however, is convinced otherwise. Especially since Mandy's ancestor was burned at the stake."

"I can't believe you guys told her."

"Mandy thought it would make things easier." He
-ed the woman wrapping a blood pressure cuff
ound Ty's upper arm. "It worked."

I remembered Mandy's excitement. "But not in the
ay she thought."

He nodded. "But beggars can't be choosers. Mom's
-ared of being turned into a frog, that or getting a
w wrinkles from an aging spell, so she's agreed to
eep her mouth shut."

"Lucky you."

"We could always tell her your boyfriend there was
warlock before he was turned."

"Oh, he's not my boyfriend. We're just having
x."

Just sex, I reminded myself again.

Which didn't begin to explain the tightness grip-
ing my chest.

Then again, Ty and I were friends. It made sense
at I would be concerned over his well-being. It wasn't
ke I was afraid for him or anything like that.

It's just that Ayala was still out there, still trying to
in my life, and she wasn't going to stop until I
opped her.

"I need you to do something for me," I told Jack as
plan started to form.

"This isn't going to work," Jack told me an hour
ter. We'd left Mandy with Ty and headed for Mandy's
partment and a final showdown with Ayala.

"She didn't recognize your voice, did she?"

"She's never heard my voice."

"Exactly. And she's never been to this apartmen before?"

"No, but it's an apartment. Not a lawyer's office.

"But you told her this was an informal call, right That you're just a hardworking professional trying t do what's right despite a bunch of pushy werewolves If said werewolves are your clients, then it make sense that you couldn't invite their enemy to you office. You would have to meet her on the side." motioned around Mandy's immaculate living room "Here. Stop worrying. It'll work. She thinks you're pretentious born vampire just like her and that you'r betraying your client's trust because, hey, pretentiou born vampires stick together."

He looked doubtful. "She's managed to frame yo for *murder*. She's smart. Too smart to fall for a scan like this."

"If she thinks that Brian the werewolf left her shitload of money in his will and his family is tryin to keep it from her, she'll come. Money motivate people."

People being the key word. But Ayala wasn't a per son. She was a vampire with all the attributes tha come with being a denizen of the undead, includ ing superior intelligence. But—and this is what I wa counting on—she was also female. In her own twistec way, she'd loved Brian. I'd seen it in her eyes.

When they hadn't been gleaming with a crazec light, that is.

On top of that, she was greedy.

"She'll be here," I told Jack. "Did you call Remy?'

He nodded. "He's on his way."

"Good." I retrieved the small tape recorder that Mandy used during her autopsy assists from the pocket of her lab jacket—right where she said I'd find it—and slid it into the pocket of my grimy but still fab Diane von Furstenberg.

"What if you can't get her to confess?" Jack asked as I settled on the living room sofa.

"She'll confess."

"And if she doesn't? What are you going to do then?"

"I'm going to kick her ass."

"And what if she kicks your ass first?"

I gave him a determined smile. "At least I'll go down with a fight."

Ayala showed up exactly thirty minutes later. Jack answered the door. "Sorry I had to have you come here," he apologized as he ushered her into the apartment and closed the door. "But Brian's relatives are adamant that you know nothing about the stipulations of the will. They're paying me quite well, but I took an oath and I feel obligated to do the right thing."

"That's admirable of you," Ayala said as she followed him the few steps toward the living room. Thanks to his luscious scent, she'd tuned in to him first and so she hadn't even noticed me sitting in the corner. The moment her gaze touched me, however, she came up short.

"What are *you* doing here?" Her gaze swiveled back to Jack. "You're not a lawyer."

"Finally the vamp senses kick in," I said.

"What about Brian's will?"

"There is no will. I mean, maybe there was. I didn't check. But if there had been, he obviously didn't leave anything to you. Why would he? You dumped him and practically killed him."

Her gaze narrowed. "What do you want from me?"

"I want to help you. It's obvious you have some serious anger management issues, Ayala. While I'm not an expert on the subject, hacking someone to pieces is usually a clear sign of inner aggression."

"Toward you. I hate you."

"Good, good. Get it off your chest." She gave me another strange look. "Confession is good for the soul. I bet if you let it all out, all the sordid details about what you did to Keith, you'll feel much better."

"I feel fine."

"Now, but you're sure to have nightmares for years. You *hacked* him up, Ayala. Into tiny little pieces. There was blood everywhere. And I bet he screamed. I bet he begged." Okay, so I was making myself a little queasy. I fought down a rising wave of nausea and plowed forward. "I bet he even *prayed*."

"Not as much as you're going to," she said a split second before she pulled a gun from her pocket and fired off a shot at Jack. He flew back against the wall and slid toward the floor. I knew he wasn't permanently injured, but it still shook me. Long enough for Ayala to pounce.

In a flash, she leaned into me. But it wasn't a gun that she pressed to my chest. It was a letter opener, the tip sharp and lethal.

This was *it*. I cast a frantic glance at my brother. While I knew he wasn't mortally wounded—already his body was expelling the bullet—he was still bleeding profusely, his arms and legs limp. Pain contorted his expression and gripped his body.

The sweet scent of toffee-covered peanuts filled my nostrils (I know, gross, right?) and my stomach jumped.

"I thought you wanted me to suffer," I told her, stalling for time. Where the hell was Remy?

"I told you back at the cabin, I changed my mind," she told me. "I want you dead."

Maybe so, but *I* didn't want me dead.

In a split second, I brought my hand up and smacked her upside the head with enough force to throw her back several inches. Before I could gather my strength again, she lunged.

I ducked and rolled, crashing into the coffee table. I was about to smack her again when the door crashed open and Remy arrived. He had a gun of his own. One shot and she crumpled at my feet, temporarily of course, but it was long enough for Remy's men to surround and seize her.

"I guess she wasn't the perfect one for me," he said, coming over to me. "And to think we had such a good time."

I glared at him. "Don't even think about asking for your money back."

His eyes twinkled. He grinned and, despite my undying *like* for Ty, I actually felt a strange warmth in the pit of my stomach. "You can owe me."

Epilogue

♥ ♥ ♥

"We need more ribs," Mandy declared as she burst through the swinging doors that led into the massive kitchen. "They're eating *everything*." She dropped an empty platter on the marble island cabinet where I stood arranging a mountain of hot wings into the shape of a baby carriage. "And snarling. And one of them even growled at me."

"They're all about to pop." It had been eight and a half months since the night of the full moon and I had twenty-eight pregnant werewolves sitting in the adjoining living room.

I'd left Evie to handle things at Dead End Dating and roped Mandy into cohosting the Big Event aka a group baby shower for Viola and the NUNS. Evie had been hurt at first, but I'd convinced her that I simply couldn't concentrate unless I knew I had someone competent to take care of things in my absence. That, and I'd kissed ass with a gift card for Neiman Marcus.

The growling was tame compared to what might happen if they got too excited or too upset, and I couldn't afford to lose a great assistant. Mandy, on the other hand, was practically family. And a doctor. And, therefore, fully armed with a syringe full of sedatives should things get a little wild.

I topped off the display with saucers of ranch dip for the wheels and slid it toward her. "This will keep them happy while I carve the rump roast."

She glanced down and her harried expression softened for a few frantic heartbeats. "Totally cute." Her gaze shifted to mine. "You're so good at this catering thing."

I shrugged. "It's all about the connections. In this case, a butcher over on Third Street who sells bulk."

She eyed me. "How are you with flowers?"

"I can hold my own. Why do you ask?"

"It's just that I'm so busy with my schedule and Jack's never planned this sort of thing before." She gave me a hopeful smile. "It would be so great if you could help with the wedding plans. Jack really wants his family involved, and your mother doesn't seem to be taking a big part in things."

The only thing my mother was "taking" as far as Dr. Mandy was concerned was a double dose of Valium whenever the newly engaged couple showed up for the hunt.

"I mailed her invitation samples last month," Mandy

went on, "so that she could have some time to look at them before we saw her."

"And?"

"She sent them back with 'Doesn't Live Here Anymore' scribbled across the envelope." A desperate light fueled her gaze. "It would mean so much to both of us. Please."

No. Between drumming up new business and searching for mates for my current clients (Rachel the were-Chihuahua and Esther the made vampire, to name two), I'd barely had time to organize the baby shower. A *wedding*? With tons of frilly tulle and sprays of pink roses and a big frosty wedding cake?

"Okay." What can I say? I'm a sucker for desperate. "Now go before they start gnawing off body parts." When she gave me a startled expression, I smiled. "Just joking." *Not.* "But you might want to hurry. As a precaution."

Determination gripped her expression. She nodded, hefted the platter, and headed back through the swinging doors.

"One rump roast ready to go." Lloyd came up next to me and set a roasting pan on the counter. "Extra rare."

What's up with that, right?

Well, since I didn't know my spatula from my meat fork (for obvious reasons), I'd brought along Lloyd to man the barbecue pit. Besides, it seemed only fitting that he help out since he'd had a hand—or at least a fairly important body part—in what was now happening.

Even more, Lloyd owed me. While his weekends weren't overflowing with dates, he *had* launched a brand-new stud service. See, one of the NUNS was having twins (the female with the Alpha Doody fetish). Turns out that bald men are bald because of a mega dose of testosterone, and so Lloyd had not only shot a bull's-eye, he'd nailed it twice.

To make a long story short, Lloyd was booked for every lunar eclipse for the next ten years.

"Thanks." I slid the slab of meat onto a giant white doily. "What about the brisket?"

"Coming right up." He headed back to the monstrous barbecue pit that puffed away on the back patio.

Remy's patio, to be exact.

Fairfield's finest had been kind enough to offer up his house for the Big Event. In addition to saving my ass during the showdown with Ayala, that is.

Which meant I *really* owed him.

Luckily, I hadn't had too much time to think about what that meant, or what he could possibly want from me, or the fact that at any given time he might decide to collect.

I'd been too busy worrying over (a) my fledgling business, (b) a pack of hormonal werewolves and—and this was the biggie—(c) an MIA bounty hunter.

That's right. MIA. As in nowhere to be found.

One minute Ty had been fighting for his life at the cabin, and the next he'd gotten an urgent phone call. Just like that, he'd hauled himself out of bed and headed back to the city with total disregard for my safety.

Okay, so maybe *total* was pushing it a little.

The fight for my freedom and my integrity *had* been *fini*.

After Remy had shot Ayala, he'd handed her over to the authorities, along with her tape-recorded confession. She'd had an immediate date with the big D (that's daylight, not Dior) since the cops who'd taken her into custody were a secret organization of very powerful born vamps who dealt with those of our kind who compromised the anonymity and safety of the rest.

Ayala was now history. The SOVPBV (we're talking covert vampires, not ad execs) had cooked up a story, complete with real evidence, and fed it to the human authorities. My name had been cleared and I'd even managed to snag a new born vamp client. He goes by the name Agent X (I'm *so* not kidding, and I've got his signature on the DED profile to prove it) and he's *mucho* hot.

But that was beside the point.

I'd had exactly one message from Ty during the past eight months, and it hadn't included an apology or a dinner invitation or a heartfelt thank you for the best night of his eternal existence. Rather, he'd asked me to drop by his place and pick up his mail.

I know, right?

I might be slow in paying my bills (my human client list had suffered because of my two weeks of notoriety and I was still trying to grow my rep with everyone else), but I could certainly put two and two together.

Obviously, Ty hadn't had nearly as good a time in bed as I'd first thought and he just wasn't that interested.

That, or he'd been abducted by aliens.

Hey, it could happen. While I hadn't spotted any little green men myself, I'd never seen a pregnant werewolf, either. I now had twenty-eight gathered in Remy's living room.

Beam me up, Scotty!

A loud crash punctuated the thought, followed by a howl that would have curled my hair if I hadn't used a straightening iron before leaving my apartment.

"Lil!" Mandy's voice carried from the other room just before she ducked her head inside the door, a worried expression on her face. "Could you come out here? We've got a situation."

"They don't like the wings?"

"The furniture. It's not comfortable enough." Her gaze collided with mine. "They're in labor."

"Which one?"

"All of them."

Uh-oh.

If you fell in love at first bite with
Dead and Dateless,
read on for a sneak peek at

Your Coffin or Mine?

by

KIMBERLY RAYE

the next delectable novel
in the Dead End Dating series!

I was being followed.

If that wasn't creepy enough, it was dark out, I was all alone, and I was standing in a smelly alley near Times Square.

Talk about a Wes Craven flick.

For me, however, it was just another day in the life of a fantabulous five-hundred-year-old (and holding) born vampire. My name? Countess Lilliana Arrabella Guinevere du Marchette, but my best buds call me Lil. Because of my BV heritage, I ooze sex appeal, and since it's oozing out of a totally hot package (great body, great face, kickin' highlights), I've had more than my share of stalkers. Like the rest of my kind, I attract the opposite sex en masse.

Okay. So en masse might be stretching things a *teensy* bit. I haven't actually had an official date in . . .

I can't actually remember the last time (fix-ups DO NOT count, Ma), and I was sorta, kinda dumped recently by a megahot bounty hunter after our one and only night together (sniffle).

But neither of those is due to a lack of hotness on my part. The Dating Deficit? My choice. Really. I've given up meaningless flings in favor of finding my eternity mate, settling down, and populating the species.

As for the bounty hunter . . . I'm sure (fingers crossed) he'll soon realize what a babe I am and come begging for forgiveness. I, of course, will tell him—as would any female who'd been dumped with not so much as a *Later* scribbled on a Post-it—to go bite himself.

At least that was the revenge fantasy I was currently tuning in to. In between numero uno—I rip off all of his clothes and we make like jack rabbits—and three—he rips off all of mine and we make like jack rabbits.

I know, right? It was one measly night. I should get a life (or an afterlife in my case) and forget all about him. And the way he kissed. And touched. And tasted.

Yes, I'd tasted him, *too,* but not during sex. I'm weak, but not *that* weak. The tasting had occurred before the sex.

I'd been staked, and he'd been trying to help me recoup my strength. I drank from him, and since then we've had this mental connection thing going on. He could send me thoughts and vice versa.

Not that he'd sent me anything in the past months. No desperate apologies. No sweet nothings. No flowers. Not even a measly *IOU for a night of hot, wild, primo mattress-dancing.*

All the more reason to push him completely out of my mind and get back on track, right? Right.

So, um, where was I?

Oh, yeah. Dark and creepy alley. Me being followed. No biggee.

Until now.

Wedge heels tapped the pavement behind me and thundered through my head as I rounded a corner and started down another alley. The sharp aroma of cheap hairspray mingled with generic body spray and 100 percent rayon burned my nostrils. I turned and caught a glimpse of a chipped manicure clutching a tiny camera before my stalker realized I was looking and ducked behind a garbage Dumpster.

A man I'd expected (see the long rambling above), but a *woman*?

While I knew chicks got off to really hot chicks every day (I could appreciate the latest Angelina Jolie pic as much as the next mature, sexually confident, semilonely woman), I couldn't shake the gut feeling that there was more to this than a love-struck groupie eager to feed her own private fantasies.

I kept staring, until she stole another glance at me. My gaze collided with hers for a nanosecond, and her stats rolled through my head like movie credits.

Gwen Rowley. Thirty-nine years old. Italian. Full

time fourth-grade teacher and part-time private investigator. Divorced mother of three. Hated men. Even more, she hated her mother who'd put her up to following a small-potatoes matchmaker when she could have been a) grading tomorrow's math assignment and then b) tailing her ex and his new girlfriend. They were going bowling. She hated bowling, too.

She retreated behind the massive metal monster, and the connection ended before I could find out the really good stuff.

Like who in Damien's name was her mother and why would she want me followed?

And, more important, had Gwen started dating again?

FYI—in addition to being a hot, happening *vampere*, I'm also Manhattan's newest primo matchmaker.

She peeked around the corner once more, camera poised, and my instincts screamed for me to shift into Supervamp mode, make like my last client fee, and disappear.

Fast.

Our species, and the dozens of Others out there, hadn't survived thousands of years by keeping a high profile. We exercised caution and kept to ourselves and avoided cameras at all cost.

I paused and made a show of adjusting my shoe (snakeskin Prada stiletto), and gave her my best profile.

Hey, we're talking *stiletto*. As in mucho P-A-I-N. I simply *had* to wiggle my toes.

And ease my own conscience. What can I say? I've got a soft spot for potential clients. Even more, I'm a jumbo marshmallow when it comes to potential clients with bossy, overbearing mothers (DO NOT get me started).

The camera clicked a few times, and I morphed from white ball of fluff into determined *vampere*. I stepped forward, my feet moving so fast that I emerged from my back-alley route a half block away, walked into the massive high-rise near the heart of Times Square, and sailed onto the elevator before Gwen had a chance to blink, much less follow.

Did I mention that born vamps are superfast in addition to being total hotties?

While I wasn't opposed to giving her a few pics so she didn't go back empty-handed, I hadn't taken a back-alley route for the great scenery. The last thing—the very *last* thing—I needed was to be caught dead (or undead) in a place like *this*.

I stepped off the elevator at the eighth floor and walked into the lobby of KNYC, a local cable network near the NBC studios responsible for several home-grown news programs, a handful of talk shows, and the recent reality smash *Manhattan's Most Wanted*.

MMW was a local version of *The Bachelor* that paired up one of the city's most sought-after males with fifty marriage-minded, crème de la creme females and let him weed them down to the One.

At least that was the idea. The last guy—a Wall

Street financier—had narrowed his bevy of bombshells down to the One Who'd Taken the Rock and Hauled Ass. She'd pocketed the cash and headed for Mexico, and the financier ended up on Dr. Phil.

Plush gold carpeting cushioned my stance and eased the pressure on my tootsies. Pale yellow walls decorated with gold deco mirrors surrounded me. Cinnamon-colored leather chairs traced the perimeter. Several tables overflowed with magazines. A man stood near a glass doorway marked *Studio A*, a headset hooked around his neck and a clipboard in his hands.

The only man in a room that otherwise overflowed with single, successful, smart, attractive, *desperate* women.

Talk about a target-rich environment.

I'd taken on several vamps and weres over the past few months, but Others were much harder to pair up than your average human. There was too much emphasis on orgasm quotients and fertility ratings for vamps, and alpha mates and lunar cycles for weres. Since I'm an equal-opportunity matchmaker—one with an addiction to MAC cosmetics and enough credit card bills to make the national deficit look like chump change—I'd decided to beef up my human client list.

I smiled, reached into my leather Prada clutch for a stack of cards, and stepped toward the first cluster of females.

I was just about to slide a card into an attractive

woman's hand—twenty-five, nurse, fed up with losers with great big egos and tiny penises—when I heard the deep, familiar voice.

"Help me."